This book is dedicated to my grandmother, Anne Merril, for the undying love she gave me in my most trying circumstances. She pushed me to be better and stayed on me to accomplish my dreams when I felt I could not achieve them. She is the spirit of this book, and without her I never would have been able to finish. I love you so much, Anne.

Acknowledgments are in order. First, Sherrie Phillips (Sherrie Berrie), for the love you have shown me. You looked over the book and put the magic on it. I am forever grateful to you for walking me through the process of figuring out how to do this thing called self-publishing. Secondly, I want to thank Sherri Williams of Sols Write House for having the patience to get me through the publishing process when I did not have a clue how to do the simplest things. You were a Godsend; I can say that much. Derek A. Waithe, when I first started this process, I had to do a lot of research. Thankfully, you were always there to give me a verse or discuss something that I wanted to add, in order to make the story realer. That was pretty cool of you, brother. Derrick Jones, you were the first person to ever read my book in full so many years ago when I had the idea to do it. I still remember meeting up in a laundry room to discuss you working on the project for me. Hey, let's make a movie. Laurie Dean (Lollie Anna), the excitement you showed me over reading this project, the love you have shown and the push you have given me can't be replaced. Thank you so much, lady. Can't wait to read what you are working on. I envy your project. Johnnie Brimmer and Martez Moore, what can I say, this story has taken on so many faces over the years, but you two were more than happy to review my work. It's guys like the two of you that let me know that I had to make this happen. I hope you both enjoy the newest version. Kelly Cole, I can't say enough about the book design you did for me. I described my vision over the phone and you had it ready the next day. Hopefully, I can be more like you in the near future. David Ortiz, for giving me the laptop to write this book on. I have worked tirelessly on this thing, and will continue to do so in the future. Clutch move you made. Thank you, friend.

The Devil's Deceit

By: Walter Martin

1 Peter 5:8

Mark 8:36

December. Night. Cold.

Gabriel Cade stepped out of his tire warehouse job in downtown Knoxville, Tennessee and prepared to walk home. The daily jaunts to and from work were usually his escape from the world and everything it had to throw at him since his thirteen-year stretch in federal prison for vehicular manslaughter ended. It was on these long walks where he found some slight reprieve from the daily grind. These were his times for peace, quiet and, occasionally, some introspective self-reflection.

He'd only had a few drinks when his superior officer in the military tasked him with taking a few drunken comrades back to the barracks. He could make it back to the destination without a hitch, he'd thought that night. At the time it didn't seem like a bad idea, but fate had other ideas.

He wasn't even drunk!

Contrary to what the breathalyzer had read, of course.

The thoughts of the crash and of his fellow marines laying helplessly on the asphalt continually haunted him during his brutal, draining stay in federal custody.

The incident happened on a hot summer night. After much prodding by his intoxicated buddies, he had foolishly allowed them to ride in the back of his personal vehicle, a small pickup truck. On the way to the barracks he was approaching an intersection when another car ran a red light, causing him to swerve and flip his truck. The small pickup skidded against the asphalt and his unbuckled allies where violently thrown from the back of the vehicle to their deaths.

It wasn't even his fault.

Contrary to what the jury decided, of course.

Cade himself suffered minor injuries, but the aftermath of what had occurred cut him deeper than any physical wound ever could have. Two of his fellow soldiers had been lost in the accident because of his negligence and could never be brought back, a fact that still gave him nightmares at night.

Though he'd explained, in depth, what had happened that night, he was unable to convince a jury to see things his way. This led the judge, an old senile man with a long military history, to sentence him to the high end of the guideline-15 years in federal prison. There was no doubt in Cade's mind that members of MADD (Mothers Against Drunk Driving) played the biggest part in pressuring the judge to be so harsh, especially during an election year. He would serve his time in various parts of the country, being flown and bussed state to state in shackles for hours at a time.

Early in his bid, there had been fights and a few attempts on his life, the results being many cold nights in solitary confinement. Thoughts of the past and present were often his only company. Cade was unsure of what God had planned for his future, but he soon realized he was not in control and had to let the Highest Power do His job, even though his faith was constantly tested.

His mind would constantly wander off to what could be in order to avoid thinking about his circumstances. A lot of times he felt as if he would be better off dead.

A small stature and bifocals made him an easy target for supremacist groups, but his heart was much bigger than they had anticipated, and his bite was that of a hungry hyena. Eventually, after enough squabbles that resulted in broken noses and blackened eyes, he had earned his respect on the yard and people stood aside, allowing him do his time his own way.

The worst part about prison to him was the lack of control. If the showers were cold you stood under the frigid water and braved the pain for the time that you were allowed to be out of your cell, or you walked around smelling like onions on a fast food line. It was free choice, yes, but hygiene issues opened the door for more severe ones behind the gate, especially when locked in a room with someone for days at a time. There were plenty of times that Cade stood under the poorly pressured shower head, teeth chattering whilst pretending to be somewhere tropical.

The imagination was a hell of a thing, yes it was.

If the food was bad you either ate it or went hungry until the next, less undesirable meal. When commissary ran low-which was the case for most incarcerated people with no money-you all but had no other option than to shove the food into the old gullet and wash it down along with any complaints you had. Cade was quick to adapt, and after only the first few months into his 13-year term, he had perfected holding his breath while shoveling random colored meats and vegetables into his mouth swiftly so that he could leave the chow hall as quickly and quietly as he had entered.

Eventually most prisoners tapped out and became institutionalized, finding daily routines to get them through, succumbing to the prison way. A terrible existence to live until release. Cade did all that he could not to allow himself to become institutionalized. He refused to live "burned out," as many on the inside called it, because he rejected the thought of prison being his normal life. He knew that nothing was completely 'burnt up to a crisp' about himself, especially during those times that his faith was strongest.

He'd always been awkward, never fitting in with crowds anywhere he went, and prison hadn't been any different for him. He was no thug or drug dealer, and he surely wasn't a badass or Mr. Popular by anyone's standards which made it hard for him to find his core group on the inside, essentially leaving him to his own world, a loner who would walk the track alone and bury his nose in books in the library. He was nothing more than a kid who had found himself on the wrong side of the gate and unfortunately, the vultures around him could smell it. The self-imposed isolation gave way to some preying upon his assumed weakness. Cade, however, was not weak in any sense of the word and the majority of the time, those who stepped on his toes or challenged him received negative results.

When a man's back was against the wall, the giant within him had decisions to make.

There was the choice to appear and back off all assailants with a fight-win or lose, life or death. Or there was a choice that he could be a coward, run and hide with the possibility of becoming a slave to another man in some way, not necessarily sexually either.

The latter was non-optional.

While away, he missed his family more than they could have ever imagined. Over the years he came up with many plans and ideas to win back their love, encouragement, admiration, and respect. He had always been determined to make everything right with them so they would be pleased with him when he resurfaced in his hometown.

Cade would always remember and hold onto some important words from an inmate serving life.

"You need to be more focused on getting your life together for *you*, rather than satisfying others and gaining their acceptance. You can't satisfy everyone, so let God deal with them and things will be greater later."

Home a year, with all the bad things behind him, Cade worked diligently towards his goals of fixing his family ties. Unfortunately, this seemingly perfect vision had become a rather difficult task, mainly because they didn't reciprocate his energy.

There were some evenings he would think about those 13 years, feeling his prison sentence had flown by at times and moved slower during others, though he knew 24 hours moved at the same speed regardless of how good or bad the days were. And there had been plenty of rough ones.

The times that moved slower were holidays and birthdays, days made harder by the fact that his whole core group of friends, along with his family, had abandoned him during his incarceration. To make matters worse, he'd only been allowed to see his daughter four times in the flesh the whole duration of his stay.

The obvious reason for the shortage of visits with his daughter was because the mother of his child held a grudge against him for leaving her alone to raise an infant child, which he wholeheartedly understood. However, for 13 years Cade had a longing for his daughter and the connection that was never able to thrive due to the separation. It was pure cruelty in his eyes from day one and did nothing to solve the problems they faced before, during or after his incarceration.

He had extensive experience working through difficult situations with Chance, the mother to his child, before he went to prison, but he never would've guessed that she would completely deny him the right to be the best father that he could possibly be, even under the conditions that had been imposed upon him after the wreck.

He'd met her and they'd begun dating while the two of them worked for chump change as waiters at a local eatery before he went into the military. They enjoyed the same music, had similar taste in recreational drugs and shortly after meeting, slept together, which resulted in Jacy-a beautiful bundle of blonde-haired joy. She was the main reason he went into the military in the first place. It had been worth the risk of his life in order to provide a better one for her, and he held no regrets because he knew if something were to happen to him during active duty his daughter would've been taken care of financially. She was just a baby-barely one year old-when the situation occurred, and soon after the incident he was restricted from seeing her.

Losing his freedom was one thing, but losing Jacy, his baby angel, left him with a thoroughly shattered heart.

Now that he was out, Cade tried his best to spend as much time with his fourteen-year old daughter as he could; while instilling some of his newfound Christian values in her along the way.

This rubbed Chance, with whom Cade lived-under her disabled mother's roof-the wrong way. She was definitely a poison, but with a lack of funds and nowhere to go once he was released from the halfway house, he decided to give it a go. The situation was temporary-only long enough for him to save up enough money to get a car and find his own place. It was quite obvious that no matter what he was doing or discussing with Jacy, heck, even his existence alone, seemed to rub Chance wrong and result in her having an attitude.

But there was only so much one man could take.

Upon his release his initial plan was to stay with his younger brother. There, he would save up the money to get settled back into life on the outside and finish the book series he'd come up with in prison. Upon completion, he would self-publish his own work-which he did-and sell them online in the case he didn't get a book deal-which he hadn't yet.

He'd sold a measly 37 copies and was an epic fail. Staying with his brother was a great idea at the time, considering no one else offered him a place to stay, but his sibling continuously brought up the past and all the pain he had caused his family by going to jail. Eventually Cade was kicked out, which forced him to move back to the halfway house. After surviving 13 years in the federal penitentiary, he had been evicted from the only place he had to live and considered himself a homeless man.

"You're a bad influence to my kids," his brother had told him. "It's better if you don't come around."

He came from a stable family and had been afforded a comfortable life although bouts of verbal and mental abuse had come with it. His drunkard of a father was a military man himself and had been very hard on Cade as well as his siblings, often going overboard to get a point across when juiced up on the pint.

The manslaughter conviction had greatly disappointed the patriarch, hence the lack of support Cade received from him while on "vacation." The rest of his family quickly followed suit, turning their backs also, leaving him feeling as if he were the worst man to ever live.

Luckily Chance's mother, Deborah, was a fellow Christian and his biggest supporter. Fresh out of the halfway house and in a time of great trouble, she offered him a spare room in her large home at the low end of the ghetto, so long as he helped with the bills and groceries. Most importantly, she wanted him to do all he could to be a part of Jacy's life now that he had the opportunity to do so.

But even just helping with bills was assaulting his pockets considering a good chunk of his money went to the court system for old fines and lawsuits against him for the deaths he had caused in the military. Plus, Chance was still bitter with him for his absence over the years and had impulsively decided to place him on child support even though he pleaded with her not to, given all the other things that he had going on in life.

I can persevere, he thought as he took in a deep breath of air outside his job, readying himself for the long but peaceful walk home. He swung his backpack around, unzipped the pouch and, removed his gloves quickly, placing them on his dry, weathered hands.

His coworker had given him the backpack that he wore now. In it was an old laptop he had gifted Cade to work on his books-a very kind gesture he would never forget for all his days. Aside from Deborah housing him, it was the nicest thing anyone had done for him since he'd returned home. In his mind the content on the computer would one day make him a rich man, someone who could change things in the world for the better.

His blessings were coming.

He was far from a perfect or deserving man and his flaws showed often, but with God all things were possible. He would have to keep that positive thinking every day from sun up to sun down in order to maintain hope in the harshest of situations.

"Without hope people have nothing," he had preached in a Bible study back in prison.

"You can always *hope* to have what you are lacking in life, and that hope is God. He will get you to where you need to be. But once you lose it-*Him*-you will lose yourself."

Cade drastically cleaned up his act with the help of his last cellmate, Dalton Ramsey, a former military marksman who found himself in prison after a stint with drugs and PTSD pushed him to rob banks. A Christian brother from Knoxville, Ramsey was something of a big brother figure to him and just what he needed at the time. When things were at their worst, inmates would lean on each other for support, and for some, their fellow cellmates were the only family they had, having been left for dead as Cade had been.

Cade promised to stay in touch with his friend from the outside, but oddly he hadn't heard a word back from Ramsey. This was strange because most people on the wrong side of the gate would jump at the opportunity for contact with the "free world," as it were called inside.

He could use a word or two from his old compadre, considering he didn't have any close associates on this side of the gate to speak to that would understand his struggle.

Exercising was his main escape while away and something Cade stuck with once on the outside, although adding muscle to his small frame had proved to be a major task.

Left alone in cells with only his imagination, he would also read books of all kinds and escape to other places, whether Earthly or otherworldly. This hobby became a love to him and soon he began writing books himself, with hopes of having a career of his own.

At first, his stories were a jumble of words thrown together in an attempt at making sense, feeble tries at horror and mystery. As he began to calm down and respect the trade, he grew into it and became better. Eventually, his niche became children books-the kind with a spiritual tone and young heroes protecting the world from evil, an idea given to him by Ramsey.

"It's best to write stories for kids with meaning," his friend had told him. So, he did. He used his time to study the Bible, using the stories he was most fascinated by to form his own stories. He created a series with a lead character and an arch nemesis led by none other than Satan himself, the negative side of all things.

In Cade's eyes, the devil definitely had a stronghold on Chance. While he was away cleaning up his life, she had become worse off, falling victim to drug addictions and living in her childhood home with their daughter. Working dead-end jobs to supply her habits until those fell through, she would steal from her mother's disability checks when times were hardest. This was not what Cade wanted his little girl to see in the woman who was supposed to be the most significant influence in her life.

Then again, what could he really do from prison? He was unable to create any type of bond with her over the years, and it wasn't like he expected her to simply turn to him or open up about her struggles. However, she could have asked him for advice and sprinkled her troubles on his anxiously available ears every now and then.

Now his voice fell on deaf ears.

There was no respect for him in the house, and he often had to hear what a loser he was from the two women he'd left alone for years. Being away for so long and now living under the roof of his child's grandmother made him an easy target. He loved his daughter more than he did himself but could not believe how disrespectful she had become in his absence. The only thing he could do for them was pray they would break the chains of anger the devil had placed on them.

His influence on Jacy fell short of Terry's, the drug-dealer/addict her mother dated. Coming around in his nice car, he would give her money before disappearing to the bedroom with Chance to do only God knew what.

The devil in Cade wanted to kill the gangly, tattooed fool, but the God in him knew it was wrong to hate any man, no matter how much filth they brought around his family.

There was also a tinge of jealousy in him because he still loved Chance and could not fully accept the fact that she hadn't been willing to give him a shot at making their relationship work upon his release. Instead, she was in a courtship with a knuckleheaded fool who would probably be the death of her.

The two men had butted heads on a few occasions, nearly coming to blows every time until Deborah broke them up. But Cade knew it was only a matter of time before he would have to put his hands on him.

He only hoped that he wouldn't go too far. Terry was a bad man who carried guns, so Cade figured his best option was to stay as clear of him as possible. He would need to save up enough money for a car and his own place-neither of which seemed to be in reach-and leave.

Upon his release, he had quickly found a job making crumbs at the tire warehouse. The job could have started out paying more, but his boss was a greedy man who knew he could take advantage of Cade's situation and pay him under market value to do back breaking work in harsh weather conditions. Surely a man who had just gotten out of prison and was down on his luck would not know any better and jump on the first offer thrown at him, right?

Desperate times could cause people to make desperate moves, and convenience was everything in Cade's world. So, naturally, he took the job. It was only a ten-minute walk away from the halfway house, and he could save money by not riding a bus while simultaneously avoiding being a burden on anyone by asking for a ride to work daily.

The work was rough, but worse than that they were vastly under-employed, causing Cade and his co-workers-five in total-to work the load of ten men. His boss valued saving as much money as he could by hiring the least amount of people in his business, all while complaining about why the jobs weren't being done quicker and more efficient.

Maybe, just maybe, Cade thought, it's because *we could use more people*!

Still, he would always be grateful for the chance to put money in his pockets and food in his stomach. The paychecks allowed him to pay off court fees and put money towards pending lawsuits as well as rent and groceries.

For now, it was a job, at least until he was able to sale more books. The stress he felt was heavier than any weight he'd lifted in prison. He fully intended to be a major success with writing but hadn't gotten over the hump since being home. He constantly had to hear about his failed attempts at success from Chance and Jacy, although if he made it...they would make it.

How could they not see that and support the dream?

"Loser," they would constantly call him. "Failure!"

Chance had some nerve to talk, he thought to himself as he adjusted the toboggan cap on his head and began his long trek home. He lived four miles away from his job, which conveniently gave him the chance to walk daily, an exercise he needed. He still did push-ups and sit-ups every day before and after work, but walking was always his favorite exercise. A bit of stress relief from it all, just him and his thoughts.

At least he still had his sanity, the one thing they could not take from him.

But he was beginning to wonder how long it would be before he lost that too.

2

He turned the corner and saw police lights ahead, slightly in the distance under the overpass beside a popular downtown bar/eatery and wondered what had happened. Although this part of town was where college kids and affluent people came to party, there were still sprinkles of dust that caused problems. Criminals, homeless people, drunken college kids, and the occasional prostitute milled about day and night going about their various activities.

Police lights never bothered him before his "vacation" at Club Fed, but now when he saw officers, he avoided them as best he could. He felt they were all against him, regardless if they were paid to protect and serve.

This was something he would have to get over, and quickly.

He could still feel the cold steel squeezing tightly around his wrist on the night of the accident, and yet again whenever he was moved from one prison to another.

As a sudden challenge to himself, he stared straight ahead and remained on his path home, directly into the lights rather than detouring to an alternate route.

"The police are only your enemy when you do wrong," he told himself.

Yeah, right.

This looked bad, Cade thought as he took in the scene. He counted at least six cop cars and an ambulance sitting beside the mandatory fire truck. Officers were directing people who were either parked in the area, or just trying to be nosey, to go around the commotion.

"Keep it moving!" a strong looking black officer with a voice like gravel instructed sternly.

Cade walked up to him and asked curiously, "What happened here?"

"You don't know?" the officer said looking down at him. Cade's face twitched and he shook his head, gave a shrug. "So, you have no information about any of this?" the officer asked.

"No," Cade answered lamely.

"Then kick rocks, with your nosey ass. Let's go, *keep it moving!*" The officer ordered him on his way.

Jerk, Cade thought with a snicker. And I'm supposed to feel comforted by these guys in blue?

He moved along as directed but couldn't help gazing in the direction of the action and saw that someone had clearly been murdered. Only time they brought out those infamous white sheets was when a life had been lost, right?

Sad, he thought, continuing to a stop sign at the four-way up ahead. Whoever was under that sheet had a beginning and now they had met a sad ending. They were someone's everything as a child and again, possibly, as a parent to child. And now that was all gone, snatched away senselessly.

Modern people were reaping what their ancestors sowed ages ago, and murder was just one of the many sins bringing humans closer to hellfire. *We were warned in the Bible, but do we listen?*

With that thought his mind switched over to the Word, but just as he began to mentally recite a verse a bum with a limp approached him.

"You got a couple dollars?" the bum asked.

Cade shook his head.

"Sorry, man. I'm barely surviving myself out here in this crazy world."

"Not so crazy," the bum said softly. He was an elderly black man with a raspy voice whose words came out painful and slow. "Once you separate yourself from it, you can live more comfortable."

I guess he's right, Cade thought. Continuing on his way, he said to the man, "You have a good night."

Leaving him where he stood, Cade crossed the street with a quickened step, obviously trying to get away.

"Come on, brother," the bum begged, hot on his heels. "Just a couple bucks. I'm trying to stay warm tonight."

"Let me guess," Cade said, stopping to look the man over, "you want me to give you some money so you can go buy alcohol and get drunk?"

The vagrant smelled as you'd think-like a combination of warm trash, a lack of showers, and three-day worn clothes. Cade gagged and stepped back from the man who had stepped closer and spoke.

"Funny you should ask. But, yes, getting drunk will keep me warm for the night-*and alive*!" the vagrant added with a toothless smile.

At least you have humor, Cade thought as he shook his head and went for his wallet. He reached in and pulled out three loose one's, and handed them to the man.

"Best I can do."

The bum's eyes lit up. "You sure, man?"

"Yea, man, it's cool," Cade said, hoping the few dollars he donated would send the bum on about his merry way. "I mean, what's a few bucks, right?" he continued, while thinking that if it weren't for Chance's mother, that could have easily been him on the streets, approaching strangers for a few loose dollars.

The homeless man looked up at Cade with an odd gaze of wonder and appreciation, his eyes exposing something of a sparkle, possibly reminiscing of a time when he was a vibrant young man, full of life and promise that merely flickered away out in the heart of the streets.

Life was cruel.

"You a noble, man," the bum said, stepping closer to Cade, causing him to tense up. The man smelled bad enough from where he was, no need to get any closer.

"I try to be. The Bible says the meek shall inherit the Earth, so, who knows, I may need *you* one day."

The bum snickered, confusing Cade. To his recollection he hadn't said anything funny.

"What's funny?" he asked the man.

"The Bible," the bum grumbled, looking away from Cade.

"You don't like the Bible?" Cade asked.

"Eh, not a personal favorite of mine. But, hey, whatever floats a person's boat."

The man rocked from side to side with a drunken stagger as he spoke. His face was stone, eye's murky, and yet he was unthreatening. Cade almost felt some kind of connection there in that moment the Bible was brought up.

Why was that?

"Well, maybe you should open the Bible up some day," Cade mustered. "Who knows, it might change your situation."

Chuckling, the homeless man scoffed, "Hasn't fully changed yours, has it? Have you gotten anything other than headaches since getting home?"

"How'd you know I just got home?"

"Your spirit told me."

Cade screwed his face. "What?"

"Mm-hm, that's right. The spirit is clearer than words, if you open up to it. And right now, your spirit is crying out for something."

"Is that right?" Cade stopped. "Crying out for what?"

"Your hearts desires, of course."

"Not unlike everyone else in this world," Cade said, turning to walk away. "Have a nice night."

About ten feet away he heard the vagabond calling after him. Hesitantly he peeked over his shoulder to see the man gaining ground.

"What is your deal?" Cade asked, annoyed, as he wheeled around to face the man under the streetlights. They were now standing in front of a restaurant which only opened at night and kept the downtown area alive with lights, music, and lots of loud conversations, as well as dancing and lively movements.

"I just wanted to say thank you for the donation," the bum said, out of breath.

"It's no big deal...you're welcome."

"You don't understand. I'm not talking about the money..." to Cade's surprise the bum produced a knot of cash. "I've got plenty of that."

"Unbelievable," Cade said, tossing his hands in the air, throwing his head back. "I've been duped by a bum. My life can't get any better."

"That's where you're wrong. It could get a lot better for you...I'm not your everyday homeless person, Cade."

"I'll say," was all that Cade could say, a tinge of entertainment in his voice. "And you know my name as well. Surprise, surprise."

"Surprise indeed." The bum smiled and pocketed his money.

"All that from begging, huh?" Cade said with obvious disgust.

"Don't knock it until you try it. It takes talent to be out here making money off the backs of others."

"That is *not* cool. Taking advantage of people isn't right at all."

"I agree, but it's a cruel world. If you don't get a little dirty out here it will eat you up. Won't even shit you out. Just let you sit in its belly stewing with regret."

"Very poetic," Cade quipped. "Why don't you just get a job? This stuff you're doing is illegal and dishonest work."

"Who defines *honest* work, Cade? You work for a man making millions off the backs of his employees, offering you no light at the end of this tunnel we call life. He's marking prices up and getting rich along the way, but he is considered to be doing good old honest American work. Knock it off. You don't want to do that your whole life. And he doesn't want you to go anywhere, because you are one of his workhorses. You really think he wants you to succeed at anything? *No!*"

I see his point, Cade admitted to himself. Why would a boss, no matter how much they liked you, want a good worker to leave their company?

"Who are you?" Cade had to ask.

"Funny you should ask..." He paused for dramatic effect. "I'm a man of many names and virtues who may just know a thing or two." He poked his head with his finger and smiled deeply as he stared into Cade, sending a chill through him.

"This is weird. You know things about me. Did somebody put you up to this? Are we being filmed?" He turned to look around.

"The camera of life is always rolling. You are never without eyes to watch you."

"Nice retort for a drunk."

"Now that you mention drunk, how about you let me buy you a drink?"

"I don't drink anymore," Cade said, thinking back to his wreck, that life-changing day. He hadn't had any alcohol since early on in his prison bid. Back in those times he was simply trying to drown his sorrows, but along the way he straightened up and found the Lord, had been living for Him since. He had every intention to continue doing so.

"Come on, one drink won't hurt you."

"Not my thing anymore."

"Ok, I see...this goes back to you saying something about the Bible. You a spiritual man, huh?"

"I try to be. Figured you would know that though."

"Jesus turned water to wine," the bum went on, ignoring Cade's sarcasm. "You should know that the Bible states that it is okay for you to have a sip for the sake of your stomach and illness."

"Yeah," Cade confirmed. "First Timothy. You know some of The Word, huh?" He couldn't help but hide his enthusiasm now, the Bible being one of the things he liked to talk about most in life.

"I know the whole Bible quite well. I still don't care for it though. Too many different interpretations, and it's a bit overrated to me. But I'll say this...whatever you are holding over your own head is not going to be judged on whether you have a drink or two."

"Right," Cade agreed. "But still..."

"How about this: I'll have a drink, and you come with me."

"What is the sense?" Cade said. "Why would I want to do that?"

"Have whatever you want, food or drink. I just want to show my appreciation to you for showing a good heart tonight."

"You do that with everyone that donates to you? Take them for food or a drink?"

"No."

"So why me? What did I do to deserve such an honor?" Cade said, his curiosity authentic.

"Nothing," the bum said stepping even closer to Cade. "But...I have something I want to share with you."

"What could you possibly have to share with me?"

The bum smiled that same smile, but this time there seemed to be some knowing in his eyes that Cade had missed.

"Funny you should ask..."

3

After several minutes of back and forth with the homeless man and his pleas for company, Cade finally submitted to his requests and turned to walk with him in the direction of the bar/restaurant on Jackson Street.

The business sat on a corner, the road straight ahead leading to the college campus, and the middle road that veered off to the right leading Cade straight to his dilapidated home on University Avenue.

The third road, which was to the right, led straight into the teeth of the homeless section of town where bums and addicts alike spend their days under the bridge. They would saunter up to the Rescue Mission for a meal during the day, ducking and dodging harsh living conditions in attempts to stay alive during the night.

Such a terrible way to live, Cade would think. But it could happen to anyone, so he didn't judge.

On weekends he would use his free time to do charitable work at the mission where, on numerous occasions, he met people who had been much different in their past life, many in better position's than he had ever been.

He'd met doctors, a former prom queen and various other people who hadn't been born homeless, causing him to realize that life had dealt them hands they could not play. But in the end, choices had to be made, and they made theirs, just as he had made his most recent one to join the toothless vagrant for whatever they were about to indulge in.

It was on these days, while working at the mission, that he had met and became quick friends with a preacher named Gil. He was a soft-spoken, big-hearted survivor of a deadly drinking habit that led to a painful divorce, which in turn, led him to his spiritual self-a life saved by grace. Gil now spent his days raising his two young daughters with his new wife and praising the Lord while doing all he could to help those in need. Cade stuck close by his side in order to draw strength from his positive energy.

The pastor was a big supporter of his writing, and apparently the only person who truly believed in him. Chance's mother wished him well, but Cade could smell the doubt in her. Weekly, he would bring the Gil excerpts from his books to critique. The feedback was always both phenomenal and spiritual.

"I know a changed man when I see one," Gil would preach to him. "The Lord has done miracles for you and He will only continue."

His friend was always there with encouraging words and Cade could not be more grateful. He was always there to remind him that God was working on delivering his blessings.

So, when would those blessings come? Waking up was the first of each day, true, but at some point, Cade wanted to see results for the actions he was taking, although he wasn't just doing God's work for rewards.

He often wondered if he was being impatient or simply chasing the wrong things. Did God have other plans for him that he wasn't seeing?

Walking into the eatery, it was no surprise Cade and the bum caught side eyed views from customers who clearly wondered what was going on with the two of them. It wasn't every day that the street people waltzed into a business such as this one.

Inside was no Met Gala, but the patrons of the restaurant were dressed well, especially in comparison to the rags the bum wore. Cade's beat up work clothes-black jeans and a dingy, matching coat-didn't exactly blend him in with the crowd either. He nervously clutched the backpack slung over his shoulder.

"I'm uncomfortable here," Cade expressed, as they made their way to the bar, all eyes on them. "I feel like everyone is watching me."

"They are. Not in the way that you would have them watch you though. You know, with admiration. Instead, they look down on you because of your appearance and who you are with, which is common in a judgmental world."

Cade had once read that there was no such thing as bad press…as long as the attention was on you, the crowd was under your control. He could not disagree with that quote any more than he did in that moment. As far as he was concerned this was the epitome of "bad press" and he was a bit embarrassed.

"It's all good," the bum assured him with a toothless, sly side grin as they each took a seat. "You're with me. You're good."

"What's that supposed to mean? I don't even know you."

"Do we *really* ever know anyone?"

This caused Cade to pause for a slight second. "I guess you're right," he responded, thoughtfully. "But it doesn't seem like anyone in here knows *you*."

"Oh, they know me well, actually." The bum said with confidence. "That's why they act the way they do. If the shoe was on the other foot, you would stare, too, wouldn't you?"

Cade opened his mouth to speak, but before he could get out a sound, the bartender was there to greet them. He was a big man with a red face and curly brown hair. The collar of his shirt was sweaty, as was his forehead.

"Help you gentlemen?" he asked, eyeing them with suspicion.

"I'll just have a double of something really strong," the bum replied.

"I bet you will," the tender said with a chuckle.

"Get this weekend started off right," the bum replied quickly.

"First off," the bartender said, leaning on the counter with his large palms, staring down onto the vagrant as people in the room watched on and silently cheered for the anticipatory eviction. "Who's paying for these drinks?"

"Funny you should ask," the bum said, producing the money he had shown Cade. He threw a hundred to the tender whose eyebrows arched to his hairline. "Keep the change off the tab."

This seemed to please the hefty man who checked the bill for authenticity with a marker.

"And for you?" he asked Cade. "Same thing?"

"No," Cade stopped him. "I'm not having anything other than water."

"Water, Cade?" the bum said incredulously. "Really? You are sitting at a bar and you order water?"

"Yes, water. I told you this before we came in here. Don't act surprised."

Nodding, the vagrant leaned into Cade and whispered, "I know all about the accident that sent you to prison. It wasn't your fault. So, I'd say it's about time to quit denying yourself a simple drink because of that one night."

"How do you know about that night?" Cade asked with a tinge of concern.

"Funny what you can learn eavesdropping at the rescue mission when someone is spilling their testimony to people trying to motivate them to change their lives. Why would you try to save everyone else's life when your own is in shambles?"

The two men shared a knowing glare. Cade nodded matter-of-factly, fully understanding how this man had known so much about him. There were so many homeless people walking the streets, it would be easy to forget a specific face, but for them to forget someone who had done a good deed for them was less likely.

As far as him trying to save others while his own life was falling apart, that was between he and God. Jesus had sacrificed much more than he had, so he knew he would be fine.

"Ok, well, still," was all Cade could formulate.

"You could use a drink," the bum prodded. "This I know. The spirit talks to me, remember?"

"I hear you..."

"So, what's it going to be?" the frustrated tender said, done with the moment the two men were sharing. The bar was filling quickly, and he had no time to wait on the seemingly indecisive duo, despite the hefty tip left in advance.

"Tell you what," the bum said, "make two of those drinks and set them right here-" he slapped the bar "-if he drinks, he drinks. If not, more for me."

"I'm sure you would love that," the tender said with a shrug before shuffling off to fix the drinks.

"He's not very nice," Cade said, eyeing the man.

"Loosen up some," the bum said, tapping Cade on the leg. "You're missing out on a good place being all tense."

"I suppose you're right," Cade acknowledged as he looked around the room. This *was* a nice establishment, he had to admit. They had done well with the design; the lighting was low enough to create some solace but still well-lit enough to see the faces of others in the crowd, bums and low life individuals included.

He'd previously ventured into the place in his imagination, visualizing it in his mind while walking to and from work. All fantasy, but now he was here with the most unlikely of company.

Life was full of these little surprises, wasn't it?

The drinks arrived and the tender sat a glass of water and an amber colored beverage in front of Cade. He simply stared at it, the desire to knock it down his throat dancing inside him, his resolve holding strong.

"I don't drink," he told himself. But the bum had been right; the accident was never his fault in the first place, so why should he not be able to enjoy a drink here and there to bring the stress down?

Because the Bible can provide me that which I need in tough times, was the answer that came from somewhere deep inside him.

"You boys aren't into anything bad, are you?" The tender asked suspiciously. "Awful lot of cash you carrying."

"There's no need to do any unsavory acts when you are in the presence of a best-selling author," the bum said, pointing to an obviously embarrassed Cade. "This is my friend, and he writes books. They're very good-"

"Ok, that's enough," Cade interjected. "This guy doesn't want to hear anything about my writing."

"Oh, no, it's cool," the tender said, his interest peaking. "Best-selling author, huh? Could've fooled me. I'd love to read your work. What's your book about?"

Was that a challenge? Cade wondered. Was he being questioned of his abilities because of his appearance and who he was with? Or did the bartender actually want to read his work?

Sensing Cade's unease, the bum spoke again. "Even has his laptop in the bag." He pointed, for the emphasis, to the pack slung over Cade's shoulder.

Laughing at the comical situation the tender simply turned and moved down the bar to the next customers, who were no doubt as entertained by the appearance of Cade and his company as anyone else in the building.

"Uncalled for, man," Cade said to the bum, his eyes a steely gaze, similar to the look parents gave to children after multiple times telling them to sit down and behave.

"Why?" the bum said, taking a sip of his drink and making a sour face. "You are an author, right?"

"Yeah, but...not like you made it seem. Best-seller? I haven't been able to sell anything." He looked away in defeat.

"Well, you won't be a best-seller unless you start moving like you already are one. You need more confidence when the subject is brought up. *Damn right you're an author!* What the mind can conceive, it can achieve-"

"Yeah, yeah, yeah...enough with all that law of attraction stuff. I know about it. I read books in prison on it."

"Then why not apply it to your daily life? It could help you."

"Who's to say I don't use it?"

"You... in your actions daily."

"Not as easy as you make it sound-"

"And it's not as *hard* as you make it seem. You are losing faith in yourself daily, and the little bit you do have left is shaken. It's all because of the life you live and the people involved in your day-to-day interactions. They make you feel like you are less than what you truly know you are, and they don't exactly respect your opinion on anything.

You will never be what you want with that attitude or with those people in your life. But, I'm here to change all of that and make you a believer in something more than that Bible in your backpack."

"Oh really?" Cade asked. "How can you help me when you are homeless?"

"Help can come from anywhere," the bum said. "Your first mistake would be to think otherwise. But who said I was homeless? Is that what you assumed?"

"Awe, man, I don't have the patience for all of this. How do you know so much about me? I didn't tell you what I have in my bag, so how do you know?"

"I told you already. I may know a thing or two."

At that moment Cade's attention was drawn to the entrance where a tall, handsome man with a strong jaw-line was walking in with a stunning, well-endowed brunette by his side. They looked like money, and moved with the confidence it brought.

I know him, Cade thought.

Being gone for thirteen years could make anyone's memory foggy, and more than once he'd run into people he knew from high school-friends and foes-that looked so much the same, yet so different. Easily done, with adding a few pounds here and there, or, as in this particular man's case, money and a pretty lady.

Some people had obviously gotten better.

But...who, exactly, was he again?

"I'll tell you something," Cade said, shaking back and hopping from his barstool. "I've had my fill of this. Shouldn't have come in here in the first place. Don't know what I was thinking."

"Where are you off to so soon?"

"Funny *you* should ask, considering you know everything else."

The bum was quiet now...

"I'm going home, where I would have been by now if it wasn't for you."

"You consider that place home? You're better off out here in the streets with the rest of these bums."

"Oh, so you know about my home life as well?"

"Yep. I know about Chance, her mother...Jacy..."

Cade squared up, ready to pounce on the man. He didn't know whether to assess him as a threat or just crazy, but either way it was a dangerous situation for random people on the street to know about his home life.

"I know everything," the bum said calmly, not in the least fazed by Cade's attempt at being gruff. "Please, sit back down."

"I don't want to sit down. I want to know who you are and how you know so much about my life. I don't recall telling you anything personally, and there's only so much one could learn by eavesdropping."

"Calm down."

"I am calm, but I won't be for long if you don't tell me who you are."

"I'm not sure you are ready to know who I really am," the bum said before turning his drink up and finishing it without so much as a squint.

"Not sure you can handle it."

Feeling emboldened, Cade said, "Try me."

"Okay," the bum said as he slid Cade's drink closer to himself. "You really want to know?"

"Wouldn't have asked otherwise," Cade replied.

The bum mulled this over as he eyed the rim of the glass he now held in his hand. As if speaking to someone in the distance he gave Cade an answer that made him want to run right out of the room.

"I'm the devil."

4

"*Wow*...." Cade said, leaning against the bar and shaking his head at the bum. "Can't say I saw that one coming."

"*I know, right!*" the so-called devil exclaimed. "Awe, man, I had to get it off of my chest. Thank you for being so cool about it. Didn't know if you would accept me after all you've heard about me in your life."

"Accept you?" Cade laughed. "I don't accept you as the devil. Either you are crazy or you are the devil, but either way, I want nothing to do with whatever game you got going on here. I'm out." With that, he turned his glass of water up and drained the glass.

"Thanks for the drink. If you see me again just walk the other way. If you come near me or my family, I will hurt you," he said as he turned to walk away.

As he moved through the crowd, he glanced at the mystery man and his date, trying hard to remember him.

"Being rude doesn't look so good on you," Cade heard the man calling after him. As he was about to push through the doors, he caught the bum's raspy voice. "Have a good cry in the shower tonight!"

This made Cade stop in his tracks, cringing at the cackles he heard around him, elicited by the comment the man back at the bar shouted out.

Oh, it's like that?

Cade turned slowly to face the man who merely looked off at the television on the wall, nursing his second drink.

He made his way back to the bar, his face solid.

"I figured that would bring you back," the bum said. "Pride is something else, isn't it?"

"Indeed, it would seem so," was all Cade could say as he sat down.

"It comes before the fall of all people, that pride."

"Why are you bothering me?"

"Bothering? Hey, man, I'm not trying to bother you. I want to make your life *better*!"

The bum took another sip, cool and causal, as if they were just two friends having drink after work. Nothing to see here, folks.

"How do you plan on doing that?" Cade asked, immediately regretting the question.

"Funny you should ask. There's a simple answer to that question, my friend."

"I'm not your friend."

"You should be."

Silence fell between the two of them.

"I haven't told anybody about..."

"The crying in the shower? I know. Too embarrassing? Makes you feel like less of a man if people know that you cry? No shame, everyone does it. Those who keep it inside are more dangerous to themselves than they know. You're not in prison anymore, Cade. If something hurts, let it be known. You laugh when something is funny, so why not be able to cry when something is painful? You have these emotions for a reason."

This was true, Cade thought. *Finally, something they fully agreed on.* His life *was* in shambles, and he readily admitted this. He'd served thirteen years in prison for something he felt he didn't need that kind of time for, and life wasn't working out how he had envisioned it would after he was released.

Chance, the woman he had once wanted to love forever, was an opiate junkie living with her disabled mother. To make matters worse, he actually depended on *them* for a place to live.

His daughter all but hated him and there had been no opportunity to even attempt to build the bond that he so desperately wanted, regardless of the fact that he was actually *allowed* to be in her life now days. And even though he could see Jacy every day while residing with her mother and grandmother, the two barely spoke. When they did, it ended in an argument or Cade being dissed simultaneously by her and Chance.

Yet, some of the most heartbreaking news that he had heard since coming home was when he learned that his mother had been diagnosed with Type-2 Diabetes and was now physically deteriorating. This was a total surprise, considering no one had ever stayed in touch long enough to tell him anything or offer any type of updates about his loved ones while he was away.

Nothing was going right, and late at night, when he was alone with his thoughts in the shower, he would cry out silently to the Lord for forgiveness and a chance to make things better.

So far it didn't seem as if he were being heard from above.

"I know about it," the bum said over his glass.

"I know." Cade shook his head, half shamed, half in wonder of how this man could know so much about him.

Because he is Satan in the flesh, he chuckled to himself. *Never. That was as likely as—Tommy.... Tommy Lawrence! That's who he is!* Cade thought, realizing now who the mystery man was that had walked inside the restaurant with the arm candy at his side.

The two had known each other very well in past years, even spending nights at one another's houses in elementary school. As the years passed and Tommy became more popular than Cade in high school, they had split-he, of course, ending up on the federal side of things after graduation and Tommy, star athlete that Cade could only dream of being, going off to college on a basketball scholarship, becoming a big fish in Knoxville's small pond.

Cade had never been big on sports but he could vaguely remember something about Tommy playing pro-ball overseas after a short stint in the professional league in America.

"Hold on..." he said before the bum could utter another word. He turned in the direction of his old friend, who was now being tended to by a skinny waitress with a pixie face and tight ponytail, leaving the bum in his place to nurse his drink.

"Tommy Buckets, is that you?" he asked as he got closer to the man's table.

Buckets was a moniker he'd picked up in high school, one that stuck after he developed a deep range jump shot that seemed to sink through the net every time the ball left his hands.

Cade wore a foolish grin on his face that made his excitement to see his old friend more than obvious, but it quickly evaporated when the pretty lady spoke.

"Can we not go out one night without all the fans hounding you?" her voice wasn't harsh or rude, and maybe she even meant to be comically sarcastic, but Cade knew her words were meant to hit home and push him away. Her perturbation was clear to see and he instantly felt uneasy about approaching them.

"Babe," Tommy Buckets said. "He's just a nice guy wanting to say hello, I'm sure."

"No, no," Cade stammered. "We went to school together, for years. It's me, Gabriel Cade. Remember?"

Buckets looked him over and realized that he did, indeed, remember him. Cade had been a scrawny kid who barely had a friend and could never get a date. He was the type to easily forget, his claim to fame-being the guy who barely graduated high school because he was always fighting, getting dismissed from class, or searching for his next high.

Gabriel Cade, a bona fide loser if ever there was one.

"Oh yeah," Tommy said, seemingly unimpressed. "You're the military guy? I remember you. Finally made it home I see."

"Um, yep. Yes, I have," Cade replied with a nervous chuckle. "Luckily. It's been a year now, but who's counting, right?"

"I'll take your word for it. How much time did you do?" Tommy asked, more interested than he should have been, but then again, many people were when in the presence of someone who had done a stretch.

Cade was hesitant, he didn't want this common exchange of pleasantries to turn to prison talk, as it did with so many curious people. Typically, he was asked a barrage of questions about his stay in "Club Fed" and they were usually the same ones: how was the food, did you get into fights, when did you get home?

Common folk talk. Talk he was tired of.

Leave prison in prison. This was his motto when he walked out of the gate. He didn't even look back when he got on the bus to leave, because to him, looking back symbolized a connection to that place, one he did not feel like he had.

"Thirteen years," Cade said, only loud enough for Buckets and his guest to hear.

"Whoa!" Tommy exclaimed, looking at his date, who was clearly unimpressed, her nose

buried in her menu. "That's a long time to be locked up."

Cade's face burned hot enough to fog his glasses up with steam. Tommy Buckets had always been known for being the most arrogant, brash individual at any event, but he could only hope that the man had changed and wouldn't make a spectacle of the situation at this moment.

"Yes," Cade said sheepishly, scratching an itch that suddenly appeared on his neck. "That's all done now."

Quietly sensing this was a sensitive subject Tommy switched his tone, happily redirecting the subject to all the success he was having with real estate and contracting.

Of course, the city still loved and supported him.

Everyone loved a winner.

"So, what are you doing with yourself these days?" Buckets asked Cade.

"Working...paying bills," Cade replied, hoping Tommy would not delve too deeply into his personal life.

"American dream," Buckets said, his sarcasm not lost on Cade one bit.

Get out of here while you are ahead, Cade thought.

"For now, it'll do. I'm in the process of trying to publish a whole series of books. Maybe things will look up soon."

Or later, a voice in his head said. He'd sent his books to a small number of publishers, who all denied him an opportunity. Because his funds were lacking, always being drained by Chance and the court system, self-publishing was looking like his only option. Being able to publish his books himself still didn't change the face that he didn't have the funds to market his product properly-as the failure in sales of the first book release had already shown.

"Books?" Buckets said, his date giving Cade a once over, as if to say, *Who, you? Books?* "Any offers?"

Scrunching his face, Cade had to admit that he had no offers yet and that things had been tougher than he had imagined from a prison cell. He would always tell guys behind the fence that failure was all in their heads, that they could do something great with themselves once they were home. Now he was beginning to question his own words.

Life was tough!

"Probably hard to get any positive results from anything running around with company like that," Tommy said, nodding over Cade's shoulder toward the bum at the bar.

Cade gazed over his shoulder and immediately turned back to explain himself.

"Oh him? No, no, no, I don't run with him-"

"That explains why you're with him." Buckets interjected.

"Not exactly with him," Cade said sheepishly.

"I hope you don't think that type of company is the kind you can succeed with. I mean, you would think that after all that time you would clean up your act-"

"Now wait a minute, man. I just met that guy tonight. As far as cleaning up my act, I became a God-fearing man in jail. I'm a Christian now, and I live for Him," Cade proudly stated, as he pointed up with both index fingers, to emphasize who *He* was.

Tommy wasn't moved at all and his date uttered, "You and everyone else that goes to jail."

Laughing, Buckets added, "I have a friend over at the DA's office, and he's brought more people to God than any preacher I know." His date joined in now with his laughter and Cade could tell that walking over to their table was a mistake and that he had quickly become the object of their entertainment.

Some people *don't* change.

"You killed people and went to jail for it," Buckets said, serious again. "And now you are at a bar having drinks with a beggar. I see great success in your future, buddy."

"Nobody really knows what happened that night but those who were there."

"They had a jury trial. The facts were presented, man."

"It's a long story."

"Well, unfortunately I don't have time to hear it," Buckets said, shutting Cade down. "Maybe you should put it in your book. See you around." Buckets picked up his menu and began scanning his options.

There it was, Cade thought. *The dismissal.* It took everything in him to remain humble and composed. Anger built up deep inside and his bowels burned with rage and hate.

You know better than to have these feelings, a voice said to him.

Yes, but wouldn't it feel so good to crack his head open with whatever you can get your hands on? a second voice asked.

Was that Satan's voice? Cade thought, as he turned to walk back to the bar and to the bum who was-

No longer there!

Great. Just great. A disappearing bum act to top off the humiliation he just had to endure.

He moved to the bar and the bartender who was in the middle of conversing with a handsome couple.

"Hey, where'd that guy go?"

"You mean your homeless buddy?" the tender asked snidely, eliciting laughter from his customers. "He said when you got done politicking, he would meet you outside." He pointed to an untouched drink on the bar-top. "He did leave that for you though. Said you would probably need it."

Cade spun on his heels and gazed out of the glass front of the building and saw the bum across the street, waving to him.

Who is this guy, really?

Satan?

No, can't be. That type of stuff only happened in the Bible or movies, right?

As he began to head toward the exit, he heard the bartender say, "Don't come back in here, with or without that guy. You got that?"

Right.

Did everyone have a bad attitude tonight? Cade asked himself, pushing through the door and crossing the street to the vagrant.

Before he could speak, the bum opened his mouth and uttered, "Sell me your soul, and you will never have to worry about people looking down on you again in life."

Sell me your soul, Cade heard again, although he was sure the man had only said it one time.

Was this guy serious?

"Okay, man," Cade said, perturbed, "this whole devil act is over and done with. I'm going home. You got your drinks-"

"I don't like how your old friend talked to you," the bum interrupted, taking Cade by surprise, obvious by the look on his face. "I mean, who is he supposed to be? "

"You must have a good pair of ears to have heard the conversation from the bar."

The bum held Cade's gaze, not a blink in his eye.

"I am who I say I am."

"Right, the devil," Cade said, a thought coming to him. "Lucifer should be spiffy, shouldn't he? All I see is an alcoholic."

"Maybe that's what I want you to see. Maybe, just maybe, I came to you in the flesh as reflection of how you feel internally."

"Whatever. You don't know how I feel inside."

"I've been on point about you thus far, haven't I? I even knew about you crying in the shower."

He had a point, Cade had to admit to himself. Crazy as it sounded.

"You see, Cade, when I come to people in the flesh with an offer it will either be in the way that they actually feel about themselves-hence this presentation-or I will come to you looking like your greatest desires. Either way, you shall be motivated to make a change in your life. But it's nice to know you think of me as being *spiffy*, as you say. I'll see about changing this attire to appease you."

Cade groaned and began his walk home.

"Just go away," he called out to the bum who followed closely, laboring with that painful limp. *"Please go away!"*

"Shoo, fly, don't bother me!" the bum sang aloud, finding the utmost humor in his antics.

Cade shook his head and pushed forward, crossing to the street that lead him home. The night was young, and all he wanted to do was exercise the day away, get something to eat and punch out a few lines on his laptop. He only hoped that after what had just happened in the last hour he could focus on his task.

His ego had been touched twice tonight: once by the bartender, and again by Tommy Buckets.

Damn them. *Damn them all!*

His jaw tightened as tears formed in his eyes. *Why is the process so hard?* he asked himself.

"Do not follow me home!" he said, wheeling around to face the bum.

The aggression with which Cade approached him didn't seem to bother the beggar.

"Listen," the bum said, scratching at the side of his head, which was covered in a ragged cap, "the people in your life may take you for granted, and they may not give you the respect you feel you deserve, but while they look at you like a loser and don't realize what a good man you are...*I do.*"

"*Ha!* If I'm such a good person why is my life hell right now?" Cade asked, stopping to look off the bridge into the distance at the interstate.

Waving the comment off, the "devil" said, "Hell is nothing more than what you make it. It's a mind-state. The Greeks at least had that much right with their Elysian Fields belief."

"No, Hell is an eternal lake of fire and torment. I didn't make it that way."

"Eternal fire, huh?" the "devil" said, thinking this over. "Have you ever been there? I mean...can you back this theory up with anything other than what you have been taught to believe?"

Cade was unable to form words in his throat.

"Didn't think so," the self-proclaimed devil said. "According to the Book of Genesis, no one was meant to die until they supposedly ate of that tree-the one that didn't exist, of course. Which means there is no Hell, because there was no need to create such a place for people who weren't meant to die to begin with. You're a writer, man. Use your head."

"Hell wasn't created for people. It was created for the devil."

"Whatever. You don't find it funny that Hell is so easy to get into, but Heaven is so hard to get into? They say only a few will get in, which leaves a lot of people to burn, if your Hell is real."

Cade listened attentively, unsure of how to respond to something as logical as what the man had just said.

"Surely no one will burn in any eternal fire. That place is merely a fable, Cade. People are too scared to end up there so they just accept the concept that Heaven is the place to go. But I assure you that Hell is just a low level of Heaven for those who want to continue living their lives the way they choose to, in the spiritual world."

Cade laughed aloud. "*Really!* You expect me to believe that trash?"

He began walking again towards home, slow enough to entertain the bum, but at a steady pace so as to get where he needed to be. Once he got to the stop sign at the end of the road, the bum's time would be up.

"No trash at all," the bum said as they passed a still train down below the bridge. "Hell is for those who don't want the party to end. It's for those who have lived painfully here on Earth and want to live the life they wanted all along. Gamble, have sex, get high, do whatever you desire there. Why suffer here on Earth just to be punished in the afterlife for not getting things right? That's stupid."

"I can't believe I'm actually listening to you. I'll tell you what...since you know so much about Hell, how 'bout you do us both a favor and go there."

The shoulders of the bum dropped in feigned defeat.

"Now, Cade, that's not nice. I bought you a drink and just got done telling you what a good person you are. In fact, aside from an old lady who is trying to end on good terms with God, you are the only person to give me anything today."

"All that money and you're telling me only two people were that generous today? I'm sure there were more."

"What world do you think you live in?"

"In that case, I don't *even* want to know where you got all that money. And you are *not* the devil, so stop with the act already."

"You don't believe me?"

Cade made a funny face and spoke in a condescending way. "What could have possibly given you that impression? The fact that I just said it?"

Searching the air for an answer the "devil" replied, "Yeah, that could be it. But I can prove I'm Satan."

"Ah, now you're talking." Cade wagged his index at the bum. "Ok, let's have it. Prove it. Turn yourself into a serpent right now."

"Why a serpent?"

"Because you were a serpent in the Bible, right, Satan?"

Chuckling as if he knew some great secret that Cade should be in on the bum said, "The whole serpent thing is nothing more than a figure of speech, Cade. It was an allegory, like most of the Bible. If you look closer at the Book of Genesis, you will see that the Lord cast the serpent to its belly. Which means it was never the slithering reptile you think of."

Cade contemplated this, knowing the verse the man spoke of, right after Adam followed Eve's advice to eat of the tree in the Garden of Eden.

"Never really thought of it like that."

"That's why you don't get paid to think," the vagrant quipped. "But now you have a new perspective on it-and perspective is everything in life. Go ahead and digest it, let it stick to your ribs."

"Figure of speech," Cade said, his finger pointing at the man, "I see what you just did there. Doesn't mean I agree with you on the whole serpent thing."

"That's the problem with religious folk-"

"I'm not religious. I'm spiritually connected to God."

"Whatever. You have *no clue* what you are talking about. The word 'religion' is Latin. It means *to reconnect* with God, and these funny, man-made rituals people do-singing, praying, fasting, or anything else that is *not* mandatory for salvation-fall right in with trying *to become one with* the Lord. *Religious.*

Aside from that, I just gave you something very logical to think about and you don't seem to care for this information, even when you know it has more logic than what you have been brainwashed to believe."

"Who you calling brainwashed?" Cade asked, insulted.

"The Bible is a poetic book, nothing more. There are biblical serpents all around you in this modern world. You just have another name for them now."

"And what name is that?"

"Humans."

"Touché'."

"Yes. And their venom can be much worse than any snake bite."

"You mean *us*, as in you and me. Humans, flesh and blood people."

Sighing, the man said, "I am but a spirit in a capsule. The human form cripples me."

"I hear you."

"I know you do, and that's what I want-for you to hear me out. People are so caught up in the image of the devil-dragons, snakes, smooth operators, even blonde headed white men with blue eyes. Ever heard that in prison?"

In fact, Cade had, many times, mostly out of the mouths of members of the Nation of Islam, a group he didn't care much for as a white man.

"So, let me guess, you want to offer me the world and everything in it-*if I sell you my soul.*"

"If it takes that."

"Even if you *were* the devil, my soul isn't for sale."

"You're better than anyone I've ever met then. Everyone has some kind of price, even though most people won't admit it. I know the truth. Sex, drugs, revenge, and, of course, the greatest deal maker of all-*money*. All prices. People are tempted by small desires, but what happens when the big guns come? I'm talking fame and fortune beyond their wildest dreams?"

"Quite the game you got going on, man," Cade surmised distantly. "Quite the game indeed. What's next? Are you going to take me up on a mountain top and tempt me like I'm Jesus? Do you want me to curse the name of God, like Job was asked to do?"

"I never tempted Jesus. Why would I do that? Even I knew that He couldn't be swayed. If He were God in the flesh, why would I tempt *Him*? What would be the point?"

Cade listened to the man ramble on.

"Oh, and one thing is for sure..." the bum said. "You are no Job, my friend. I'm still pissed about how that played out."

"Wait a minute," Cade said. "You're telling me that the Bible is lying about Jesus?"

"That's exactly what I'm saying. Every third letter of the phrase Holy Bible spells *lie*."

Cade thought it over. "Did you think that up all on your own?"

"As a matter of fact, I did. But it's the truth. Unlike these filthy preachers keeping all these elaborate lies alive. Who is any man that sins to bring the word of *God* to the people?"

Cade sped up his walk, moving ahead of the "devil." It was time to get the hell away from this fool.

Up ahead was a stop sign where he would make a left and be home free. This was where the two would have to part ways, but if the bum knew about what happened in his private life, then he probably knew where he lived.

"I'm not going to wake up tomorrow and see you in my front yard, am I?" he asked, half joking, half serious.

No reply.

"*Am I?*"

Stopping abruptly, Cade realized that he was now standing alone at the stop sign, not a single breathing body in sight.

What?

"*Hey!*" he called out to the wind.

The only response he got was the sound of passing cars in the distance.

Spinning around frantically, he searched for the man that had accosted him for money only an hour ago, but he was nowhere to be seen.

Okay, this is strange, Cade thought as he walked backwards, clutching the straps of his backpack and scanning his surroundings in amazement.

Well...

The bum's voice played over and over in his head as he turned and continued on his way home, relaying everything that he'd said.

The devil?

Ha!

Imagine that.

Yet, still, after only a short time with the man, Cade couldn't shake the thought of him.

He had a strong feeling he would see the vagrant again.

Surely he wasn't done speaking his piece, and that was exactly what Cade was most afraid of.

Maybe he was just some crazy old drunk who was well read in the Bible, and in the process of losing his mind on the streets, thought he was the devil. If that was the case, he wouldn't be the first to lose his noodles out here amongst the dregs of society.

Who knows?

All Cade could do now was hope that they would never see each other again.

As a Christian, the best he could do for the man was pray for his soul and hope that the preposterous thinking he was trying to spread would evaporate from his mind and put him back onto some sort of path of normalcy, whatever normalcy was nowadays.

The devil...

5

When Cade got home, he promptly washed down a granola bar with a cup of water, to give himself a bout of energy, to get through his daily calisthenics workout that included jumping jacks and sit-ups. Then, he took a quick shower and ate dinner before spending time on his laptop perfecting his new book. He would end the night with prayers and Bible study before shutting his eyes.

All by ten o'clock, every day.

He didn't have enough money to splurge on a gym membership, but the prison system had taught him to work with what he had, and what he had was self, in every aspect of life.

He opened his eyes the next morning, having slept like the dead-the whole world and the problems that it brought along with it, left out in the cold.

With any luck, those problems had died off in the frigidness under the night's empty sky.

He could only wish to be so lucky.

Watching the morning news, he caught the story of the murder on Jackson Street the night before. A lawyer was stabbed multiple times, left to bleed out, and found by a group of college kids making their way into the bar beside the parking lot.

Sad, Cade thought. The man had left behind a wife and kids. Now what would they do without him?

The devil had such a stronghold on the world and caused mass confusion among the people who inhabited it.

The devil!

His mind flashed back to the hobo he'd met only hours ago. Some kind of character he was with that claim.

Collecting his thoughts, he dropped to his knees and gave thanks to God for waking him up to see another day. No matter how hard life got, he had to remember that he still had a life worth living. When he woke up, he had to acknowledge that he had new opportunities ahead of him.

In the midst of asking for blessings his nose caught a whiff of Deborah's cooking down the hall. Every Saturday she would make a large breakfast for the family as a reward for making it through another week.

I need these prayers to be answered, he thought, getting to his feet. Indeed, he knew some were answered sooner than others, but his patience was wearing thin.

He pulled on a shirt and moved into the kitchen through the living room, the old, dusty floors grieving under his bare feet.

Any of the joy he had at the thought of having a pleasant meal with his daughter and Deborah was washed away like debris in the sand once the waves pulled back into the sea when he saw Chance and Terry sitting at the breakfast table.

Chance was wearing a pair of dirty jeans and an old sweater. She was blonde as could be, slim from drug use, and her eyes were low from a long night with lots of drugs and little sleep.

Next to her was Terry, the antagonist in Cade's life story. He was shirtless, with numerous fading tattoos on display. His blotched, drug-ridden skin matched Chance's own sheet of corroded flesh. His oily hair was straight back in braids, and Cade couldn't help but want to knock his gold teeth down his throat as he chewed a biscuit.

Chance was no longer the person he had fallen in love with so many years ago. She had been so vibrant when they first met years ago. Being that Cade had never been much of a lady's man back then, she was a catch for him-one he would have done anything for, in order to keep her around. She had been all he needed in those days.

Now she was just a fish he wanted to throw back into the water.

"Good morning," Deborah acknowledged him from her place at the stove. "Hope you're hungry."

"He's always hungry, mom," Chance drawled.

Sniveling, Terry said, "It's all that walking back and forth to work he does. That boy done worked up an appetite! Right, Gabriel?"

"Yeah," Cade said reluctantly, secretly hiding his disgust from the room. "Sure."

Why even hide his feelings? Everyone in the home knew that the two didn't like one another, and if Cade had *his* way, Terry would be sitting where he had just come home from a year ago, rotting in a cell for the rest of his days.

He hated to think that way about anyone, but Terry was scum, the dirt on the bottom of a shoe that had no laces and a flapping sole.

The worst.

He sold drugs on the side to support his habits along with Chance's, supplying Deborah with a few bucks here and there as a show of gratitude for not throwing him out or calling the cops to come get him when he was overdosing in the bathroom of her home, or worse, throwing some kind of fit that kept the whole house up at night.

Some of the fights between he and Chance were physical, but never life-threatening. However, she was still the mother of his child, so if and when that time came, Cade would be prepared to kill Terry.

Cade took a seat across from him, their eyes locking in a challenge, bait for one another to take. Terry was bigger than him, sure, but Cade was positive he was too slow and out of shape to take the fight. With this thought, he smiled inwardly.

Terry was all show-a frightened child malingering and portraying a gangster, yet he was nothing more than a junky, one of way too many running the streets of Knoxville, Tennessee claiming to be a hustler.

But the biggest problem wasn't Terry himself, rather the issues he would have to deal with if the two came to blows. Clearly, there would always remain the greatest severity of tension between the two men, especially while residing under the same roof. If Cade was to act on this tension at any point, he knew he would ultimately be forced out of the house shortly thereafter because the pressure that Chance would put on her mother. Chance's manipulative demeanor, quick anger and constant demands to do so would be too much for the old, disabled lady, and Cade knew her would be told to leave whether Terry instigated it or not.

And he was still on probation, which meant violent acts could be considered a cause for violation in his probation officer's eyes. His PO, a hardened lady with whom he had to check in once a month, would not be so quick to see his side of things.

Otherwise, he wouldn't be so passive. Hell, he might have slapped the biscuit right out of Terry's mouth just to see where things went.

Deborah was pouring coffee for Cade when Jacy walked into the kitchen. She was groggy and tight-eyed like most teenagers tended to be on Saturday mornings. Her long, blonde hair hung in tangles around her sweet face and in that moment,

Cade was struck by how much she looked like a younger version of her mother.

His heart sputtered every time he gazed upon what he had been a part of creating. He greeted her, only to get sleepy teenage grumbles in response.

"Mornin', baby girl," Terry said, to which he received a warm response-a strong hug and a kiss on the cheek.

Cade's own cheeks burned red, and he in that very moment he wanted to jump over the table to strangle the life right out of Terry. Why was he in competition with this man for the affection of *his* daughter-his own flesh and blood? Sure, he didn't make great money at the warehouse, but he worked for it. And what little was left over from his checks went towards her. He was trying to instill some semblance of morality, but the length of time he was away didn't make that an easy task.

He was now able to give her what he hadn't been capable of giving for so many years-his presence.

Unfortunately, Cade was fighting an uphill battle. Terry had been in her life much longer and had been more of a father to her than he had, even if he was a bad influence. Parenting is a lot like a job in that showing up is often more than half the battle. Jacy didn't share Cade's opinion of Terry. The drugs, the theft, the laziness-none of that mattered much to Jacy, simply because Terry had always been there. One day, Cade thought, she'll understand.

"You know, I'd like a hug and kiss sometimes," Cade said, unable to bite his tongue.

Rolling her eyes, Jacy said, "Whatever."

"Jacy," Deborah admonished, as she made her granddaughter a plate of food, "honor your mother *and* your father."

"Father?" Chance snorted. "Hell, Terry's more a father to her than Cade is. His attendance record has *certainly* trumped ole daddy's over here."

"Momma's got a point there, Gabriel," Jacy added cynically.

He hated when his daughter called him anything other than dad. People hardly called him by his first name anyway, and hadn't since his youth, but to have his only child disrespect him in such a way was a show of the time they lived in.

The Bible prophesized this would happen.

Cade glared at Chance, pain and anger obvious in his eyes. Not like she cared much. The disdain his daughter felt for him was a direct result of her, coming from all the lies she had filled Jacy's head with over the years. They were the kind of lies that would easily sway a child's thinking to one side of the parental see-saw, especially in his absence.

How could he defend himself if he wasn't around?

Silence filled the room like water in an empty cup, and though no words were spoken, everyone knew what was being thought.

No one had any respect for him, and whenever possible, they would all let it be known.

The pain his daughter and Chance felt at his absence over the last decade was obvious, and they weren't going to let it die any time soon. They struck at Cade's heart and pride whenever the opportunity presented itself.

In a way, he understood. He'd left Chance to raise a child alone, and he'd left Jacy to grow up without her father. Why wouldn't they hold a grudge?

Deborah rolled her eyes, knowing where this conversation was going. Couldn't everyone just eat breakfast and get along for once?

Nope. Not around here.

This household was chaos. Every day Cade tried to wrap his mind around a way to get away from it all.

If only he could sell his books.

If only...

"You have to excuse your dad," Chance said to Jacy. "Now that he is home, he wants to be a father."

She looked to Cade, daring him to retort as she dangled the bait in his face. This wasn't the first time she'd done this, and he was sure it would not be the last.

"I always wanted to be a father," he replied, his pride not letting him avoid the situation, even though he knew what she was doing. "You wouldn't let me. No visits, no pictures, no nothing. You alienated me from my child."

"Right, blame it all on me."

"No one else to blame it on."

"Yeah, Cade, there is. *You*! Don't commit a crime and you wouldn't have to worry about not seeing your daughter."

"Chance, we all know that he was taken away from us and was unable to do much of anything," Deborah said to her daughter. "But he's home now, and he's trying."

"Trying?" Chance snorted as she got up to get coffee. "With what, those dumb books he's writing? They don't even sell. He's living a pipe dream, momma. What he needs to do is get up and find a better job."

Cade looked off, his focus through the window and into the sunny winter day.

Take the high road, something deep inside him said.

"You know," he said calmly, "I would get a better job, but I don't think I want you having even more of my money to get high with."

Jacy's spoon stopped mid-air and eggs spilled off as she looked on with surprise. There was a twinkling bit of mischief in her eyes that reminded Cade of himself when he was her age.

She wanted to see a fight.

Yeap, she was *his* daughter-not Terry's.

Typically, he would take Chance's abuse and keep it moving, his head tucked between his legs like a wounded animal. He knew she harbored pain, and he knew some people had to express themselves multiple times before they got over it; but today he felt emboldened to buck up on her for some reason.

Her eyes burned deep into him.

"You're a loser," Chance said harshly. "You always have been, and you always will be. You think you have what it takes to be some big shot author, but you barely know your daughter. You spend more time doing God's work for those bums at the mission than you do with her. I know I have faults, but no one here likes that whole 'my-shit-don't-stink' Christian attitude you've had since you got home. We get enough of that around here already," she added, shooting a glance at her mother.

"*Amen!*" Terry said.

"Why don't you shut up?" Cade said to Terry.

"Make me shut up, boy. You wanna come for me?" Terry questioned instinctively as he stood up and leaned on the table with his hands.

Cade's adrenaline moved like interstate traffic, extremely quickly coursing through him. He wanted to pounce, so badly wanted to pounce, but remained quiet.

"I thought so. I'll knock your whole head off."

Jacy grunted. "Such a chump, dad."

"*Jacy!*" Deborah said.

"What? He lets mom talk to him however she wants to and he scared of Terry-"

"I'm not scared-" Cade said before being cut off by Terry.

"You should be. This ain't prison. It's different out here. Tough guys get dealt with quick in these streets."

Was that a threat? Cade wondered as he sipped his coffee.

"Get a real job, bum," Chance spat at Cade.

Bum? Cade thought.

"Get a job in general," Cade shot back, unable to bite his tongue. "You live off Terry and your mother's disability checks. I'm the bum? I have a real job. I *really* clock in and they *really* pay me to do it."

"You hate your job and they pay you shit! At least Terry makes his own way out here and don't have to answer to anybody."

"We'll see how long that lasts."

"Long as I want," Terry spoke up. "Unless you go off snitching."

"*I think everyone should just calm down,*" Deborah yelled.

"I think he needs to take life more seriously," Chance said.

Deborah looked at her child. "You're one to talk."

"Whatever," Chance mumbled. Looking at Cade, Chance continued, "All I'm saying is I think you can do more. It's not our fault you got all drunk and killed those boys. You took those people's babies and left your own to grow up without you."

"The worst part of it all is I left her alone with *you*, so she could watch you destroy yourself."

"I don't want to hear all this," Jacy said as she got up and took her plate to another room.

"Uh-oh," Chance called after her. "Somebody has a sensitive side. Guess you are your daddy's kid."

Again, Terry snickered as he munched on a piece of sausage.

Again, Cade wanted to pounce.

"How many times do I have to tell you I wasn't drunk that night?" Cade said, reflecting vividly on the night of the incident, hearing the sirens in his head.

He shuttered every time the subject was brought up, and he figured Chance knew this, which was why she blatantly disrespected the fact that he never wanted to talk about it, or prison in general.

"Right..." Chance said with disregard. "Which is why the system sent you away for all that time. Guess they got it all wrong, huh?"

You have no idea, Cade wanted to say. Over the years he had seen so much injustice in the system; there were plenty of men doing extensive time, numerous years in prison for small amounts of drugs that didn't even add up to a small side of mashed potatoes. In recent years, a handful had been released on clemency, having fought for their freedom and receiving the blessing of God to walk out a free man.

But in his case, there had been no such miracle. He lived by the" No Regrets" rule, meaning his life was in God's hands, and whatever happened was for the good of the Lord. He was a writer, but God was the big dog of all authors.

Whatever He writes, I will follow.

Because it built character, he would continue to live by this rule. It had made him the man he was now. Had he never gone to prison, there was no telling what his life would be like. Maybe he would be like Chance and Terry, or possibly a rich and famous man. Or maybe he would have ended up in the streets like the bum he had met the night before.

The bum!

Where did he disappear to last night? Was he on drugs? One thing was sure, a mental case like that had no business walking the streets freely spewing hatred for the good book.

Never mind that. Cade just hoped to not ever see him again.

He opened his mouth to speak when there was a knock at the door, causing everyone's attention to peak.

"I'll get it!" Jacy called out, footsteps heavy on the floor as she moved to the front of the house.

"Anybody expecting a guest at such an early hour?" Deborah asked, eyeing Chance and Terry with suspicion. In true addict form, they each had a number of friends with similar interest stopping by at all times, mostly at night, when the freaks and zombies came out from their holes and divots under rocks.

They both shook their heads and looked to Cade who simply shrugged.

A moment later Jacy walked into the kitchen, a grin on her face as she leaned against the doorjamb.

"It's for you," she said, pointing to her father.

"Him?" Chance said, sounding more surprised than Cade looked. "Is it a cop? He damn sure doesn't have friends."

Cade shot her a look as he began to stand from his seat.

"Apparently he does," Jacy replied, giggling. "A pretty cool one, too. A guy named Lucifer. That can't be his real name, is it, Gabriel?"

He froze in a half rise from his chair, looking deep into his daughter's eyes with a fear she could sense immediately, causing her grin to vanish.

His mannerisms didn't go unnoticed and Chance asked, "What's wrong with you?"

"Uh, nothing," he lied terribly as he moved beside Jacy and quietly said, "you said his name was Lucifer? Is it a homeless guy?"

Jacy snorted, "Homeless? Not dressed the way he is. And he was driving a sports car-"

"Awe God!"

He quickly moved past her and through the living room to the front door.

Nothing, no one.

Imagine that, another disappearing act.

"No one's here!" He called out.

He turned back to see everyone standing in the hallway, expecting some kind of explanation. Before he could formulate one, the sound of a car horn blared from outside.

He stepped out on the front porch, followed closely by the nosey group in the house, engulfed by the repeated honking of the horn, over and over and over again.

A bright red sports car sat in front of the house. To Cade's dismay he knew the driver.

There he was....

"Satan."

6

His heart sunk and his throat tightened as if someone's hands were trying to suffocate the life out of him right there on the porch.

What...is...he...doing here!

In front of the house, leaning against a shiny red Lamborghini parked in the middle of the street, was the man from the previous night-only he wasn't a bum anymore, just as Jacy had said.

But how?

The two locked eyes in a moment of recognition.

The "devil" wore a charcoal suit, a far cry from his duds the previous night. His hair was cleanly cropped, and even from were Cade stood on the porch he could tell that his teeth were pearly white like snow, due to the huge smile on his face-that felt eerie in a strange way.

"Gabriel Cade!" the "devil" called from where he stood. *"My main man!"*

No, No, No! I'm not your main man. Not today. Not any day!

Quickly, a barefoot Cade took the steps two at a time and approached the man, stopping short to examine him in wide-eyed wondered, marveling at the change of his appearance.

This can't be real, Cade thought, as he eyed the people moving about on the sidewalks of the neighborhood, their watchful eyes on the fancy car.

"What are you doing here?" he asked.

"You know what I'm doing here. Got spiffy for you too."

"Nice suit," Cade begrudgingly acknowledged.

"You know my brand," the man said, holding open the suit jacket to show the designer label. "They wrote a book on it."

This isn't real, Cade thought with a frown.

"And check it out..." the man added, shaking his leg and stomping twice, "fixed my limp."

Forget the limp, Cade thought. How had his voice gone from scratchy to smooth as caramel without a hitch? That was the real question. Last night was no act-the man he met was real, and he *did* walk with a limp while talking with a rasp.

"What are you doing with this car?"

"Speeding," the "devil" said with a toothy grin.

"You know what, I don't even want to know where you got this thing."

"It's mine. Yours if you want it."

"Dude, you are drawing way too much attention. If you don't leave now," Cade said, teeth gritted, "I'll call the cops."

"Really, Gabriel? You snitching on people now? Imagine what the guys back in prison would say if they got wind of that?"

"I don't care what they would say! You need to leave, now!"

The man chuckled as he waved over Cade's shoulder, causing him to turn and see everyone from inside the house on the porch, watching intently. Terry wore a shirt now, leaning on the rail, aiming a disparaging look right at Cade.

"Hello!" the "devil" called to them.

Cade's stomach flipped.

"Hi," Deborah called back, her arm around Jacy. "How are you?"

"Marvelous!"

"Ok," Cade called out to the group on the porch. "Nothing to see here. Just going to talk to him a moment and he'll be on his way."

With that, Chance began to step from the porch. Cade stepped to the stairs to meet her with no hesitation.

"Go inside," he said to her, his distress obvious.

She scrunched her face and asked, "Who is this guy, really?"

He paused, searching for an answer that would suffice. "A salesman," he lied.

She eyed him with suspicion.

"What kind of salesman?" Chance questioned, not believing him.

"Uhm, vacuum."

"We don't have carpet," Chance responded.

"It's not nice to lie to the lady, Gabriel," he heard the man call out from behind him. He frowned and hung his head in shame as Chance's eyebrows arched.

She said, "Nope, it's not nice to lie, Cade." Pushing past him with her shoulder, she left him standing in place as she approached the man leaning against the fancy car, his hand already extended to her.

"*Put your hand down,*" she barked. "Who are you, and what do you want?"

"I'm a man of many names and virtues."

"Whatever. You a Jehovah's Witness or something?"

Cade came up beside her just as the man spoke.

"Jehovah's witness? Not me. If anything, I'm a backsliding, filthy sinner."

"Well, join the crowd," Chance spat. "I backslide, front slide, side to side slide, all of that stuff."

"In that case, we should be friends," the well-dressed man said. He had such a cool confidence about him, and that made Chance stand straight, shoulders thrown back in defiance.

"I don't know you to be your friend."

"Oh, you know me. Everyone knows me."

"Is that right?" She asked, standing akimbo, expecting an answer that would suffice.

"*No!*" Cade interjected. "You two don't know each other."

"Would you shut up?" Chance barked at him, causing his face to flush.

The "devil" crossed his arms and chuckled at Cade's expense-standing there barefoot, with no jacket, visibly cold and thoroughly shamed by the chastising Chance gave him.

"I see she's as hard to handle as I've heard," he said.

"Heard? What you heard about me?" She turned to Cade. "You been telling this fool about me?"

Cade's tongue was in a knot and he could not formulate a single word, his cowardice on full display.

"You just going to let her talk to you like that, Gabriel?" the man asked. "You've got to handle her better than that, man."

Cade looked at the man in the suit with dismay, knowing that he was purposely pushing buttons in Chance, who was now sizing him up with the look of a predator ready to strike.

"Handle me?" she said. "Let me tell you something. No one can *handle* me."

"I beg to differ," the man said, tilting his head to the side, calmly adding, "you aren't wearing that sweater cause it's cold out. You're hiding something."

She opened her mouth to speak but was cut off by the man as Cade watched on desperately, wishing this would all end.

He had no idea who this man really was. How had he switched his appearance so quickly over night? One thing he did know was the guy had a strong confidence, but Chance's bite could break through his exterior and straight to his bravado.

"I'd say that the dope running through your veins is your master, and I see a puppeteer standing right there on that porch." He pointed to Terry, who tensed up, and grimaced at them.

"Hey stop-" Cade started before Chance's hand met his face with a vicious slap, causing him to back up a few steps.

"Have you been telling him my business?"

"No," Cade groaned, holding his face with one hand, his other up to prevent being hit again. This was not the first time she had hit him, but what could he do, fight her? "I don't know how he knows so much about us."

Again, the man laughed at the scene playing out in front of him. Chance scowled at him with venom in her eyes.

"Funny?" Chance asked him.

"Hilarious," was the only response she got.

Turning to Terry she waved for him to come from the porch and Cade's pulse spiked.

This was about to be bad.

"We'll see," Chance said to the man, who was unmoved by her threat.

"Indeed, we will," he calmly replied.

Terry stepped from the porch and came to a standstill in front of the man, arm around Chance's shoulder as Cade stood off to the side, anxiously awaiting what was to come while silently praying to God that this would not go the way that it appeared to be going.

"What's up, baby? You got a problem you need daddy to take care of?" Terry inquired, while kissing her on the cheek and eyeing the man leaning against the car, with both suspicion, and grit as he bared his gold teeth.

"I want him to leave," Chance said, nodding to the "devil." "Like, yesterday."

"Enough said. Scram, homeboy." He removed his arm from her shoulder and sized up the man in the fancy suit.

"Not without him," "Satan" said without flinching.

Chance and Terry turned to Cade whose face was suddenly drained of all color.

"This your boyfriend or something?" Terry cackled. "You a fruit?"

"At least he's dating up," Chance added, provoking more laughter from her boyfriend. "Done got you a rich one?"

The "devil" was stone faced, not the slightest bit entertained.

"This is the life you want to live?" he asked Cade. "Under the roof with a couple of junkies who don't even respect you when they should be praising you?"

"Junkies?" Terry repeated, insulted. "Man, who you think you are, coming around here all fly and running your mouth like you're a big dog or something?"

"I am fly though, right?" the "devil" said, dismissive of Terry and anything else he had to say past the compliment.

Terry raised his shirt, exposing a pistol on his waist. "Anybody can get it around here. You want some smoke?"

Chance smirked as if the game was in hand, but to her surprise, the man calmly pulled a cigar from his jacket pocket and lit it with a fancy lighter.

"I want all the smoke you can offer," he said, taking a long drag and blowing the smoke in Terry's direction. "But be careful...tough guys get dealt with quick out here in these streets. Isn't that what you told my boyfriend earlier?"

Terry mulled this over and suddenly pulled the gun from his waist and stuck it in the man's face, drawing no reaction from him, which made him even more frustrated with the situation.

Who the hell was this standing in front of him?

"Whoa!" Cade exclaimed. "Come on, Terry, is that really necessary?"

Terry turned the gun on Cade.

"Terry, no!" Deborah yelled as Jacy let out a squeal.

"Say something else and get shot! *"* Terry said to Cade, whose lips sealed together like the licked flap of an envelope.

"He won't shoot you, Cade," the "devil' said calmly. "You and I know damn well he is a coward. He's just trying to scare you."

Terry turned the gun back to the "devil".

"That's right," the "devil" said. "Aim that piece of shit .22 at me."

"You don't think I'll pop you right here?" Terry said.

"I don't think, I know."

Even in the cold of the day, Terry could feel the heat from the challenge the man presented, sweat beading on his forehead as he held the gun tightly.

"I'm going to call the police." Deborah called from the porch.

"No need," the "devil" assured her. "Nothing's going to happen here."

"You don't know me," Terry said.

"Oh, but I do," said the "devil" eerily. "Pride is the head of all sins, and it comes before everyone's fall. Right now, you would rather take a chance of going to jail or having me hurt you just to put on a show and look tough."

Terry fidgeted, cracked his neck and flexed his shoulders.

"That's right, look at you, all scared right now like a little *bitch*."

"I think you two better leave," said Terry.

"That's all I wanted to begin with," the "devil" said, looking to Cade for a response.

Terry turned his head to look at Cade as well, a mistake he would regret immediately.

With the swiftness of tornado wind, the "devil" snatched Terry's pistol-toting hand, pulled him forward, and relieved him of the weapon as he swept his legs off the ground with a quick kick, sending him to the cold dirt, flat on his back.

Tossing the weapon up into the yard and looking down on him the "devil" said, "I'm not scared of you, and I damn sure don't have any probation on my back to violate me if I whoop your head. Isn't that what's holding you back, Cade? You do like to be called by your last name instead of Gabriel, right?"

Yes, he did, and there was a good reason for it too.

Cade looked into the man's eyes, his pupils begging for him to leave. He had caused enough trouble so far, and he couldn't afford anymore.

Terry struggled back to his feet and squared up with the "devil". He took a wild swing, missing badly, the "devil" making a smooth parrying move to avoid it, sliding to his right and stepping away from the car.

Again, a swing. Again, a miss.

Again and again, more misses.

Deborah and Jacy, moved from the porch pleading with them to stop the foolishness as Cade and Chance stood back. Terry was sweating now, his breathing labored as he leaned on his knees.

"Pathetic little man," the "devil" said to him humorously as he leaned against the car again.

"Come on, Terry, what happened to all that tough talk you had for me a second ago?"

Terry looked up at him, weakness and defeat in his eyes.

"Just leave," Chance said to Cade. "And take your friend with you. Don't even bother to come back."

Cade was at a loss for words, but the "devil" quickly stepped in to be his reasoning.

"You don't think he really wants to be here, do you?" he said, facing Chance, his attention no longer on the wheezing and defeated Terry. "You are the biggest headache he has had to deal with since he came home. He could do no better than to leave, which is why I am here."

He turned to Cade. "You coming with me?"

"No!" Cade whined.

Suddenly, Terry, having caught his second wind, lunged at the "devil", attempting to wrap him in a bear hug. Problem was, he left himself open, allowing for his throat to be gripped by a strong hand that lifted him off the ground, leaving his feet dangling and kicking for the grass below him.

"Put him down!" Jacy screamed fearfully, yet amazed how any man could lift another with one hand and hold him there as if he were nothing more than a piece of material to be examined.

"What do you say, Cade..." the "devil" said. "You think I should throw him on the roof?"

"No!" everyone said in unison.

Chance stood frozen in shock, having met the "devil's" eye and catching a glimpse of something that made her step back.

Cade pleaded for the man to stop causing trouble.

"All I ask is that you listen to what I have to say," the "devil" said without looking at Cade.

"You don't like what I have to share then I will take you anywhere you want to go, and I will leave you alone. Promise."

Cade thought it over as he looked up at Terry whose eyes were clinched tight. His face was flushed red and spit hopped from his mouth as his lungs struggled for air. Oh, how he would love to allow the man in the suit to choke the life out of him and be done with the filth that he was for good. But that wouldn't play over too well with the cops when they came for an explanation.

What could he say?

The devil did it?

Then there was the fact that he was a forgiving Christian man, and he could not just stand by while another man had the life snatched out of his body, no matter how much he disapproved of him as a person.

But this was surely an incredible site to see! Cade thought. To think, big bad Terry manhandled like the child he knew he was. Admittedly, he liked the way the man operated, so smooth and debonair, but this had to be wrong.

Still, he admired that attribute, and he wanted so much to be as sure of self as the man-whoever he really was.

"Let him go, man!" Cade voiced.

The "devil" looked to him now. "Go get a jacket and some shoes, and get your ass in the car."

Cade's eyes met the three women of the household, all unsure of what to do, scared to approach someone who so easily embarrassed a man they all feared.

"*Okay!* Just put him down."

Smiling a devious smile, the "devil" said, "Whatever you desire. You say the word and I gotcha."

With that, he let Terry fall to the ground, a defeated man.

Chance hurried to his side as he heaved air into his lungs. Deborah held Jacy close as the two of them watched on.

"Go," the "devil" calmly said to Cade who looked to his family one last time before heading inside to retrieve some warm clothing.

A moment later he returned, nervous as ever about where the man would be taking him, wondering if he were in any kind of danger.

But why would I be? Cade thought to himself. He'd come as a defender to him, a bully to the bully in the household.

The "devil" tossed him the keys to the car and said, "Drive."

"No," Cade said, tossing the keys back. The "devil" let them hit the ground without attempting a catch.

"That wasn't a question."

Moving to the passenger side of the car the "devil" lifted the door to the sky and disappeared inside.

Cade turned to Chance and Jacy who were now helping Terry back up the stairs and into the house. Deborah could only shake her head at him as he searched for words deep within him, finding none, his sorrow spoken with his eyes.

"You may need to get your things later. I don't think you have a place here anymore."

"Deb-"

She held up a hand and cut him off, "Won't be safe for you here. Terry will want blood."

She was right, he thought, as he watched her turn and move into the house. This would no longer be a safe place for him to lay his head, and it was all because of the man sitting in the fancy car.

He gritted his teeth, yet smiled inwardly at the thought of how easily Terry had been put in his place, assisted into the house like an elderly.

But he was going to be homeless now, just like so many of the people he had tried to help since he had been home, even though he wasn't in the best position to help anyone.

Now he would possibly be living with them.

This was his reward?

God, where are you at? Why is this happening to me?

With no immediate answer coming to him from above, he decided to get into the car. At least he would be out of the cold for now.

He had close to five hundred dollars saved up in his bank account, but of course that would only get him so far. Half of that wouldn't even be good enough as a down payment at most apartments worth living in. Even though he would make another small check in the coming week most of it would be garnished, leaving him with only so much to add to his meager savings. Not to mention he would have to get accepted for an apartment, which, if he didn't because of his background or lack of credit, would be at least forty dollars down the drain for an application fee.

He could not afford to get denied by multiple spots.

His chest tightened at the thought of how his life had crashed over the years, and how much worse it could possibly get now. He wasn't the worst person in the world, so why the punishment? There was no way he could fathom why his life was what it was, but he knew his faith was being tested.

Where would he go? He wondered as he snatched the keys from the ground and moved to the driver's side door.

"Ok," he said aloud to the man in the car as he pulled the door of the car upwards towards the God who was not answering him back at the moment, "you got what you wan-"

He stopped short of finishing his sentence, his heart nearly jumping from his chest.

It was no surprise the man was gone, again.

7

"Come on!" Cade yelled as he leaned inside the car, exasperated, hands on the seat as he shook his head in wonder of how this day could get any worse.

Why does he do this?

Who was this character?

You know who I am! Came the "devil's" booming voice from nowhere.

Cade wheeled around quickly, hitting his head against the roof of the car. As he held the back of his skull, the laughter of the missing man played constantly in his head like a popular radio song.

Yet he was nowhere to be seen as Cade scanned the neighbors milling about on the cold but sunny day, scatterings of people sitting on their porches or congregating at the corner store a block over.

Nowhere!

"Gabriel," he heard from behind him.

He turned to see Jacy standing on the porch. The two shared a silent moment before she stepped from the porch and handed him a piece of paper.

She patted him on the shoulder. "I know you mean well," she said before turning back to walk inside.

"Jacy," he called to her. She turned to him. "I love you so much. I'm sorry I haven't always been here for you, but I will do everything that I can to make things better for you."

"I know you will."

With that show of confidence in him, she warmed his body enough to forget about the weather, if only just for a few seconds.

As she walked back into the house, he looked at the piece paper she had given him, a smile appearing on his face. On it was a Bible verse that he had written down and slid under her door, something that he had done every day since moving in. While studying his Bible at night, he would find a scripture, write it down, and slide it under her door so that she could start her day with the Lord's promises. He wanted to sprinkle her with small doses of The Word, knowing she was only a young lady and could not digest everything that he had learned over the years in one day. So, a verse a day would suffice.

But his daughter had given him the verse this time. Romans 8:31.

Just as he was about to read it aloud to himself his cell phone rang in his pocket.

The number read 666-666-666

What the...?

Looking around again for the man he timidly answered the phone.

"If God be with you, who can be against you?" came the voice of the "devil", smooth as ever, quoting the verse that was written on the paper. "I'd say right about now the whole world is against you, my man. You're newly homeless and without a friend or family member to turn to. For all your efforts to help people and be a good man, your God doesn't answer your prayers."

"Why are you doing this?"

Chuckling on the other line the "devil" replied, "How many times do I have to answer your dumb questions? How about you start asking the *right* questions?"

"Here's a question for you then: if you're the devil, how could you have actually choked Terry with your bare hands? The devil isn't supposed to be able to touch people physically."

"Who in the world told you that? And why would you believe such nonsense? Can you show that to me in the Bible? Show me where it tells you I can't physically touch what I want to."

No response from Cade.

"I thought so. As I said, ask the *right* questions, like what will I do for you if you sell me your soul."

"I do *not* want to sell you my soul, and you are *not* the devil. What you did out here today was *not* cool. Now, thanks to you, I have nowhere to go!"

"Tell you what, Cade...open the trunk."

"Why?"

The "devil" let out a sigh. "Questions, questions, questions," he said.

Suddenly the trunk-located at the front of the car-popped open. Cade jumped back, both startled and confused.

"You like that, huh?" "Satan" said as Cade continued to look around for him.

He had to be around here in order to open the trunk. Or did he? Electronics weren't what they were when he had left for prison, and he was still trying to figure it all out.

"I know what you're thinking..."

"Do you?" Cade asked as he moved to the front of the car and discovered a bag sitting next to a suit that was equally as nice as the one the "devil" had on.

"Indeed, I do. You're thinking... 'why would God allow the devil to come and tempt me to sell my soul.' The answer to that is simple. *He didn't.* You see, nothing in your life is scripted and already foreknown. Things just happen and play out the way they do. I'm here to help a man in need. Will you let me help you?"

"No!" Cade said, slamming the trunk closed. "Now come get your car and get out of my life."

"Here you go, acting all tough again. I understand. Truly I do. But didn't I just hear you tell your lovely young daughter you would do everything you could to make things better for her?"

"Stay away from my daughter," Cade warned.

"Anything you ask. I told you, say the word, I got you."

"Then leave me alone as well."

"Anything but *that*," laughed the "devil."

Placing a hand to the side of his head while leaning against the car, Cade cried out, *"Why?"*

"You know what," the "devil" snapped. "I don't really think I want to help your ungrateful ass anymore. All you do is whine. How'd you ever survive in prison anyway? I will take your blessings and give them to someone who can appreciate them. *Now, bring me my car!*"

"No, you can come back and get your car, yourself," Cade snapped back.

"Do you want to end up like Terry?"

Cade thought about that for a moment.

"Bring me my car," the "devil" repeated, enunciating each word loud and clear.

"I can't. I don't know where you are," Cade said honestly. "Besides, this car is not in my name, and I don't have the insurance-"

"Cut the excuses, Cade. Check the dash. Everything is taken care of. Get in the car and drive it to me. Drop it off, but take the bag in the trunk with you and have a nice life."

"What's in the bag?" Cade asked.

"A million bucks." The "the devil" said, sensing Cade's brows raise and laughing heavily. *"Sike!* Fooled you. If you want to know what's in the bag you will have to open it yourself."

Cade's shoulders slumped.

"I don't know if I really want to know."

"Trust me, you do. Hey, have I done you any wrong or harm yet?"

Cade had to admit that he hadn't, at least not yet.

"Now," the "devil" growled, *"bring me my damn car!"* The boom in his voice caused Cade to drop the phone to the ground. He hurriedly scooped it up, only to find that the line was dead.

Great! I don't even know where he is.

As soon as he processed the thought a message came through on his phone. The "devil" was waiting for him at a prominent country club across town.

Cade frowned. He did not want to walk into the country club dressed as he was, and expressed this in a return text.

That's why you have a suit in the trunk. Wear it! the man replied via text.

Got it all figured out, huh, Satan? Cade thought.

Yes, I do, came another text.

Fear gripped Cade like a lover with a hungry heart. This was too much for him to take in. First, the dirty, toothless man had appeared out of nowhere the night before. After asking for and receiving a few dollars from him the guy had pulled out a huge wad of hundred-dollar bills. Not only did he somehow talk Cade into going into the fancy eatery after that, but he also made fun of him in front of a room full of strangers and then disappeared. Once the two were reunited outside, the man continued to tell Cade more and more about his life, mentioning things that only Cade himself knew. Less than 24-hours later, the man showed up at his house in a brand-new sports car, introduced himself as "Lucifer" to Jacy, was decked out in a designer suit, looking like a million bucks, and was sporting all his teeth. While at his house, the man showcased moves that

Cade had only seen in the movies while putting Terry in his place and refusing to back down, even with a loaded gun in his face. Apparently, he could read minds as well.

Satan?

No, absolutely not!

He moved to the passenger side and opened the dash. Just like the "devil" had said, the title and proof of full coverage insurance, all in Cade's name, was located in the drawer.

Eye's bulging, he moved to the front of the car, and opened the trunk again. He grabbed the bag and opened it, a great smile appearing on his face.

"No way!"

Now this all made sense to him. Everything was so much clearer to him now, but this new bit of information still didn't explain how the man knew what he was thinking at any moment. Nor did it explain how he was able to lift Terry, one-handed, above the ground the way that he did.

He would have to take this up with him when he arrived at the country club-because he was surely going now.

First, he would need to find a place to change into the suit.

His whole mindset was different now, and he could not get to the exquisite edifice soon enough. The excitement he felt at the moment was nearly too much to contain.

"Thank you, Lord!" he bellowed, as he started the car and took in the whir of the engine. In comparison to most vehicles, it made a beautiful sound.

"Hallelujah," he cheered

Chance stepped out onto the front porch and watched him in wonder, clearly vexed as to what was happening. The two of them met eyes and

Cade turned his music up loud and threw her a peace sign as he pulled off.

This day wasn't going to be so bad after all.

8

When Cade arrived at the country club, he had to circle the lot in order to find a parking spot. In the glove compartment, he found a parking pass, which was apparently law here. Pulling into an open space, he eventually found and displayed the pass in the window, sitting quietly in new ride that appeared to belong to him according to the name on the title. Looking out the driver side window, he took in the scenery carefully.

A packed house, he observed, as people milled about outside, conversing with cronies as they made their way inside. Cade caught a few people gawking at the ride he was in. Most likely, they were wondering who he was.

Make way, he thought, as he stepped from the car, crispy in his suit, feeling like he'd just won the lottery.

Had he?

From what he'd seen in the bag in the trunk, it would appear so.

He stood in wonder and amazement at the massive structure that looked like an old Scottish castle. Yes, this was where the big dogs played, where the old, arrogant, better- than-thou money came to congregate on a hilltop overlooking the Tennessee River.

Oh, hell yes, they did!

Pulling out his phone, he sent a text to the 666- area code number and got a quick reply, almost before he could even hit send.

Come on in!

He moved cautiously to the entrance, uncertain of how he felt about being there, knowing he didn't belong. He wasn't a member, and could only hope the man in the suit was really there to meet him.

At the entrance he was met by a young attendant.

"Morning, sir" he said to Cade, who only gave a silly smile in return. "Just in time for the Christmas party."

Christmas party?

Great. Just great.

Of course, the man picked this particular location as a rendezvous spot. And, of course, he would choose to bring Cade to the highly prestigious club on a day when the place would be packed with most, if not all, of its members, all celebrating the birth of Jesus Christ.

What is this guy's angle?

He was pulling tricks out of his sleeves left and right and Cade was having a hard time wrapping his head around everything. He had drastically changed his appearance in less than 24-hours, had all of his teeth suddenly, had strength unlike anything Cade had seen before and Cade was still dumbfounded on how the car's hood popped up on its own. Not only that, but the cell phone, the sudden inclusion at the country club, the registration and insurance for the car were both in his name and waiting on him in the glove box, and a perfectly fitting suit was folded up next to the bag in the trunk.

How?

The man had some explaining to do. But still, after looking in the bag...

Upon entering the country club, Cade stopped and drew in a deep, long breath. Looking around in awe, he was intrigued at the site of the historic building and wanted to be sure to take in all the details. He was especially fond of the beautiful wood used throughout, taking note of the intricate details in the carvings, sure that most of the wood was original.

But what did he know? He was nothing more than a pheasant from a small part of town called Fountain City, a bum who came from working class folks, nothing in comparison to the "Who's Who of Knoxville."

Taking a guess at what he should do next, Cade moved to the desk just ahead of him and spoke to a pretty, full-chested blonde with high cheekbones.

"Hi!" she greeted him, with a huge smile.

Um, what do I say? He wondered.

Before he could utter a single word, a strong hand gripped his shoulder.

"There you are," came the voice of the man in the suit—the self-proclaimed devil in the flesh. "Didn't think you would ever get here. Got me in here with all these rich white folks feeling nervous."

Cade's rose his eyebrows as did the woman the counter.

To the lady the "devil" said, "Did you know they wouldn't even let black people join here years ago? Now that my friend has written a book and gotten rich, he's opened the door for a nig-"

"Okay!" Cade abruptly said, thoroughly embarrassed. "That's enough."

"Yes," the "devil" said, "enough indeed. Go ahead and check us in. It's your name on the list, not mine."

Skeptical, Cade said, "My name?"

"Well, yeah, I'm not a member here. I wouldn't give y'all a dime," the "devil" said to the lady. "But, hey, to each their own."

Blondie at the counter was unsure how to react so she remained silent, holding the smile on her face best she could.

"I'm kidding, sweetheart," the "devil" said. "I've bought a bunch of memberships for people here."

Cade leaned in and growled through his teeth, "I'm not a member here, and I'm damn sure not rich."

Tilting his head, the "devil" said, "You sure about that? What'd you find in the bag?"

The silence between the two men was like meat on a sandwich, thick.

"What did you find in the bag?" the "devil" asked again, causing Cade to produce a paperback book from beneath his suit jacket.

The book had his name on it, along with own his personal design that he'd come up with while incarcerated.

"Looks good, doesn't it?"

"Yeah," Cade responded. "I would expect that from a publisher."

"Publisher," the "devil" said to himself, humor rolling off his tongue. "No... not quite."

Cade's stomach turned and he said, "Come on, man, knock it off. My book is online. How else would you know what it looked like? You probably took it upon yourself to do the book and now you're here with an offer. That's why you're acting like the devil, because of the theme of my books, right? It's actually kind of creative."

The "devil" remained silent as Cade smiled dumbly.

"Right?" Cade asked again.

"I've already established my offer, and it has nothing to do with that dumb ass theory you just created on your way over here, or the books-which I hate-considering you have my minions and I losing to God in all of them. *Foolishness,*" the "devil" added, tossing his head in the direction of the lady at the counter who watched them with deep curiosity, "Go ahead and check us in. You're a new member, so they don't know you yet. But trust me, they will."

"You're so full of it."

"After all I have done for you so far in life, I still haven't earned your trust?"

"All you've done for me?"

"That's right. Every sin that has ever given you pleasure, you owe me a debt for."

"Here you go again with the devil act," Cade said, annoyed. *"Stop!"*

"No act."

"Whatever."

"Yeah, whatever. Everyone loves those famous seven sins."

"Don't you mean seven *deadly* sins?"

"Can't be too deadly if you're still alive. I mean, is evil really so bad when the whole human race embraces all the so-called 'bad things' I encourage them to do?"

Holding his eye Cade looked for a sign, as if he were really any good at doing such things.

The "devil" nodded to the desk once again.

Moving in that direction, Cade checked in with the lady who scanned for his name in a large book, a very vintage way of doing things. To his surprise he received a warm smile from her.

"Have a good time, sir," she said to him. "Merry Christmas."

He bid her the same and turned back to see the "devil" smiling at him.

"I'm just saying," the "devil" said with a shrug.

Cade came to within a foot of the man, "I'm not doing this."

He tossed the novel to the "devil" and walked past him, feeling his eyes watch him the whole way.

Outside he berated himself for coming this far and asked the Lord for forgiveness. What was he to do? He'd saved Terry by agreeing to hear what the "devil" had to say and had been kicked out of his home in the process.

And now, all of a sudden, he was a member of the oldest, most prestigious country club in the city?

He didn't know how this day could get any crazier for him.

As he approached the sports car outside, he was sent into a frenzy of chills that had nothing to do with the temperature. The "devil", arms crossed, was waiting for him by the red vehicle!

"You said you would hear me out, Cade," he said calmly. "Surely a good ole Christian man such as yourself isn't a deceiver, are you?"

Spinning on his heels, Cade looked to the entrance of the country club and back to the "devil", once more to be sure he wasn't losing his mind. He knew he wasn't, but there was no explanation for how the man in the suit had beaten him to back the vehicle.

None!

This was not happening. How could he have beaten him to the car?

"Like I said," the "devil" continued, moving closer to Cade, "listen to what I have to say. You either accept it or you don't, but if you don't...I will leave you alone."

"For some reason I don't believe you."

"Only one way to find out, my friend," the "devil" said with a smile, holding his arm out in the direction of the massive building. "After you..."

So, there were no other options here? Cade thought. This man was a step ahead of him in every way.

Or was he just an ordinary man?

Could this truly be the devil in the flesh?

Gritting harshly, Cade begrudgingly turned to lead the way back into the social club. After all, he was a member-one of the boys-and could waltz back into the building whenever he felt, no questions asked.

But he did have some inquiries for the crazy magician following closely behind him.

His stomach turned and he wondered what kind of mistake he was making as the sun beamed down on him like a sign saying, *Get out of here now!*

There was something fascinating about a person who could go from being a bum one minute and a seemingly affluent individual in less than twenty-four hours. He was drawn to him.

And that could spell trouble.

9

There was a heavy crowd dressed in casual attire, but none fancier than the two of them when they walked into the elegant dining room with its stunning view of the river through a massive wall of glass.

Cade couldn't help but notice all eyes were on them as they made their way to the end of the bar.

"Feels good, doesn't it?" the "devil" said, taking a seat.

Confused, Cade asked, "What feels good?"

"The adulation. Nothing like last night when we walked into that restaurant and people gave you shady looks because of the company you kept. These are the *big* money people."

Cade looked around, took it all in, and nodded his agreement. "Yeah, that's something, isn't it?" he said.

"Yes, something."

"That just goes to show that love of money is the route to all evil. People care more about wealth than health."

"The latter part of your statement is true," the "devil" said as he flagged the bartender. "But it isn't the love of money that is the route to all evil. It's the lack."

"The Bible says-"

"I don't give a damn what the Bible says!" the "devil" hissed.

Cade held his gaze, unsure of how to respond.

The bartender arrived and the "devil" calmly ordered a bottle of their most expensive wine.

"Bring my friend here a sparkling water."

And then the tender was gone as fast as he came.

"You see, Cade, the *lack* of money is what drives people to do the heinous things they do in this world. You have to understand that as time goes on, we come into more knowledge. The people who wrote the Bible were mere men, with little knowledge of self. The things they were saying were good and inspirational for the time, but it's a new day."

"I don't believe the men who wrote the Bible were mere men. They were inspired by God himself."

"And that, my friend, is a misconception you have to overcome. All the men who wrote the Bible are dead and gone. They're never coming back. Why? Because they were merely men who breathed air just like you. They were a bunch of crazy authors, just like you.

But as I said, lacking drives people to extreme measures. Even the rich people in this room have lacking issues. Life is gravy when you are up, but when it begins to wither, so does the fun and comfort they have built."

"So, they go to all ends striving to get as much as they can to ensure they never fall from their place up above us 'small people," Cade concluded, to which the "devil" nodded.

"You better know it."

"Gentlemen, would you like a couple of menus?" the tender asked, as he placed two empty wine glasses on the table and began to open the bottle of wine that the man had ordered.

Cade opened his mouth to speak but the "devil" said, "Yes" before he could utter a word.

"You could use a really good steak," he said to Cade. "Plus, your breakfast was cut short."

"Thanks to you."

"You owe me thanks for more than that."

"Whatever, you are not the devil," Cade said, looking off into the crowd as he sipped his water from a glass that appeared to be cleaner than any he had ever drank from.

The Country Club. Nice touch.

"We will see," the "devil" said.

They said nothing for a moment and then Cade turned to him and spoke. "So, let's say you are the devil, which is insane. But if so, why did you come to me?"

"Don't ask why, ask why *not*."

Cade rolled his eyes.

"The things I will tell you," the "devil" continued, "are very unconventional, but I believe you can handle them."

Menus were placed in front of them and the "devil" asked, "Do you still like your steaks medium?"

Cade looked up from his menu and replied, "Lucky guess."

Chuckling the "devil" said, "I know you, man-better than you know yourself. And I know all your desires. I can help you attain them."

"I'll get my blessings from the Lord."

"Same way you been getting them? It's taking long enough, isn't it? Humans are the only species on Earth with the brain capacity to create the problems they have in life. They are always looking to something other than themselves to solve their problems when the answers are right in their face."

"God's delays are not his denials. He has a time and season for everything."

"Me too. That's why I'm here-it's Satan Season. You have paid your debt to society. You are trying to live a righteous life and you go to church all the time to praise a God who won't entertain anything you are saying."

"Well, things are supposed to be this way starting out. I mean, after all-" he leaned in so as to not be heard, "I'm a felon."

"Only if you let them label you as one," the "devil" retorted. He explained to Cade that there were worse people than him who didn't bear the title, and plenty with the word attached to their name who weren't criminals.

"You're no criminal, Cade," he said. "You had an unlucky night and had to pay for it with years of your life. But even now you are suffering the backlash for it. You're practically still in jail. Still having your check garnished..."

"It's fair. I took those peoples kids away from them."

"Not intentionally. Wouldn't it be nice to have enough money to just write the families of those soldiers a fat check and be done with the whole situation?"

"Yeah, but that's not the case."

The tender reappeared with silverware.

"Could be," "Satan" said. "And for the record, *fair* is a place they judge pigs. The world is a cold place, so what are you going to do to avoid being a victim of the chills?"

"Awe, man, you're crazy-"

"Not the first or last time I will ever be called that-and by better people, if I might add."

"You're a bit of an arrogant jerk."

"You haven't heard the news about me? How beautiful and confident I am?"

"Not you, but the devil, yes. I know he was thrown from heaven and will suffer in hell for eternity because of that arrogance. I know he is the deceiver and enemy of mankind," Cade said through the "devil's" raucous laughter that drew more attention than they needed.

"Thrown from heaven!" Satan announced loudly, embarrassing his company.

"Keep your voice down," Cade said.

"Thrown from Heaven," the "devil" repeated. "That's funny, considering I freely left that boring place that all of you humans seem so interested in going, even though you have no true knowledge of it. I know the verse you speak of. 'Oh, Lucifer, how you have fallen from the stars and been cast down to the earth.'"

"Isaiah 14:12. I've read it," Cade said, feeling satisfied with himself for keeping pace with the man. He had spent many nights reading his Bible, working diligently on becoming a better man.

"That's right. But that's not talking about any devil you refer to. The fact that Lucifer means light-bearer is lost on people, although I have brought so many to the light. The Lucifer you speak of is the Prince of Darkness. I see a contrast there. Since you're so well read-as you portray-have you seen that they call me 'The Morning Star' in that book and Jesus the same exact thing in 2 Peter and Revelation? Which one of us is the bad guy?"

"I'm not so sure about all that."

"I know. Most of you are fools. You understand only what you want to understand when you read the Bible. But here's something of an appetizer for you to chew on before your steak gets here," the "devil" said while looking deeply into Cade's interested eyes. After adding an unnecessarily long dramatic pause, he continued on with the conversation by asking, "What makes you think that I am beyond being able to go back to heaven?"

"The devil could never get back to heaven."

"On the contrary. God's eternal love and forgiveness doesn't extend to me? I am one of His *original* creations, Cade. My relationship with God is rocky, sure, but I'm closer to Him than any human. And, most of all, I don't blaspheme the Holy Ghost-I wouldn't bash my Father in Heaven. Last I checked, that was the only unforgivable sin."

Cade shifted on his stool, uncomfortably, "That's what the Bible says. But you do blaspheme."

"By definition most people do. I'm just doing me, like the rest of mankind. Are you all doomed to Hell?"

"See, that's just fancy talk to confuse people."

"Not at all. Isn't it strange that you are expected to forgive all the sins of men, but your God doesn't? He supposedly creates an eternal place of torment, and I'm the bad guy?"

"Whatever."

"Religious people are funny to me. I give you a fact that should change your thinking on something you have been taught, but you refuse to accept it."

"This is non-sense."

"No, my friend, it isn't. You have to ask questions in this life, or you will be left in the wind as the world progresses."

"You're telling me that the devil can go back to heaven after all of this time? After all the trouble he has caused in the world?"

"Yes. In fact, I am the *true* savior of the world, not Jesus. If I were to ask for forgiveness and go crawling back to God, there would be no more sin, no one to tempt you. Then what?"

"In that case, what would happen to hell?"

"Not even I know the answer to that one."

"Oh, you don't know something for once?" Cade quipped.

"I know God created me, and I was in heaven. I left, yes, but He and I aren't enemies. Man is the author of our beef. I don't ever speak badly of Him, and I never will. I speak truth. There is a big difference there."

"I can't believe I'm still listening to you."

"I can. You are drawn to this truth I speak. Most people can't stomach it, but you've done well so far. Speaking of stomaching, here's our food."

Their plates were placed in front of them and Cade's eye's widened at the sight. The smell of the steak was like freedom at the gate of the prison when he was released.

"Can't find much better than this place when it comes to food. You really can't. Eat, you look famished."

Placing his fork and knife to his steak Cade had a thought as he watched the "devil" take a large bite.

"If you're the devil why do you need to eat?"

"I'm entertaining dumb questions now, Cade?" the "devil" retorted, mouth full. "Ask me something that has substance."

"Excuse me," said Cade sarcastically.

Turning his focus to the food on his plate Cade took his first bite of the best steak he had ever placed in his mouth. And yes, it was cooked medium, just as the man across from him had suggested he would eat it.

He loved it.

"So, you're not a publisher?" Cade asked, placing his knife and fork on the plate.

"Not in the least. Although, I had my hand in the Bible, if you want to count that."

"Hand in the Bible? How is that?"

The "devil" gulped from his wine glass, hurriedly, before offering his rebuttal. "It's full of murder, sex and every other thing you human's call a sin, right?"

Cade replied, "Yes."

"Need I say more? The whole Bible is about me. How to get *me* behind *thee* shall I ever confront *thee*. And people have the nerve to act like I'm chopped liver or something. I'm someone important, you know? Someone you should know."

Cade scanned the room slowly, trying to take it all in. This place was absolutely incredible, so much better than he had ever imagined.

"I know you would like to think that you should give all thanks to God, but you need to know that He doesn't have a hand in all your blessings. I've got my thumbprint on some of them. Rappers make millions of dollars to promote violence, sex and drug use. What do they do? Thank God for that success, when in reality they should be thanking *me*. Even porn stars thank God, but you and I know that hot air isn't the only thing they're blowing."

Cade chuckled in spite of himself and said, "Touché."

"Just saying. Everyone who appears to be blessed isn't necessarily a 'good' person. Everyone sins, Cade. Even the Pope. So, it can't be that bad. After all, it's God who created all things anyway-sin included. You were born into a world full of it, have been treading in it like a pool your whole life, which is why it comes so freely. You are no saint, by far."

"Listen, man," Cade said, his head beginning to hurt as he listened to what amounted to foolery in his eyes, "you say all these things...but you're *not* the devil. Maybe a well-read atheist or magician-"

"A magician, you say-" the "devil" interrupted. "Ok, you want to see magic, do you?"

"Well, no-" Cade attempted to say, but before he could finish the "devil" snapped his fingers, causing explosions of glass on every table around them. People shrieked in horror as their fancy clothes were stained with expensive wine and food, shards of crystal falling around them everywhere.

"Oh!" Cade exclaimed, hopping from the bar stool and taking in the chaos.

"Oh!" the "devil" mocked. "Boy, I think it's time you take me a bit more serious, because you are about to miss out on all that I have to offer. And frankly, you are getting on my damn nerves," the devil said coolly, getting to his feet and facing Cade-whose suit was unstained, as well as his own. "I am who I say I am."

"Well then, I want nothing to do with you. Or any of this," Cade added, sweeping his hand around the room at the mayhem.

"I get that impression," the "devil" said. "So, you would rather deal with a Jesus who has shown you nothing of what you have been taught about Him?"

"Says who?"

"Says you. Look at your life. All you do to be a good man, the life changes that you have made, all the praying, all the reading and memorizing of the Bible, and *this* is what your Lord has brought you home to?"

"I can't allow the way my life is to interfere with my personal relationship with God."

"Personal relationship?" the "devil" said with disgust. "You haven't even met God. How are you going to say it's a personal relationship?"

Cade turned his gaze away from the "devil" to focus on the crowd of people as they wailed and scattered around hectically, demanding answers for why their glasses had burst spontaneously.

"The Bible is the number one selling book of all time, and it's star won't even show up for a book signing to explain which one these big groups of fools that claim Him is right and which group is wrong. Just leaves you crying for miracles, looking like a fool and suffering. Me, on the other hand, I'm always around when you need me. Just call and I'm there."

"That's a lie. The devil isn't omnipresent like God. He doesn't have that ability."

"Is that something you've been told, or something you can prove? Can you show me in your little Bible where it says that?"

Stumped, Cade said, "No, it's what I was told."

"Exactly! You Christians are so comical! I simply ask you to show me something you believe in, but most times you can't even find it in your own authoritative book that you swear by. Instead you lean on faith."

"What's wrong with faith?"

"For one, the Bible even tells you that faith without work is dead. And yes, I can show you were it says that-"

"I know what it says," an irritated Cade interrupted.

Smiling and pushing on the "devil" said, "Faith is the belief in a God that has no beginning, one that you can neither see nor prove exists. Why would you ever have such a thing?"

At that moment a male attendant appeared at their side.

"Mr. Cade, would you and your guest like to retire to another room while we sort through this impromptu situation."

"You know my name?" Cade asked the man who appeared to be taken aback at the question.

"Yes," he replied with a smile, "I do. You are a member here."

"What do you say, Cade?" "Satan" said. "How bout we continue this conversation elsewhere?"

Before Cade could speak the attendant said, "How are you two the only clean people in the room?"

"God's will," the "devil" said, looking at Cade who obviously was not entertained by the sarcasm. "In fact, that's exactly what I was about to discuss with my friend here."

"I suppose," the attendant responded. Turning to Cade, he asked "Sir, would you like to be moved?"

Cade shifted his eyes to the "devil", looked deep into him without a single blink of the eye.

"You sure you don't want to hear what I have to say?" the "devil" asked.

Silence, uncomfortable silence, was the only thing that stood between the two of them.

Again, the attendant asked, "Mr. Cade?"

"Ok, yes. Why not?" Cade said.

Why did I agree?

"Very well. Follow me."

The attendant turned to lead the way out of the room, leaving all the frantic activity to those stained in the morning's meal.

"Good choice," the "devil" said to Cade as they crossed from the room to a long hallway leading to an elevator. "Down below we go," said the staff member as the doors slid open. "You may order food, wine, cigars, whatever you please."

"Exclusivity at its finest," the "devil" said as they boarded the cart.

"That it is," the attendant agreed. "You'll like it down here."

And like it they did.

The elevator doors opened to a beautifully lighted room, crafted of oak and ruby carpeting with a large bar directly ahead of them. There were pool tables and card game areas, blackjack and poker dealers at the ready, a true man cave if there ever was one.

"Enjoy, gentlemen," the attendant said to them, stepping back onto the elevator and disappearing.

Moving to a private seating area with a glass table, Cade said to the "devil," "Better make this quick, because I've about had enough of you."

"Then why did you come down here?" the "devil" asked as he took a seat.

"I'm asking myself the same thing right now."

"Give me an hour and you'll change your way of thinking."

"That's what I'm afraid of."

"No need to have any fears," said the "devil."

'So you say," Cade retorted.

"I have to admit, Cade, I thought you would've tucked tail and ran out of here by now, but it seems your curiosity has gotten the better of you."

"Guess I'm fortunate *not* to be a cat."

Chuckling the "devil" said, "Good one. You have the witty dialogue of a writer."

"Would you gentlemen like a beverage?" a middle-aged waiter asked, coming to a stop at their table.

"Just a bottled water, thank you," the "devil" answered. "Same for my friend." When the waiter was gone, he said to Cade, "No sense in drinking alcohol alone. That's no fun."

"Oh, pity you," Cade said sarcastically. "Say what you have to say about God's will so I can leave."

"I caught your ear with that, did I?"

"I'm here, aren't I? Still listening?"

"That you are," the "devil" said, leaving the air open of words a moment, for affect.

"God's will doesn't exist."

"Doesn't exist? God's will does exists."

"Then what is it? Tell me the great plan that God has for mankind?"

"I'd say God's will is whatever He wills, whatever He allows to happen."

"If you believe that, then there is no reason to ever be mad or sad. Why argue with God's will? You don't even have the right to feel joy over succeeding in life because you did nothing more than play the role that was written for you."

"I don't think it works that way."

"Again, that is why no one has ever paid you to be a thinker, Cade. You really ought to use your head and ask yourself is it God's will or His predestined plan for a small child who is without sin to die from a brain tumor? For kids to be molested by the very ones that they trust the most? Or for a healthy, non- smoker to die from lung cancer?"

"I can't say," Cade said, looking away. "All I can say is that it's God's will."

"Just going to stick with that, huh?"

Cade shrugged.

"You only have two purposes in this world. That is to love and procreate."

"That sounds stupid."

"It would to an idiot. Love fulfills God's law, as it says in Romans. And in order to continue life on earth you have to have babies. What other reasons you have for being here?"

"I'm pretty sure there is more to it than that," Cade objected. "People are meant to be things in life, they have a purpose."

"Then it must be your purpose to live the way you are now. So why are you always whining?"

"That's not my calling. I have a higher purpose than this- *God has a bigger purpose for me*."

"I understand," the "devil" said, shaking his head despondingly. "The Bible says to train a child in the way that they should go and they will not depart from it. I see you are a good little puppy boy when it comes to what the lost souls have taught you."

"Lost souls have taught me nothing other than what I shouldn't do. By watching them, they have taught me how to avoid an eternity in hellfire."

"You know nothing of what you have read in your Bible. You know nothing of what is literal and what is simply an allegory. Most people read the Book like it's a bedtime story, quickly and without understanding. But as long as they do that small act, they feel they have done their soul some kind of justice."

"Well, that's not me. I'm close to God. He is in my heart and He gives me understanding of what I read."

"Oh, bullshit!" the "devil" said loud enough to draw the attention of a group of men playing poker nearby.

Cade's face burned red as he growled, *"Keep your voice down!"*

"I don't have to take orders from you. I don't even obey God. Who are you to tell me what to do?"

"Jerk," Cade mumbled.

"Do you truly believe, or are you living in blind faith, hoping for things that you know in your heart are not going to come to pass from simply waiting on God to bless you? Seems to me you are as much a skeptic as a believer."

"I'm already blessed, and highly favored at that."

The "devil" groaned and waved off Cade's statement as if he were swatting a bug.

"You call the life that you're living highly favored? You are officially homeless and barely make enough money to survive because everyone else is getting your paycheck. On top of that, your daughter barely respects you and nothing is happening with your books. All this after doing a thirteen-year sentence for something that wasn't even your fault? That's a blessing?"

"Blessings go beyond all of that. All kinds of people in the Bible went through situations similar to mine. And to be honest, if I hadn't let those guys ride in the back of that truck that night, I wouldn't be here now."

"And you probably wouldn't know anything you know now. But what I know is-" he waved to the waiter who had stopped by their table only moments ago. "I think I will have a drink, because this guy is driving me crazy with his buffoonery."

Cade rolled his eyes as the "devil" ordered his drink on the rocks. "I have my faith in what I have read in the Bible. It's all I have. It's my rock."

"Yeah, well, your faith-that rock-is slowly crumbling. You and I both know I'm telling the truth. I see all of your doubts as well as God, your Lord and Savior, does. I see the pain and anger you have for your family and friends after they left you hanging in prison. You hide it behind an aggressive determination to succeed, but I see inside you and know you never really fully forgave anyone. The heart doesn't lie."

Cade shifted in his seat, a strong feeling of unease coursing through him as he thought of those lonely, cold nights in unfamiliar territory. He may have been around thousands of other inmates, but he was alone in that world.

He did harbor feelings of anger, admittedly, and he was beginning to have doubts about God, wondering where he stood in his spirituality. Life didn't appear to be heading in the right direction, although he was trying to live as faithful as he could. He spent time fasting, tithing, and praying, among many other things he was advised to do by so many if he wanted things to change for the better.

Times were supposed to get hardest before the blessings though, Ramsey would remind him when they were stuck in those small jail cells.

The waiter came to their table with a tall glass bottle of sparkling water, two glasses and "Satan's" strong drink.

"You keep drinking around me as a reminder of why I ended up in prison."

"I'm actually tempting you with a visual."

"So, what is it you want from me?" Cade asked.

"It's not about what I want. It's about what *you* want. I'm just here to provide it. But you will have to do a few things in order to get it. First things first, stop praying and believing in a God that is *not* on the same page as you. All you have to do is allow me to prove that everything you hold as truth is nothing more than a big lie dressed up in pretty clothing."

"Lie?"

"All lies. No need for you to masquerade like all the hypocrites of the world who carry themselves the same way they did before they were believers. What's the sense?"

"I can't judge them for that. There's a progress to being people of God. What they do is what they do. It's on them. I have to work on my own sins. Narrow is the path to salvation-"

"And wide is the path to destruction. *Whatever!* I know more scripture than you. Stop with the quoting before I embarrass you."

"That supposed to scare me?"

"If that fool back at your old home made you scared, I definitely will."

Cade thought of Terry and what condition he was in now.

"My favorite types of believers," the "devil" went on, "are those who pray and pray for forgiveness of sins and run right back to the ones they ask for strength to defeat."

"It's a struggle."

"That's a lame excuse. People work harder to avoid jail than this hell you speak of. I'll say this; when people go to church it's one point for God because they showed up, and two points for me because when they leave, they are, for the most part, the same people they were beforehand for six days after until the next Sunday sermon. Yourself included. Had sex since you been home?"

Cade frowned, thinking back to the sexual encounters he'd carried on with a chubby woman from the halfway house. She was fresh out of prison, as was he, and the two of them, having raging hormones, began a fling. It was all too common in co-ed places like that where everyone had their mind on one thing.

Satan was the accuser.

Cade watched him with content as he turned his drink up, shook the ice in the glass when he was done, apparently satisfied.

"You can work on sin all you want, but it's a part of you and everyone else walking this earth. You know that, right?"

"No one's perfect."

"Actually, you are perfectly imperfect. Everything in this world has contrast so don't expect too much perfection. Do you really believe people were meant to be flawless in the beginning?"

"I do, right before the fall and the serp-" Cade caught himself, remembering what the "devil" had said about the serpent being cast to its belly. He'd read the verse himself the night before and now the subject was being revisited.

"Yes, the fall. The tree of knowledge of good and evil."

"Oh, let me guess, that didn't happen either?"

"Nope. Just a story."

"Man, you are something else," Cade said, exasperated.

"It's an allegory for the way that you fool's kill yourselves off with every bit of knowledge you gain. The food you eat-humans are naturally vegetarian, you know-to the cars you drive. Alcohol, drug, and my personal favorite, technology, will destroy you all one day. Robotics will turn on all of you and erase the human race from the planet." At this moment, he held up his glass and sarcastically dedicated his next sip by saying, "Cheers to humans loving the things that destroy them! And, it all comes with the knowledge of how good it makes you feel!"

"That's not what the story says."

"Jesus said a lot of things that weren't actually what He was saying. It's called a parable, Cade. Learn to actually understand them. And while we are on the subject of the Garden of Eden, there were never only two people on this Earth, my friend. Hate to break it to you."

"Adam and Eve started civilization. The Bible says so."

"Ok, if you say so. Tell me, who are the people spoken about in Genesis if they only had two sons?"

"I know what you are talking about," Cade said, speaking of the other people in the chapters-Cain's wife in Nod, the people who were warned not to harm a hair on his head, a sevenfold punishment to come if they did.

"The Bible can't detail every little thing happening in the world," he continued. "Couldn't fit it all in."

"I wish I could be so naive," came the response of the "devil". "But I challenge you to think otherwise. If you read Leviticus and Deuteronomy it clearly tells you not to have sex with your brothers and sisters. If it were wrong in those books it would be wrong in Genesis as well. Therefore, there had to be more people roaming the Earth at that time, and they were not of the same bloodline. Never were there only two people to begin with."

Cade sat still, listening to logic and hating himself for it. It made sense. It challenged his core beliefs, and that was treading in the area of danger.

"Am I getting through to you?" the "devil" asked, sensing he was.

"I'm not exactly sure who you are, or how you pulled off the stunts you have today-"

"I can do that type of stuff I did earlier all the time in order to convince you of who I am. But it's more fun to debunk all that you have been taught about the Bible your whole life. You have to know that I know more about the Bible than any man walking this Earth."

"You are just a mortal man like the rest of us. Obviously, you are well read, but whatever has made you go astray in life, you have to know that God still loves you and His grace is still upon you."

The "devil" laughed. "Grace is a whore that I never was fond of. And I'm not interested in God's love either. I know Him, He knows me. We have an understanding, as I have told you once."

"It's not too late for you to be saved."

"Please tell me you are not about to try to witness to me. It will never work. You have been reading your Bible all of, what, a few years? I'm *mentioned* in the Bible. One thing for sure, there are many religions with many different Gods, but they all have the same me."

"Yeah, as a nemesis."

"That's what man says, but they don't know me. I'm sure people say things about you that aren't true also. But, hey, I'm used to it. Someone has to be the bad guy. Might as well be me."

"The one who makes the world a worse place."

"On the contrary, ole fatuous one. Even the molesting, thieving preacher will tell you that I can't make anyone do anything, although it appears I can when it comes to them. I only tempt people to do as they please, whether it's considered good or bad in the eyes of man. I am all for your pleasure. I've helped killed presidents, a few civil rights leaders, and I even helped start slavery and homosexuality. All unnatural acts of God, but hey, if it makes you feel good, I'm all in. People control their own thoughts. I just prod you along to do-"

"Bad stuff!" Cade barked.

"Depends on who ask. Don't be judging people for killing or being gay just because it's not your preference. Who are you supposed to be? Tell me, if everything is God's will as you say, then maybe you should be mad at *Him,* for *He* is the one who created all things, sin included. Stop giving Him a pass, because all the suffering you see in this world is *His plan*!"

"Now that's a damn lie," Cade said, bolting from his seat and standing over the "devil" who sat back in his seat, giving a golf clap, thrilled that he was able to get a rise out of him.

"There we go, Cade. Show some emotion. You said so yourself that God's will is whatever He will allow to happen. Shot your foot on that one, huh? Tell me, why pray if everything is already done in God's masterful plan. It's not like He's going to change His mind on anything."

"God is the All Mighty. He can change His mind at any given moment. You saw Him do it all the time in the Bible."

"Wrong, you uneducated fool. According to James 1:17 the Lord doesn't change. I know *personally* that He is stubborn, and that is why I had to get away from Him. The Bible has many contradictions, Cade. People who are far smarter than you have found them, my friend."

"People over-think things, especially highly educated people. There are naysayers all over the world who just sit around trying to find the bad in the Bible. It's pathetic, actually."

"What's more pathetic, accepting anything that you are given as truth, or finding the truth for yourself? Some people accept the teaching of having free will while God has predestined all things. Even worse is, they truly believe that God has written all things, yet He will intervene for them in hard times."

"He will. He hears prayers and answers them accordingly."

"If that's the case.... you're saying your perfect God makes mistakes. I mean, why write something divine and change it later?"

Cade shifted and said, "Don't know, but He did it-and still does it. Like in the Bible when He flooded the world and said that He regretted making man."

"First of all, there was never any flood. Get that out of your head. People say it can be proved, but let me assure you, *it never happened!* Noah was never the only righteous person on earth. Are you kidding me? Furthermore, do you really think that God has regrets of His own plan? Are you saying He's a fool?"

Frustrated, Cade wagged his finger at the "devil." Feeling his frustrations mounting, he quickly composed himself and sat back down before he caused a scene.

"Why are you getting so angry, Christian? People don't like when you tell them the truth, but I would rather be realer than all of you. That's why I'm hated. No different than modern day poets and rappers, hated for telling the truth-*the real truth!*"

"Just shut up already," Cade said, balling his first.

"Ask yourself, Cade. Why would God create a hell, for sinners, when He was the one who allowed it all to happen in the first place? Are you the type to ask no questions at all of what you read and are taught in these money hungry churches?"

"You're wrong. The devil is the originator of sin."

"God allowed sin to be unleashed on His perfect world to begin with. Am I really the originator? Are you going to take me back to the story of some fallen angel who took a third of the angels with Him? God's will? His plan? Doesn't make sense to have sin in a perfect heaven, Cade. That story could not possibly be talking about the devil in Heaven."

"The story of the devil's fall is in revelation-"

"And that book is a prophesy of things to *come*, not a reflection."

This made Cade seriously wonder. Had there been sin in Heaven? Surely not in the most perfect place, right? If that was the case, would that void the story of the devil in Heaven?

This wasn't the first time his mind had visited the subject of sin in Heaven. If one thing in the Bible was void, should it all be? Or was the story truly and simply misunderstood?

This crazy man said the devil could go back to heaven.

Cade revisited the subject.

"Oh, I was there alright. Just didn't get kicked out like you think I did. Those are misleading stories in your Bible. What sense would it make for God to create an angel that He knew would turn on Him? One that He knew would be thrown to Earth and eventually drag most of His prized creation to an eternity of suffering."

"Don't know why-"

"That's because it is a lie. Every third letter of the phrase Holy Bible spells *lie*," "Satan" brought up again, proudly.

This was all becoming too much to digest at one time and Cade began to feel sick. Shooting to his feet, he flagged down a passing waiter.

"Is there a restroom here?" he asked, half-breathed.

The waiter pointed to the corner and Cade moved toward that area swiftly, without uttering another word, leaving the "devil" behind.

10

In the restroom, Cade splashed his face with cold water and breathed deeply.

What am I still doing here? He asked himself aloud, over and over, while starring in the brightly lit, wall-sized mirror.

He could not believe the things that had come out of the man's mouth, not only the vitriol towards the Bible, but his claim altogether of being the "devil" had his mind twisting, lost within a labyrinth of words spoken so smoothly that he couldn't help but be confused at the moment.

Did he truly believe that he was the devil?

Maybe he was...

But that couldn't be possible.

Then again...it happened in the biblical times. So why not now? Why not to him?

A more important question loomed in Cade's mind: Would he be able to get rid of him? He'd come to him as smooth as wind the night before on a downtown road, and had found him at his home the next day.

He knew so much about him.

"Why God?" he mumbled. "Why me?"

"Why not you?" came the "devil's" voice from the doorway.

A chill ran through Cades' body as he turned to see the "devil" locking the door and inching closer to him. His spine straightened as he stepped back and braced himself against the sink, fear gripping him like a lover from a long-lost time.

"No need to fear me," the "devil" said plainly. "I'm not here to hurt you, although I've been hit with the image of a killer and destroyer of mankind. All I do is push you to do as you already please. But if everything is in God's control, why praise Him and say He is working in mysterious ways?"

"He does. I serve a glorious God."

"Tell that to the parents of innocent children who die. Tell that to the person who praises Him wholeheartedly and ends up on the other end of a gun barrel. Everyone should *hate* Him. Instead you reserve that powerful emotion for me, the *true* good guy, the one who wants you to be happy with everything you do."

"Everything is not good-"

"But the things they call a sin make you feel that way. They just call me the bad and Him the good. More slander on me, but I can handle it. I am all for the fleshly desires of man."

"We must die to the flesh."

"Only way to do that is to die in general, and you don't want to do that because you are too scared to die. But if you truly believe in the promise of the Heaven that they have put in your head, you would have no issue with dying and going to that place."

"People are scared to die because we are meant to live. Whenever God sees fit to call my number, then it's my time. I will be ready to go."

"No one has a death date set in stone, you idiot. Again, God has not predestined anything, because if *when* you die is known, then *how* you die is also. Which means if you blow your brains out and go to hell, it was His plan?"

"No, you had free will."

"You're not digesting a word of this, I see. Not because you can't-you just don't want to."

"That's because what you speak is non-sense."

"I'm here to give you all that you desire and you repay me with slander. It's okay. I have thicker skin than your God. I won't turn you into a pillar of salt for your insults."

"Maybe all I desire isn't exactly what you think."

"Sure, it is. You want money, just like any other red-blooded human being."

"See, that's where you are wrong. It's not money I'm chasing. I want to be successful and still give the glory to God in the process."

"Glory to God? Please. You know damn well that riches and fame come with the type of success you would like to have with the books you are writing. I see inside you," the "devil" added, placing an index to his temple. "You desired prosperity before you ever desired living for God."

"Got a comeback for everything, huh?"

"I do. I'm the most savvy, quick-witted individual that you will ever meet. It gets no better than me."

"You sure talk like you are the devil."

"In the flesh, my friend. A blessing you can actually see for once in your life."

"I've seen plenty of blessings in my life. God waking me up every day is a blessing. Jesus dying on the cross for me is the most important blessing of all."

"*The Lord isn't waking anyone up, Cade.* You think there's a great big list of the people He will bless with a new day or great prosperities? Faith without works is dead, says your Bible. If you don't do for you, He damn sure won't. Most people are so sincere in their prayers, and they get nothing in return. Just pray and wait on God like fools."

"God's delays are not his denials. But sometimes people ask amiss and when they don't receive the blessing they seek, faith is lost. I saw it all the time in prison when guys prayed to go home and continued suffering day after day. I was one those men, until I found God."

The "devil" tilted his head and placed a single hand at the top of a stall door, coolly crossing one leg over the other.

"So, since your life isn't amounting to what you desire," he said, "are you asking amiss?"

Running his hands through his hair Cade said, "Sometimes I ask myself that same question."

"Trust me, I know. I love to see the doubt in your heart."

"Yeah, well, doubt or no doubt, I still side with the righteous decisions of the Lord All Mighty. I am nothing but a human. How could I possibly understand something so divine?"

"You can't, so quit trying. It's only going to get worse if you keep on dealing with Him."

"The righteous cry out-"

"And the Lord hears them and delivers them out of all their troubles," the "devil" finished for him. "So, you know a few scriptures. Good for you. *I don't give a shit!*"

Wow, Cade thought. This guy really was well versed in the Bible. Finishing verses? He had to admit that he was impressed. But still, the devil he was not.

His mind immediately traveled back to prison, to his teacher of the Word, the man he had studied with in and out of the cell, the man he studied with day and night.

Ramsey.

His friend would know what to do with this so-called "devil." Or would he? Cade himself knew verses, but he was nowhere near as well-studied as Ramsey when it came to the Bible. How could he hold a candle next to the gust of wind that his best pal was?

Why had he lost touch with me over the last year? Cade wondered. I'd love to tell him of this experience. His ammo was running dangerously low in that quiet bathroom. Everything he threw at the "devil" was shot down and quickly responded to as if the things that flowed from his lips were already known before being said.

What now? he wondered.

Everything that the "devil" threw back at him was clearly logical, though he didn't want to concede to any of it. He was a Christian man, and that he would remain, no matter how much sense the well-dressed non-believer standing in front him made.

Is my faith really as shaky as he says?

"I am a walking talking miracle that is happening to you right now, Cade," the "devil" said. "You should take heed of this and accept your blessing."

"Miracle? Blessing? Cut it out." Cade leaned on the sink, and looked himself deep in his own eyes.

"The miracles you believe in are ones you didn't even witness," the "devil said, obviously offended. "They say a sea was split, that Jesus walked on water and raised people from the dead. How much of that did you actually witness to say that any of it is true?"

"Are you saying it's not true? What about people surviving sickness and tragic accidents? You don't think that was God intervening on their behalf?"

"I'm saying people who believe in all that stuff weren't there to actually confirm any of it. And that is the faith I am telling you to get rid of. It's for the blind."

"We see miracles all the time, man. You have to let go and let God, because He is always going to look out for His people

"Damnit, Cade, Preach hard, son!" Laughing, the "devil" added, "All you know is what you have been given in this life and what has been implanted into your vulnerable little mind. Nothing more, nothing less. You run with it like you came up with it yourself. That's hilarious to me. While His people are suffering here on Earth, mine are living it up."

"Yeah, for now. Sin for a season is cool, but what about after?"

"What do you know about the afterlife? You have never died to see what it is like. But if you must know, my people will still have everything once they die."

"Whatever."

"I told you about hell last night, my friend. The gate to the party is always open. None of the lake of fire claptrap is even in the Old Testament. So, where did it come from all of a sudden? They made it up to scare you, and it is working damn well. Some people are so petrified they are more motivated to avoid Hell than getting into Heaven."

"People say they have died and seen Heaven and Hell. I believe them."

"Yes, but the Bible says in 1 Corinthians 2:9 that no one will know what God has prepared for you, and that includes Heaven. Pull it up on your phone."

Hesitantly Cade pulled his phone from his jacket and retrieved the verse.

"Funny how all these people say they've been there, but the Bible-their authoritative book-says otherwise."

"I've never read this..." Cade said.

"Big surprise!" the "devil" joked. "As you see, it's there. And what you can believe is that all the people who say they have died and seen Heaven are complete liars, a big brood of vipers. For all

they know they saw Hell and didn't even know it. There's no white light at the end of any tunnel, no purgatory, no long naps. Just a quick transition from here to either Heaven of Hell."

"No one is in Hell or Heaven until the end of time."

The "devil" tossed his head back in agitation. "The end of time is when you die and separate body and soul."

Frustrated, Cade gripped the phone tightly and sucked air into his chest as he began to pace back and forth in the small space he was afforded.

"I know it hurts to hear the truth, Cade. But the truth shall set you free, as they say. And once you are free, you can serve me and have all that you have ever wanted in this life. Just toss that first commandment out the window and proceed to do as you please."

"Do as I please?"

"It's simple. All you have to do is live your life the way you want to. Sin as much as you want. When people see all the fun you are having, they will want to join. That is how I continue on. If you spell evil backwards that is what you will do when you are with me."

L-I-V-E.

"At the end of your life you will have lived, and if you spell *that* backwards, you know what you get?"

Cade thought about it....

Lived....Devil!

Strange how that worked out.

"That's right..." the "devil" concurred. "Religion is all one big trick in order to keep you in control and live the way they want you to."

"You say they? Who are *they*? Illuminati or something?"

"I figured this would come up. Illuminati just means a group that is smarter than most and take advantage of it-you have that in high school. There's no group of people buying up souls for success. You haven't even seen your soul, so how could a person sell it to another human? That's just stupid to think. They don't let the church control them, so they are painted as bad people."

"Going with the devil has bad consequences."

"Not everyone is scared of the Hell you have been taught about. In fact, some find it quite comical; the notion of a Hell that an all-loving God has created for His degenerates."

"Nothing funny about hellfire and brimstone. Sounds pretty damn scary to me."

"That's what the powers that be want you to think, but they haven't been there either to tell you what it is like. Yes, there is a Heaven, and there is a Hell...but the latter is nothing like what you think it is."

"So, who is in Hell?" Cade had to ask, his curiosity getting the better of him.

"Every kind of person you can think of. There are so many trans-generational cults out there that engage in ceremonies to honor me. They're into some deep stuff-they'll kill you if you expose them. Many of them are closet devil worshipers, only because of what society will think of them. So, they put on the mask of soccer moms, teachers, cops and even preachers-*lots of those.* They know better than to deceive the people-"

"For Christ's sake-"

"*No, for my sake!* Now you can make a decision to accept my offer right here, right now, or you can go on about your business and live your miserable, worthless life. I don't have to beg anyone to do anything for me. I have seen and done it all. Do you think you're special? You have nothing to offer me."

"I have my soul to offer."

Standing to the side he allowed Cade a clear path to the door, his escape, if he so chose to take the option.

"I don't need it. Go on and serve your biased God."

"Biased? What's that supposed to mean?"

"You believe He has a chosen people. The Jews, right? You believe that He blesses some with more than others. That would make Him biased, right? Why hasn't He given you all those blessings? Why should you have to suffer here on Earth just to get to Heaven?"

Cade stood silent, no words forming in his mind. *Why should I have to suffer?* He wondered. He did the things he was supposed to. Granted, he was not perfect, but who was? He would never claim to be better than anyone walking the Earth, but why wasn't his life shaping up to anything he had imagined before he had come home.

There was a process to all things, yes, but he could not see the light at the end of the tunnel for the life of him, and he was beginning to lose faith in all things Biblical.

He was sure the "devil" knew this, and that had to be the reason he had come to him.

Wait! He halted his thoughts. *Am I admitting this guy is the devil?*

No! Do not fold or cave in.

But what if...?

"So, in short, you are telling me that the Bible is false?" Cade asked, stepping closer to the "devil".

"Not all of it. I'm saying that the Basic Instructions Before Leaving Earth-*Bible*-are a bit warped. Yes, God has spoken to many men, but a whole book full of crazy stories that most people can't understand was never in His plan. That book is not all His work. His words can't be reduced to paper or any book written by man. Yes, it's filled with lies, though it's not a complete lie."

"Not a complete lie," Cade repeated to himself.

"That's right. Part truth, part lie, part allegory, mostly written in a way that people can't even understand. 1 Corinthians 2: 6-8 even says so. It's written in a mysterious way. Who really has time for that?"

"You got to have the Holy Spirit to understand The Word fully. That's why prayer doesn't always work-because people don't know how to pray with the true faith of a mustard seed."

"You can only have the Holy Spirit if you are pure in spirit, Cade. There is no one person on this Earth that fits that criteria."

"Not true. People catch the spirit all the time."

"That gibberish that people do in church?" the "devil" said with a smile. "You can't be serious."

Frowning, Cade said, "The Bible mentions speaking in tongues."

"*And?*"

"The Bible has stood the test of time. That is saying a lot"

"Ever heard of The Crusades?"

"The what?"

Shaking his head and tsk-tsking, the "devil dived in on Cade, "Oh, child of mine. You are but a babe in this world. The Crusades, the bloodiest time in history of man. Of course, the Bible has stood the test of time…when people were killed in the name of God! You really ought to expand your horizon when it comes to reading. The Bible is not the only book on Earth."

Cade's mind waged war against itself as he listened on.

"And as you know, Christians are not the only religious group that think they have been spoken to directly by God. Every one of them has laid claim to Him. Why? It's one big competition between them-the Jews, the Christians, the Muslims, and any other of the million different belief systems out there that can't seem to get along and love each other as God would have them do. It's all a joke, nothing more than a big Ponzi scheme. I suggest you remove yourself from all of it because they are all going to be punished in the end."

"I can't speak for any other group-"

"*Well, I will!* They are a bunch of loons. Moses and all the rest of them were crazy as hell. All the spectacular things God can do and you want to believe that He simply burned a bush?"

"I don't want to hear this?"

"Well, then leave. I'm not stopping you by any means. Go on and get away from me. You're ugly anyway."

Unable to formulate a response, Cade slowly stepped toward the door, unlocked and pulled it open. He stood there a moment looking the "devil" in his eyes, finding no emotion whatsoever.

"You will regret your decision," came the words from "Satan."

Without a response Cade stepped through the threshold, leaving him where he stood.

11

The following days where trying for Cade.
Kicked out of the home he had become
accustomed to since being released from the
halfway house, he was forced to stay in the shelter
on Broadway. A pauper himself now, he got
acquainted with the type of the people he had
personally tried to help when he was in a better
position.

Now he was a part of that group; someone who
had no sure home to lay his head at night, walking
amongst the living dead day and night.

He had nowhere to go, no family or friends to
turn to. Not even his pastor friend Gil would open
his doors to him, for he had three young children
and a wife who would disapprove.

Perfectly understood, but why God allowed
these things to happen he would never know. As
he prepared himself for a new day he began to
wonder, *what is it that I believe in?*

Wasn't God was supposed to take care His
own? The ones who admired Him and praised His
holy name should have more of a hedge around
them, shouldn't they?

So why was he now without a home?

Why did he have to go through these things?
Was there something bigger at play in his life that
he just could not see at the moment?

People in the Bible had gone through similar or
worse circumstances, but reading about them was
a vast contrast to actually living it.

As the saying went, 'the struggle was real.'
With that struggle, doors would close…but more
would open.

Conveniently enough the shelter was not far from his job and his walk to and from work was shorter than that of the one he had while living under the same roof as Chance.

There was a plus after all.

Go, God! He laughed, in spite of himself.

He found himself revisiting the same plan that he originally had when he first got out and his brother kicked him out, to save up some money and find a *cheap* place to live, if they would have him. Gaining housing was no easy task for felons, and just as he found out before Deborah allowed him to move into her family home, each denial due to credit or background checks meant another thirty to fifty bucks out the window with every burning application fee.

No man in his position could afford to get denied ten times, because the money from his checks continued to be garnished.

Walking down the sidewalk on an early morning jaunt to work, he held his head low in defeat and shame of what his life had become in the first year out of prison. Granted he hadn't been home long enough to accomplish the things he truly desired, but at the same time he was a believer in patterns, and his current situation was not the most likely path to success.

As a homeless man, Cade had plenty of time to reflect on his time both in prison and living with the chaos crew he no longer had to deal with. Admittedly-although he was without a place to live-he felt relieved at the fact he didn't have to deal with their poison, knowing that eventually they would have brought him down in some fashion.

But…he missed his daughter!

He wondered if she missed him also, or even thought about him at all now that he was no longer visible in her day-to-day life.

In his days at the shelter, he also had plenty of time to recount everything that the "devil" had spoken to him in the previous days. He hadn't seen him anymore-as promised-and that was a big surprise. There was nothing to be negotiated, so why would the "devil" stick around?

For the same reason he would tempt all of humanity until the rapture and the end of time, Cade thought.

He could not fathom why the man had accosted him on that dark street only five nights ago, but everything happened for a reason. At least that's what he thought before their chance meeting.

Maybe the "devil" had been right, that nothing was planned or happened for any reason other than happenstance. Maybe life *was* just one big coincidence, and people were stuck on a God that was far too busy to direct the lives of each and every individual walking the face of the planet.

Maybe.

But then again, maybe not.

The "devil's" words played over in Cade's mind, haunting him, every hour of every day. He was clearly well-versed in the Bible, more so than Cade at his current stage of his Biblical studies, and it showed.

"Satan" had come to destroy all that Cade believed, and had done quite the job up to the point of him leaving the restroom at the country club.

He'd needed to escape, absolutely had to get away from him.

Otherwise he might have fallen to the temptation...

Still there was the lingering thought of an

eternity in hell. The devil came to steal, kill, and destroy everything that Cade had been taught to believe. His mind could not be untangled from the very notion that if he were to sell his soul, he would find out in the hardest of ways possible that it was true what they said of the devil and hell.

Go back to Heaven!

Was he serious?

The nerve.

Cade continued under the overpass on Broadway and passed the day park were most of the homeless community congregated during the hours of light, simply milling about until their next meal at the rescue mission. He came to a stop light in front of a corner store to his right. Up ahead across the bridge he would come to the same eatery he and the bum had gone into to have drinks less than a week ago.

He could still visualize the particular evening vividly, clearly hear the "devil's" raspy voice and slow, painful words in his head. Unfortunately, he could even smell the combo of warm trash, a complete lack of showers, and 3-day-old worn clothing which encompassed the elderly man's personal space upon that first chance meeting. It was precisely these detailed flashbacks that had changed his route to work, simply to avoid the street where the two had met altogether, in hopes of erasing the new destructive thought process and unwanted sensory overloads that the street held.

The new pressure he faced daily was getting out of work in time to go find housing rather than taking days off and losing pay. The shelter would only allow a certain amount of time before they reviewed a person's case and asked them to leave. Luckily, as long as he could continue showing that he had full time employment, he would be able to buy himself some much needed time.

He'd explained this to his boss recently, who was anything but concerned or sympathetic to his situation.

"You make problems for yourself, you fix them," he had told Cade earlier in the week.

Great.

He simply could not grasp the concept of being a heartless individual. Did people not realize that in due time the tides of life would turn? That reaping what you sowed was a real thing indeed? How one treated people in their younger years could come back to haunt them in the elder stage. Honestly, he could see nothing but trouble in the vile owner's future.

It was said that patience was a virtue, but how many were so virtuous to begin with?

Lord knew he tried.

His thoughts were broken at the sound of commotion to his right where a group of homeless people gathered about watching an older man yell back and forth with a young lady of about twenty. Even from his standpoint, he could see that her body was withered from drug use and her clothing was extremely dirty, tangles of blonde hair falling around her face.

He immediately thought of Chance and how she had transformed in the years he had been gone from society. Her path was the one of least resistance, and it had been easy for her to conform to drugs in order to ease the pain of life. He'd seen it many times with guys in prison-he had even done the very same thing himself in his early years of incarceration.

But he had only gone on a downward spiral as a result, one that would ultimately lead to his destruction if he did not change his ways and turn his life over to Christ. He thanked God daily that he had not succumbed to the pressure placed on him.

The Lord will not place you in a position you can't handle, he constantly told himself.

The words played in his mind as he wondered if Chance could eventually handle her own addictive situation. He decided that everyone had to come around in their own time, if they came at all. The only way that a person would be successful at sobriety was if they wanted it for themselves.

He would continue to pray for her-had done so ever since being kicked to the curb. There was nothing more he could.

Let go and let God.

As he watched the ensuing argument between the man and woman a new thought entered his mind.

What if God wasn't the one placing people in their situations after all? What if the "devil" had been right? Did all things happen as a result of people making decisions and having consequences?

Free will.

How could free will exist alongside predestination? What choice did mankind really have in all of their existence? Were the two no more different than oil and water, unable to mix?

It irked him to think such things that were different from the lessons he had been taught in multiple Bible studies and church sermons. His beliefs were supposed to be law, unchanging, but was that essentially the problem with the world he lived in? Were people too closed minded to newer, more logical ways of thinking? There was nothing wrong with an evolved way of thinking, was there?

That's what the devil wants you to think, he could hear Ramsey saying from somewhere in a distant land.

The argument between the two homeless people was amplifying as he watched on from the corner of his eye, impatiently waiting for the chance to cross the street and go on about his day. Not minding your own business was the quickest way to die in prison and he intended to play by the same rules on the outside as well.

Suddenly the man reached back and viscously slapped the woman, causing her to fall to the ground as some of the spectators looked on as if nothing was happening. Shamelessly, others started laughing and letting out sounds of entertainment.

"Ah, man, don't do that!" Cade growled through gritted teeth.

Looking around for any sign of law enforcement, Cade felt a surge in his blood. Any other day a police vehicle would be stationed nearby, a handful of cops patrolling the area to prevent drug use, prostitution, and situations such as the one he was observing now.

The light turned red and he considered simply crossing the street and continuing on his trek to work. *Not my problem*, he thought. *Let one of the watchers break it up and mind your business!*

But he knew that wouldn't happen.

He watched as the man moved over to the lady and snatch her by the hair.

What would Jesus do? he couldn't help but think.

He wouldn't just walk off, as shown by His ultimate sacrifice in the Bible.

With that thought Cade went into action, crossing the street to where the situation was occurring, his stomach turning with butterflies as the assailant grew in size with each step he took.

Big mistake! Big mistake!

As he neared the group he called out, "You all just going to stand here and watch a woman get beat on?"

There were more than ten people that he was able to count, and not a single one responded to his inquiry as the man continued to assault the young lady.

Finally, a middle-aged man said, "We was waitin' on you to come play hero."

The man appeared to be in his forties, missing the top row of teeth in his mouth and was in bad need of bathing. His beard was matted to his face and he wore a dirty orange jacket with the hometown college logo on it.

Even though he had sniped Cade with sarcasm upon their initial meeting, a feeling of sadness crept over him as he envisioned himself out here just like one of the many in the coming years.

Who had the man been when he was my age? Cade thought to himself. Had he been an aspiring writer as well? Had he worked a regular job and paid taxes? Had a family? Was he a star athlete in high school like Tommy Buckets at some point in his life?

Had he been made an offer for his soul during his lowest point in life?

So many questions ran through his mind.

Life could go wrong so quickly. He now knew this even better from his own personal experience. Never could he have imagined that his life would go from loner in high school to promising military man, to prison and then to homelessness. Somehow, he was here though, faced with the same adversities as so many before him.

But would he fail like the man in front of him?

"Hey!" Cade called out to the abusive man who was now face to face with the woman, his hands gripping her face as profanities spewed from his mouth like blood from an open wound.

He paid Cade no mind.

"Let her go!" Cade growled as he went into savior mode, quickly moving in the direction of the man who was much larger than him.

How do I find myself in these crazy situations? He thought as he shook his head and came to a stop two feet away from the domestic abuse.

"Mind your business, boy," came the man's response.

He was about an inch over six feet, Cade calculated, and weighed about a hundred pounds more than him. This wasn't a good scenario, but...

"I said let her go!"

"You think I give a damn about what you said?" the man spat as he pushed the woman down. He now squared up with Cade who took a step back, his heart picking up speed.

"Bitch stole money from me!" the large man continued.

"I ain't stole nothin' from you!" the woman whimpered from her place on the gravel.

"Shut up!"

"Aw, man, come on," Cade said. "What'd she take? A fist full of pennies? Let it be."

The crowd laughed, and the big man's face flushed crimson. Cade knew then he had overstepped his boundaries. He'd read that sarcasm and quips were good for writing.

This was not a book though.

"Oh, you wanna be funny? You a show out?" the big guy growled.

He took an aggressive step towards Cade who slid to the side, wondering what he had gotten himself into.

"Don't run now!" the man barked at Cade as the crowd stood at full attention, anticipating a decapitation.

The man took a wild swing, Cade ducked, and nearly lost the backpack he had slung over one shoulder as he grabbed the fallen woman and helped her to her feet.

"Run!" he called to her. *"Go get the cops!"*

The woman wore a mask of relief on her drug-spotted face as she turned to run back toward the shelter where there would surely be some kind of authority figure loitering around for showman's sake.

"You crazy as hell, boy," she said to him just before taking off in a sprint.

"You better run and hide!" the goliath yelled after the woman.

Left alone with the seething man, Cade felt himself looking for an escape route. He'd saved the woman and now his first job was done.

His second was to get out of dodge and save his own tail.

"You getting the cops involved?" said the large vagrant, "How 'bout I *kill* you and give them a real reason to come get me?"

Panic set deep into Cade's bones, like cement, and he was unable to move, at least until the man lunged at him in an attempt to grab him.

Another side step as he wondered how long the bigger man would keep this up. He was slow, which made Cade figure he could run away now and not have to think about it anymore.

But, unfortunately, he was homeless now, which meant a high possibility of coming into contact with the giant again, even though in five days of being without housing he had never once seen him.

The crowd of onlookers cheered, loving the notion of having some 'real' excitement in their low-level lives.

He decided that if this fight would take place it would have to be some time down the road. Turning to run away he felt himself being pulled back, his bag being ripped away from him.

The man's long reach had finally paid off and he took full advantage of it by pulling Cade back, slinging him to the ground, the book bag in his hand.

"What you got here?" he said as Cade looked up at him. "You a school boy?"

"Give me my bag!" Cade yelled as he attempted to get back to his feet, a large foot meeting his rib cage as he did, toppling him into the gravel.

The on-lookers let out cheers as the fight finally began to escalate. The big man opened the backpack and found the laptop that Cade cherished, his livelihood.

Anger filled Cade's body and he felt hot all over.

"Looks like I got me a new computer, y'all," the gargantuan said to the group of bums who were obviously on his side.

Holding the device high he turned to the crowd to gloat. His victory was short lived as Cade put all of his weight into the man's middle section and took him to the ground with a strong football tackle, hurting his own shoulder in the process.

He straddled the giant and delivered a quick blow to his nose, partly to disable him, partly to relieve some of the stress that he had accumulated over the last, oh, fourteen years of his life-the latter driving a larger percentage of the punch.

Although he played the humble guy in Deborah's house when it came to Terry, he was no chump. After all, he had done military *and* prison time. There was a time to fight and a time to back down. *This was the time to get it on.*

Fighting back, the bum struggled through hazy vision to free himself from beneath his adversary, warm blood trickling from his nose to his neck as Cade fought with him for the laptop.

"Let go!" Cade demanded.

The host of vagrants gathered around, chanting their approval of the battle when suddenly the siren of a police car blared and caused them to scattered.

"Break it up!" came the voice of an officer who stood beside his car with his hand on his pistol, ready to draw down on the two fighting warriors as they continued on. *"I said, break it up, now!"*

Slowly Cade stood up from the top of the man, but not before he could snatch his laptop back.

"Hey!" The officer called upon seeing the move. "Both of you get over here, now."

Stepping away, Cade allowed the defeated man to regain his footing and began walking toward the officer, leaving the beastly man behind as he tried to explain the situation to the officer.

This was a terrible mistake that he could not have foreseen.

As he moved to within twenty feet of the officer, he heard a shriek come from his right, emitted from a woman who looked to have been in the streets the better part of her life.

Before he could react, Cade felt himself being yanked back by his forehead, a sharp object being driven into his chest from behind-*once, twice, three times.*

As he fell to the pavement, he heard the thunderous sound of the officer's gun going off. A nanosecond later the man he had been fighting only moments ago fell at his side with a thud, a spiritless body now.

On his back and gasping for air Cade could only wonder if he would be waiting for him on the other side of death. Would they be in different places-he in Heaven, the man in Hell?

Or vice versa.

What is Hell?

He heard the voice come to him as his chest began to tighten. His breathing became more labored as he gripped the ground with his fingertips.

He tossed his head side to side, looking for the source of the voice that had just come to him from nowhere.

He knew that voice.

But what did it matter now? He was dying. He could feel himself slipping away as his throat tightened. He looked to the sky, unable to formulate a sound other than a guttural moan, inwardly calling on the Lord, his savior, Christ All Mighty.

"You are calling out to the wrong one!" The voice came again, this time booming, full of rage. *"I can save you!"*

Coughing blood as tears formed in his eyes, Cade felt himself slipping further away as a fear he had never known gripped him tightly.

"Fine. Lay there and die, you fool!"

And that was just what Cade did.

He felt himself floating, weightless in pitch black with no sound, so very cold in a moment of nothingness.

There was no white light, as the "devil" had told him. But this was no quick transition either.

In fact, it seemed he had no end in sight.

12

So, this was death?

Have I done enough to get into the gates of heaven? Cade wondered.

Or would he fall into the pits of hell, having fallen short of the glory of God?

Wait, I have a conscious? Do dead people think?

You will have to wait to see, because you aren't dead yet.

The voice of the "devil" spoke loud and clear, piercing his thoughts like a poisonous dart.

In that moment Cade's eye opened to sunlight coming through a window as he came to. He squinted and took in a quick breath, instantly feeling a sharp pain in his chest that made him desire a restart on life.

Where am I?

Something was in his mouth, plastic. Cautiously he raised his hand to his mouth and felt what he now knew was a breathing tube.

What?

Through a haze he looked around and instantly knew that he was lying in a hospital room. He couldn't recall how he had gotten there, but as he started to come to panic flooded his body.

Struggling to raise himself to a sitting position, the pain in his chest worsened and he wondered just what had happened for him to be in such agony. It spread through his shoulders and to the back of his neck causing him to take short breaths in order to control it.

He thought hard.

The sun was bright so he figured it was morning. *What did I do yesterday? Work? Yes, of course, work.* He was always there, if not at home working on his writing. But what day was it? Had he in fact been at work yesterday?

Placing a hand to his chest he felt bandages and looked down, every movement a painful regret. *Jesus Christ!* he roared inwardly.

What happened to me?

It was said that pain was nothing more than a reminder that one was alive.

Damn that, he thought, although he was surely happy to be breathing still.

He felt heavily drugged and weak, but fully aware of the pain coursing through his body like poison.

Grabbing the alert button on the side of the bed, he laid back and waited for assistance from someone who could tell him something-anything-about what was going on and why he was here.

His mouth was dry and he was cold, the fear of breathing growing with every intake of air. Whatever drug induced state he had been put into, he wished that someone would hurry to his side and administer another dose.

This is a nightmare.

Not real. Not real. Not real.

A moment later a nurse walked into the room. His eyes darted to her with thanks and high hopes of an answer as to what he was doing in a hospital bed feeling like he had been shot. *More meds, please?*

And why am I here?

"Good morning, Mr. Cade," The nurse said. "How do you feel?"

"Terrible," he grumbled, the breathing tube making it hard to be verbal.

"Oh, well, that would be a normal feeling. You seem to be responding well to your surgery though."

"Surgery?"

"Oh, yes. You're a bit foggy right now. It's just the anesthetic. That is normally the case after such dramatic procedures."

"Dramatic?"

The nurse, a red headed, middle-aged woman with a few extra pounds let out a giggle. "You are full of questions, aren't you?"

Why wouldn't I be? Cade thought harshly, watching her disappear into the restroom. A moment later she returned with a cup of water and pressed a button on the side of the bed to bring Cade to a seated position.

Argh! He groaned, closing his eyes tightly and wishing the pain away in silence as she removed the tube.

"Your mouth must be dry," she said. "Here, drink this."

She placed the cup to his lips and he slowly drank, each swallow worse than the last. His legs shook and knocked against one another, but he could not resist the water. His mouth was dryer than a city in a drought.

"It's a long road to recovery," the nurse said, taking the water away from him and placing it on the counter. She leaned against it. "Do you know why you are here?"

Slowly Cade shook his head and quietly said, "No."

"You are a very lucky man. Blessed by the Lord indeed."

Not true! A voice rang out in Cade's head, causing him to jerk in the bed.

Alarmed, the nurse said, "Are you okay?"

"No! Why am I here? What happened to me?"

She explained to him that he had been stabbed in the chest with a screwdriver during an altercation, sustaining life-threatening damage to the left ventricle that could have left him brain damaged had it not been for immediate heart surgery.

It was then that he began to remember everything, the meeting with the "devil", the altercation at Deborah's house the next day, the country club, and then saving the homeless woman from being assaulted on his walk to work. He remembered being grabbed from behind, penetrated by some kind of object, the gunshots....

"You had a heart replacement," she explained to him. "You are very fortunate to be alive right now, considering there is a very long national organ transplant list. Even then, being on the list could be a five-year wait. Unfortunately, many people *die* just waiting for a chance to *live*."

If that didn't put a new perspective in his mind, nothing would.

How could he have possibly afforded a heart transplant? He had read in a magazine once they could cost over a million dollars, and the waiting listing was unbelievably long- thousands of people were on it, just as the nurse had stated.

So how had he been able to get a replacement so conveniently?

He asked the nurse and her face went dark.

"Money, of course," she said with a shrug. "When you have the kind of friends that you have..."

"Friends?" he asked, no clue as to what she was talking about. He wondered if the meds were messing with his hearing, but knew otherwise.

She had said friends. *Clearly* said friends.

"I will be honest with you, sir. You were brought in a day ago and had no insurance. Didn't look too good for you to get a heart. But then, out of nowhere, this really handsome black man made a large donation for your sake, and got you moved up the list. So, here you are. He must have really wanted you to live."

Cade was moved to silence. He looked away from the nurse, breathing slowly as his mind went to the "devil", clearly the handsome black man she had just referred to.

She then began to explain to him the struggle he had to look forward to over the next few months, beginning with the fact that even though the survival rate after one year was about 88% the average life expectancy for heart transplant recipients was a mere nine years, a fact that made him want to savor every breath he took, no matter how painful they were.

He could be dead soon-should have already been dead.

"How long do I have to be here?" he asked her, a tear trickling down his cheek, his nose running.

"Two weeks, maybe more," she answered, retrieving a tissue and handing it to him. "Recovery time is generally about three to six months, but I wouldn't worry myself over that just yet. We have to see how everything goes initially with your medications-there's a long list of them. We have to make sure that there is no acute cellular rejection of the new heart in your body."

This, she explained, happened when the T-cells in a person's immune system attacked the cells of the new heart, which was why he would be on a long list of medications and would need to exercise along with taking on a strict diet.

"After that we can begin to worry about how long you will live. But I'll tell you, in many cases, people live over the average of 9 years. Some go 10-15 years without any major problems. The longest survivor was 33 years, and he was told he only had five years to live. He beat the odds."

Well that was a relief, Cade thought. He didn't want to die any time soon, especially at the same hospital that he was born in.

The nurse went on to explain that he would experience tiredness, pains on each side of his chest for several weeks to come, and even the possibility of a personality change from the transplant. Scary stuff. Just the thought of it made him want to curl up and hide in an imaginary shell.

But he had life when life was supposed to have been lost, so therefore he would do whatever it took to get back on his feet and moving again.

Two thoughts entered his mind: The first was a matter of where he would stay once released from the hospital, considering the shelter would not hold onto him and supply care while he rehabilitated if he didn't have a job. His family was clearly out of the question, and there was no going back to stay with Chance, especially as a cripple after the events that had transpired only a week ago.

The second thought that ran through his mind was the "devil". Where was he? There was no doubt that he had been the one to make the so-called "donation" to pay for his heart transplant. Cade started to feel anxious, as he wondered if that would be held against him. After all, he had saved his life.

But why?

"Where is my cell phone?" Cade weakly asked the nurse. Moving quickly, she retrieve his bag of property from a drawer in the counter and handed it to him. Slowly he opened it and found that his phone had no energy.

He groaned aloud.

"What's wrong," the nurse asked.

"My phone is dead," he whined.

The nurse offered her own charger to use until his phone was fully charged and moved to exit the room. Cade called out to her weakly.

"What happened to the guy that stabbed me?"

The nurse was silent and thoughtful for a moment then said, "He was shot down by the officer on the scene."

"Dead?"

She nodded.

"Shame," Cade mumbled, shaking his head.

"Yes," she agreed. "But you had to get that heart from somewhere."

What!

The look on his face spoke volumes.

The nurse caught his reaction and said, "The Lord works in mysterious ways."

Yeah, whatever!

Left alone, Cade closed his eyes and began to drift away from the pain, away from the adversity of his life, away from it all, fully exhausted.

And then the phone next to his bed rang.

His head fell to the side and he eyed the noisy object on the table, figured it would stop ringing once the person on the other line got the point that no one in the room was interested in talking at the moment.

Instead, it kept ringing.

And ringing and ringing.

Finally, he struggled to roll over and pick up the line. Before he could say a word the voice on the other line came through the receiver.

"I saved your life," the "devil's" haunting voice came through the phone, darker than before. "I believe you owe me for that, because I didn't see your God moving to do anything about the situation, even though you say He takes care of His own. I guess Philippians 4:19 is a lie, huh?"

"Leave me alone," Cade said weakly, hanging up the phone.

He knew that would never happen. The "devil" was on his line, and would not let up until he got what he wanted.

As Cade fell back into his slumber, he thought to himself, *maybe I do owe him.*

Just maybe.

13

Everything that the nurse had told him of his stay in the hospital over the next few weeks had been a vast understatement. While trying to use the bathroom or simply moving from the bed to his wheelchair so that he could be rolled outside for sunlight and fresh air, he felt like he would topple over and die. At night, he found himself wishing for a quick death in his sleep so that he would be put out of his misery.

The steps to grieving, he knew from a suicide prevention class in prison, were depression, anger, denial, pleading and acceptance.

DADPA, as he called it.

Towards day nine in the hospital, his mind started to switch gears and he accepted that his life had been spared. That meant another person had to die for the heart to be available. Instead of crying and being angry about the hardships and issues he was facing once he was released from the hospital, he decided that he would fight on until he was back to full strength and able to get back to his old self.

While thinking about his life however, he was unsure if he even wanted to be his old self again. What, exactly, had that person accomplished in life other than creating pain for himself and others?

Wasn't it time he did something better?

Aside from accepting Jesus as his savior his life had been pretty calamitous, nothing short of mundane, not exactly the success story he would have hoped for.

He couldn't help but think that if he had died, had the "devil" not come to his aide....

Was God going to let him die? After all the Bible reading, all the changes he had made in his life in order to be a better Christian?

Would that have been the plan for his life, written by the Lord Himself?

If when you die is known, then how you die is known.

The "devils" words skipped around in his mind like mischievous kids.

So, if it was God's plan for him to end up in the hospital with a new heart beating in his chest, then it was the plan all along for the homeless man to stab him, which meant that poor man would have died in his own sin and was now burning in hell, having been shot dead by an officer, who was no doubt having flashbacks of his own from taking a man's life.

All planned?

No, it couldn't be. What kind of God would sit around devising those kinds of plans all over the world? Shouldn't He be doing bigger and better things with His time?

Cade's thought process about what he believed was now being reshaped, regrettably, but...his life was full of lessons that had shown him that maybe it was time for a change.

He wondered if the heart in his body was making him change. Was the homeless man harboring an evil organ that was now slowly making Cade vile beyond his own knowledge?

No!

This had nothing to do with organs, rather everything to do with his life and his faith that was now shakier than a bicycle ride on railroad tracks.

I don't know what to believe anymore, he would tell himself every day when his eyes opened.

The day to leave was fast approaching and he still had no home to go to once he walked out of the hospital. He'd set his pride to the side and contacted his family who all denied him a place to stay. They hadn't even come to visit him-no different than when he was in prison-but he could not stress over any of it. He needed to be extra cautious with the new muscle in his chest, so stressing was out of the question.

He refused to die here, from a literal broken heart. No, he would figure things out somehow. He hadn't heard a word from the "devil" since the last call made to his hospital room, and in a way, he felt he had failed himself by not taking the offer made to him. At least he would have had something to get out of the hospital to. His belongings that he had in the mission were delivered to the hospital, and once again he was without a place to rest his head at night.

Living on the streets after recent heart surgery was not an ideal situation, he knew. He could very possibly die out there in that cold weather and had been told as much by hospital staff, who, by no fault of their own, had to prepare him for an exit.

Other people needed beds as well, and it was not their fault he had no place to go. Their work with him was nearly done, and once it was, he was on his own. It would be his responsibility to make it to follow ups and continue taking his medication correctly if he wanted to continue breathing on earth.

You're no Job, he remembered the "devil" saying.

Job was a man who had everything-children included-taken from him, but never renounced the name of God, against his wife's wishes. As a reward for his faith, he received double what he had taken from him.

It would take an incredible person to withstand such loss and not turn on the one who had allowed the travesty to happen in their life.

Or was that just a story? Had it even really happened? Allegories and parables.
The Bible was full of them, he knew, but now he wondered if the whole book was built on stories, falsehoods and folklore to motivate people to be better, all while blinding them to their own powers-whether purposely or inadvertently-causing them to place all faith in a God who was not in the business of doing for people who praised Him and gave their all in His name.

Faith without works is dead the Bible said. But what about works without faith?

He looked in the mirror of his hospital bathroom, stared deep into himself as he brushed his teeth and hair. He ran cold fingers through his beard, which hadn't been touched since being admitted to the hospital.

Depression was his new name, and he could not shake the lingering idea that God was failing him, letting him down when he had attempted to give his all to Him. Letting him down when he needed him the most. Each day he would have to wake up and clean the wound on his chest to prevent infection, and in doing so he would be reminded of the close encounter he had with death.

Did anyone truly have the answers to God? Or were most believers merely guessing and hypothesizing, trying to come up with the best way to live life while on this cruel earth?

The latter was beginning to make so much more since to him at this new, near death stage of his life. Answers about God were hard to come by, and he now wondered what was the use of it all.

Basic instructions before leaving earth-a common acronym for the word Bible-was something he once held on to as a principle of life, but now he wondered if he had sold himself short by playing on the Biblical side of the fence.

He walked back into the room and found his phone lying on the bedside desk. Cade eyed it a moment before picking it up, feeling the weight of an object so small, yet so heavy, knowing what it contained.

Three numbers.

Numbers that could very well change his life, he thought as he punched them in. He took a deep breath before he placed his thumb on send.

He wrestled with the thought of pushing the call button as the new heart in his body began to pump harder. His breathing became shallow and tears began to form in his eyes.

So, it had come to this? Had his depression and desperation led him to lose faith in the Lord?

His thoughts traveled back to his early life, to the night of the incident that ultimately led him to hell on earth-prison.

Had God been anywhere in the picture all of those years?

He wasn't sure what he believed at that very moment in his destitute life. The only thing he knew for certain was that he should be dead, somewhere resting on a metal slab with a toe tag, cold from the cooler in the morgue, just another victim of life.

But he was alive, and it was because of....

Satan?

He'd been spared, no doubt, but should he feel indebted for the act? Is that what the "devil" had anticipated?

He held the phone up, his hand shaking dramatically.

"Mr. Cade?"

He dropped the phone, startled by the voice

behind him. Wheeling around he was surprised to see the same nurse who had allowed him to use her phone charger.

"Didn't hear you come in," he said weakly, slowly leaning to retrieve the phone. Quickly the nurse moved to help him.

"I've got it," she said, helping Cade into the bed. "You need to rest up."

Without giving too much fight Cade allowed himself to be tucked in, closing his eyes.

"You've been crying," the nurse said. "Would you like to talk about it?"

Without a word Cade shook his head side to side, his eyes never opening.

"You know, the Lord will take you through things in order to see just how much you can take right before he blesses you."

"I used to think that," Cade responded.

The nurse offered to bring him a Bible, to which he refused. No longer did he desire the Word of God, for all the reading and praying he had invested into it had only led him here, crippled and lying in a hospital bed, unsure if the heart in his body would last through the night.

So many thoughts ran through his head as he lay in the hospital bed at night, eyes clinched tightly with tears falling gradually from the corners as he thought of his daughter.

Would he ever see her again? Could he make amends before his heart failed him?

Jacy!

Would she ever grow to love him the way that he wanted her to? Between missing so much of her life and Chance planting such a bad depiction of him in her head, a rift had grown between them. Now she was more connected to Terry for being there in his absence. The very thought of him playing daddy to her made Cade sick. Being away all of her life, hidden and locked away from view, only to come home and be a failure in person didn't make matters any better between he and his daughter.

But if he could turn the tide in his favor....

Opening his eyes, he looked over at the phone again.

He was stunned when it rang right as he had gotten it into his grasp. Hesitating, he picked it up and looked at the I.D., unable to recognize the number. He debated whether or not to answer, nowhere close to being in the mood to deal with any telemarketers.

"Hello," he answered.

The friendly voice on the other end was one he did not know, but the liveliness of it made Cade want to get up and run around every floor of the hospital spreading good cheer.

"Mr. Cade, are you ready to pack up and get out of that cold, depressing room?"

"Uh, yes, but who is this?"

"The name's Vernon, and I'm at your beck and call, sir. You say the word and I got you, my friend."

Confused Cade asked, "Who are you? Why would you be willing to be at my beck and call? How did you get my number? Who sent you to come and pick me up?"

Chuckling Vernon replied, "Questions, so many questions. How about you come on downstairs and I'll explain everything to you when we leave."

"I just had a heart transplant. I can't leave here yet."

Vernon's voice suddenly went from friendly and cheerful to serious and stern. "Everything you could ever need has already been arranged, Mr. Cade. Including your medical needs. You won't even need your bag of personal property. Just leave it. Now, I can come up and help you down, or you can have the nurses bring you so we can get out of here. It's all the same to me."

"I'm not so sure I should do that." He waited a beat. "I asked who sent you."

"Your friend sent me."

"Who?"

"Lucifer."

Cade felt his heartbeat spike once again as he sat up straight in the bed, listening intently.

"Hey, that's not his real name is it?" Vernon went on, seemingly entertained. "That a nickname from back in the day or something?"

"Uh, sure, yeah, whatever. Where are you?" Cade asked, laboring as he got up from the bed and moving painfully through the room to the window, looking out to see if he could see Vernon.

"At the entrance to the medical center."

Silence was Cade's response.

"I was told to leave you here, if you so desired"

"*No!* I want to leave. I hate it here."

"I'd say so. Well, come one down, my friend.!"

"Wait, where are we going?"

"Home. I've come to take you home."

Cade waited a beat and then asked, "Is Lucifer there?"

"Oh, yes, he will be anxiously awaiting your arrival."

Anxiously, he says, Cade thought inwardly. *I bet he is!* Hanging up he moved slowly to the bedside button and summoned the nurse. A moment later she arrived.

"I'm leaving," he said, his demanding attitude taking her by surprise. "Sign me out of here."

She did her best to convince him otherwise but he would hear none of it. A doctor was brought in to suggest other options as well, but Cade shook his head.

"No. My ride is here and I am leaving. I appreciate all that you people have done for me, but it is time for me to go."

And that was that. What were they going to do, hold him hostage? He only had a couple of days before they kicked him out anyway, and he expressed as much.

A moment later he was being wheeled down to the exit by two nurses, a physician very close by with a bag of medicine in hand, giving Cade his instructions on how to take the meds the whole way, reminding him to come for check-ups.

Pushing through the exit into the sunny day the wind chill hit like a swift boxer, but he could not care any less. He was alive and the cold had never felt better. Sitting in the wheelchair he could not decide what felt better; being released from prison or the hospital, alive.

The latter, of course, once he really thought it over logically.

In the pick-up circle at the front of the medical center he laid his eyes up on a beautifully crafted car. Beside it stood a tall, strong looking man in a nice suit.

Vernon?

"Mr. Cade!" the man said. "Nice to meet you!"

Reaching his hand out he took Cade's and pumped it twice with a grip so firm Cade was unsure if he would let go.

"I'll take him from here," Vernon told the staff who could only look on in wonder of the handsome giant and his shiny chariot.

When asked by Cade where, exactly, he had come from Vernon's response was a simple "I'm just hired help."

That was enough for Cade, who was too tired to get deeper into things at the moment. The "devil" had many tricks up his sleeve, apparently, and this appeared to be one of them.

Helping Cade into the car, Vernon pushed the wheelchair to the side and began to close the door.

"All you need is your medication," he said to Cade. "You have full care where you are going, wheelchairs included."

Well, all right then, Cade thought as he sat back and buckled up for the ride-a wild ride, he was sure.

"Anything you need before we get to where we are going?" Vernon asked as he started the car. "Anything at all? You say it and you've got it."

He looked at Cade with such sincerity, making him immediately feel safe, as if he were a big brother sent to be guardian.

Cade shook his head.

"No, I just want to get to where we are going and see...." He paused a moment, realizing what he was about to say. "Lucifer."

"Say no more, my friend."

Vernon punched in the address on the GPS and pressed the gas to begin their ride to the destination, Cade staring at the screen the whole time.

"Lyons View Pike," he said aloud. "Isn't that the street that the country club is on?"

"Yep," Vernon answered. "We are going a few places down, to the Villa Collina."

"The villa what?"

Laughing Vernon said, "Just sit back. You're going to enjoy this, Mr. Cade. Trust me, it's like nothing you have ever seen."

I guess I will take your word for it, Cade thought as he rode in silence. What else could he do? He was helpless and on the fence with death, possibly walking hand in hand with the reaper. Things were basically out of his hands now.

He was no longer the writer of his own story, and rather than give it all over to God as he had tried to do only days ago, he was ready to turn his life over to a new God.

The devil.

14

The Villa Collina, it's exterior painted in Buena Vista gold with valet white trim, sat high above the river and could be done no justice by a mere description. As Cade laid his eyes upon the gargantuan of a structure, he marveled at its beauty as they moved past the gate.

The grounds were perfectly hedged, and in the distance, he could see the river that ran down below.

"Took five years to build this place," Vernon said as he came to stop under a large breezeway at the entrance of the home. "It's the largest home in Tennessee.

"Who lives here?" Cade asked.

"I'm just hired help, my friend. I do as you ask of me."

"Is this where... Lucifer is?"

"Yes, it is."

A moment later Vernon was out of the car and helping Cade just as two women with soft features dressed in casual clothing stepped from the house, one of them pushing a wheelchair.

"Your nurses," Vernon whispered to Cade. "I'd say you could use a sponge bath right about now, huh?"

Cade chuckled.

"Welcome, Mr. Cade," the taller, blonder of the two nurses said, her Russian accent sending a tingle through him. "My name is Milania and this Nadia-" she pointed to her friend. "We will be your personal nurses until you get back on your feet and moving like your old self again."

"Not so sure I want to heal if you two have to leave when I'm healthy again," Cade said flirtatiously, taking his place in the wheelchair.

The nurses giggled, blushing at his charm.

"Good one," Vernon said, giving Cade's shoulder a gentle squeeze. "Right on time. I can tell you are a writer."

Cade looked up at him. *Yes, I am a writer, damnit!* Vernon was likable, Cade thought. Very likable.

"Your guest is awaiting you," Nadia said with a smile, her teeth white as the purest snow.

"Guest?" Cade said. "I thought I was the guest here."

The nurses giggled once more, sharing a knowing look.

"A guest in your own house, Mr. Cade?" Nadia said.

My own house?

His throat constricted and he couldn't speak. He felt sweat beading on his forehead as he tried to gather himself, knowing this was all too much. He'd gone from being flat broke to a member of the oldest country club in the city to barely holding on for dear life, to....

This!

The biggest house in Tennessee!

How?

The answer was easy, and it was behind the doors of the, waiting for him to step inside and accept the offer made to him.

Cade was now prepared to accept.

Milania stepped behind the wheelchair and slowly pushed him into the elaborate manor. His breath was instantly taken away by the magnificence and beauty of the home.

A large stairway that looked sturdy enough to hold another residence loomed straight ahead. To his left, Cade saw a fancy dining room with a table and cabinets filled with intricate China and pieces of crystal that looked to cost more than he was worth as a human. Above him hung a crystal chandelier that would break his heart had it fallen to the floor below, for he had never seen something so beautiful and grande up close and personal.

"This place is so serious," Vernon said. They all took in the home together. "I'm going to love living here."

"You live here too?" Cade asked, surprised.

As well as other staff members, Vernon informed him, to Cade's delight. This included the nurses, which excited Cade all of the sudden when only a few weeks ago the thought of fornicating would have had him asking for forgiveness, just as he had after the few slip ups upon his release.

Forget the rules of man. Live life.

Why feel so bad about something that comes so naturally to all humans

A stunning young Latina woman with hair darker than oil moved through the room in clicking heels and pants so tight they would surely have to be torn off. She introduced herself as Claudia, his personal assistant and spokeswoman who would handle anything he desired. She informed him that she, too, lived in the home.

Staff members, he thought with a smile. People who worked for him now. He could and would get used to that.

Positioned close to the stairs was a beautiful piano and Cade, never having been one for the art, suddenly felt motivated to learn, picturing himself playing harmonious expressions to crowds of friends and family, his joy for life on full display.

He was deep into thoughts of harmony when a voice from the top of the stairs broke his reverie.

"I'll take him from here," Lucifer said, staring down at Cade as he slowly took the steps down.

The two of them locked eyes in a moment of knowing, the devil wearing a sly smile on his face, sensing victory in his efforts to persuade Cade into selling his soul.

Vernon and the three women suddenly disappeared, leaving just Satan and Cade in the entrance of the home.

"John 3:16," Satan said as he came to a stop on the last step and leaned on the rail. "The most quoted Bible verse of all time. Would you agree?"

Cade replied, "I can see that being the case."

"Is that right? Can you see it being the biggest lie ever told by man?"

Cade was quiet and unsure of what to say. His faith had been fully rooted in God and the belief that He had sent His son to die on the cross for the sins of all people, Jesus returning soon to save them one glorious day.

Now he wasn't so sure of that.

"I don't know what to believe anymore," he said.

"Good. That's a start that I can work with," Satan said, his face set in stone. "But you better get to know that the verse I refer to... is the biggest hoax ever created by man."

"If so, you are to blame."

"Not at all. As I told you before, I can't make you do anything. If a thought is conceived, I push you to enjoy yourself in doing the deed of that thought. You see," he continued, stepping off the stairs, "that is where God and I differ the most. I am a fan of people doing whatever they want, no matter how much chaos it causes. Please the flesh all you want. Him? Not so much."

"The world isn't exactly a better place with chaos."

"Says who?" Satan asked, insulted. "You?"

Again, Cade was without words, unable to

formulate any kind of answer that would suffice in the particular situation.

"You see, Cade," Satan said, rotating his body toward the piano and beginning a slow trek through the house, snapping his finger and causing the wheelchair Cade sat in to follow without warning, "chaos gives the world balance. Everything has to have contrast. Up, down, left, right, peace, chaos. I am the balance of this world."

Such an arrogant, devilish thing to say, and Cade was unsure how he felt about it.

Gripping the sentries of the wheelchair tightly, he could only ride and listen, partly in fear of what power the devil truly possessed.

Did he ever really stand a chance against the prince of evil? he wondered as Satan turned to lead the way down a long, decorated hallway with columns throughout, much like Greek times.

"You have all kinds of people who like to judge others on their sins, oblivious to the fact that they are no less guilty in the eyes of God than the people they shun. The Bible-trash as it is-teaches that there is no sin worse than another except...?"

"Blasphemy of the Holy Ghost."

They came to an elevator door and the devil held up a single finger, never turning to look at Cade.

"Exactly. Romans 3:23 says all have sinned and come short of the glory of God," Satan mocked preached. "Jesus was close to the bad guys, but these so-called "do-gooders" are the ones who masquerade in churches every Sunday in their pretty clothing as if it will hide the filth they are covered in beneath. Aren't you supposed to be a new person after being "saved?"

Turning to Cade he added, "Luke 12:2 tells you

that whatever is covered will be uncovered. They might as well show up to church naked. Because honestly, it wouldn't make a difference to God what you wore."

"They could if you hadn't made being naked a bad thing."

"Oh, let me guess, you still have it in your mind that mankind started from two naked fools in the Garden of Eden. We'll break you of all the lies eventually. Just stick with me."

The elevator door opened and the wheelchair was pulled inside the mirrored carriage as Satan moved forward. He placed his back against the wall, looking down at Cade who was feeble as ever.

"For God so loved the world," Satan recited as the doors came to a kiss and they began ascending, "that He sent the devil to make the world sin and drag most of society to hell. That He would let you praise Him day and night, only to end up on your deathbeds."

Looking down on Cade he asked, "Who was the one who loved you enough to save you? Where was He in your most desperate time? Hmm? Was he busy resting like they say He did on the seventh day?"

Cade tried looking away but he could not escape the shame on his face, the mirrors capturing everything and reflecting it back to him, as if mocking.

"You want to know why the Bible is the biggest con to mankind? It's because of the lack of absolute truth. One plus one will always be two, no matter where on Earth you do the math. The sun is the sustainer of life *worldwide*. But when it comes to the Word of God, the supposed most important thing in the history of mankind...too many interpretations. Which makes it ironic that they chose to write it on flimsy, easily torn pages."

"I'm feeling weak," Cade complained.

"Easy on that heart," the devil warned. "I don't like you enough to get you another one."

Cade looked up at him with pain in his eyes.

Laughing as the doors opened the devil said, "Just kidding. You're my main man. I'd kill for you to have another heart, if and when the time comes. And I mean that." Leaning in he whispered, "Why do you think I had that cop shoot the man who stabbed you? He didn't really have to do that, but we see it all the time, right?"

"You also had the man stab me," Cade said heatedly.

"Stay out of people's business next time!" Satan growled in Cade's face. "He created the thought of killing you, and I had no choice but to push him along. You know better, so the blame is on you. I had to cut you. It was only fair."

"Me to blame?"

"How I work will all come to you soon," Satan continued, ignoring Cade. "You forced my hand, but I'm on your side though, just so you know. That's why the homeless man is dead and you are alive. Besides, I wanted him more than you anyway. He was ready for hell. If you died, I might not have gotten what I wanted."

He stepped off the elevator as Cade's wheelchair spun around.

"How is that so when-" Cade was beginning to say when he laid his eyes upon a fantastical entertainment room with the shiniest floors he had ever seen.

"When what?" Satan said.

"How can I trust you when you already tried to have me killed?"

"You're not understanding me, so let me say this once more. I don't plant thoughts in the heads of people. If they envy the new fortune and fame you have, that's on them. I won't stop anyone from taking you out because that's not what I do. If that's a problem you have two options. One, turn around and enjoy your new heart, maybe go back to God and live like you were living before."

"Option two?" Cade asked, feeling he had no choice.

As if for added drama, the devil paused, moved closer to Cade and leaned in close enough that the smell of a recent cigar could be smelled on his breath.

"Hire a mean security team. That'll at least thwart any attempts on your life."

Furrowing his brows Cade could only accept the answer. Otherwise he could choose option one and take his chance with the new heart pumping life through his frail body, not knowing how far that would get him.

"What the hell were you thinking trying to save that homeless girl anyway? It's not like her life matters."

"All lives matter," Cade said.

"No, they don't."

Cade was mute, so the devil continued.

"I can see in your eyes how bad you want to side with me. All that I have told you, the new chance at life I've granted you, this house...You're only timid because you have been brainwashed, your thoughts bleached of all reason, leaving not a bit of common sense in you. People are their own worst psychologists, faking themselves out through prayers and always expecting things that will not happen."

"If it's all lies why hasn't everything been exposed and ended?"

"Oh, it's exposed all the time. You good folks down here on earth just never seem to want to accept it. People carry on with their cults and prayer rituals that steal souls, unbeknownst to the public."

"What does that mean?"

"It's means when you go into a church and pray the Lord's Prayer in unison you are secretly being hypnotized while a human sacrifice is performed right below you in the church?"

"What?" said Cade, skeptically. "You're telling me that thousands—"

"Millions!"

"Of innocent people—"

"Guilty in the churches eye, for they have sinned."

"So what? They kill them for that? Kind of backwards."

"No, they offer up their offender's soul and sacrifice them to God. But here's the catch; they don't even know if God will accept their sacrifice."

"So, they're just experimenting?"

Satan stood straight and tilted his head, his answer *yes*. Cade shook his head slowly, thinking of all the times he had said the Lord's Prayer, how many people had possibly been sacrificed within feet of him.

"Do they ever hear from God telling them who made it in and who didn't?"

"I wouldn't know."

"What do you mean you don't know? You're there to see all this stuff go down, aren't you?"

"Nope."

Cade gave an expectant look, demanding an answer with his eyes.

"I haven't seen it because it hasn't happened. I made it all up." He bellowed with laughter and pointed at Cade who held his chest in pain, wondering what he had gotten himself into.

He was sure he would find out, in due time. But for now, it was time to have some fun.

"I will be putting that one into play very soon. And I will help them run with it and make it real. Their claim will be that God gave them the idea while I just sit back and watch this world burn to the ground."

"You said you don't give thoughts."

"Little white lies, Cade. It'll come to you in due time."

Cade opened his mouth to speak but was cut off.

"*Come on and see this house!* It sure as hell beats the homeless shelter."

Indeed, it did.

15

Satan began his tour of the home, Cade too wrapped up in it all to hear anything he was saying. He would have to take a second tour on his own time to appreciate the splendor of the mansion in full.

"Why me?" came from Cade's lips.

Satan stopped abruptly, turned to face him with a smile on his face.

"Why not you-"

"Damn that!" Cade blurted, two-hand slapping the rails of the chair. "I want to know why you came to me. Of all the people in this world, you come to me. I want to know why!"

Satan held his gaze, his face serious now. Taking two slow steps to the wheelchair he once again leaned down to a face-to-face position and pressed Cade's hands to the rails-tightly-causing his face to become flushed with fear as he fought back unsuccessfully.

"I don't have to tell you a damn thing. You know why?" He gave Cade a moment to think it over. "Because you are not stronger than me. I will not answer to you or any God who claims to be above me. *I have no God.* We clear?"

Cade said nothing.

"Clear?" the devil asked again, this time with a bark, applying more pressure on Cade's hands.

"Yes!"

His hands were released and he opened and closed them as he grimaced at the devil.

"I just want you to live out your pipe dreams," Satan said pleasantly. "Isn't that what Chance said about your book writing career?"

Cade nodded aggressively. "Yeah, a pipedream."

"We'll show them, won't we?"

"That we will," Cade concurred, taking Satan's outstretched hand and shaking it.

"This is going to be so much fun!" Satan exclaimed, jumping behind the wheelchair and racing Cade through the long hallway.

"Slow down!" Cade managed to scream through the pain in his chest.

"No slowing down, ever again."

Satan pushed him down hallway after hallway of the 37,000 square foot home, which was bought in a haste for fifteen million dollars.

"Fifteen million?" Cade choked.

"Only the best for you, my man." Satan informed him. There were fifty rooms in total, and they traveled nearly all of them, each one delighting Cade more and more as they went along.

The wine cellar was a brick fortress of the finest tastes from around the world and Cade knew not one single brand.

"Don't know if I need this room," Cade said, looking up at the devil sheepishly.

"I don't care how many people you killed when they say you were drunk. This life is way too good to not have a fermented drink every once and a while. You're enjoying this!" Satan ordered.

Cade shook his head and smiled. "What am I going to do with you?"

"Everything we want to do. Whatever world you choose to create, it is yours."

In his bedroom he found a pearl colored couch made by a company he could not pronounce, further letting him know he was now in the money. Not only because he had a pricey, funny named couch-*because he had a couch in his room.* There was a sizable closet nearly the size of a small retail store as well, a suit of all colors resting on expensive mahogany hangers, the smell of new fabric heavy in the air.

Who does that? He speculated.

Rich people did that, because they had rooms the size of apartments to play around in. He was ready to play.

"Let's see the garage-" Satan began.

"Wait, wait, wait," Cade gasped. "All this excitement has me hot and barely able to breathe," he told Satan. "I want to go outside and feel the breeze on my skin."

"You mean you want to feel alive?"

Cade swallowed hard. "Yeah, I feel like I should be dead, but I'm here."

"That you are. Make the best of it."

Outside Cade squinted in the sunlight but could still see the Spanish roof tiles above him as he counted every column that lined the back of the house.

Oh, to what do I owe the honor of such a home?

They parked themselves at an outside table overlooking the pool and gazed out at the river down below, both muted for a very long moment.

Finally, Cade said, "Tell me about Jesus?" Satan looked him over with disgust. "For what?" he asked.

"There's just things that I'm curious about still. I need to be fully convinced to do this whole deal."

Rolling his eyes the devil groaned and shot to his feet.

"As if that new heart in your body isn't enough convincing! As if this house and that membership at the country club isn't enough convincing! My transition from bum to this!" he swept his body in display. "You think that shit just fell out of the sky over night?"

"No-"

"Then what is it? You're about to make me take that heart back. I bought it. It's mine."

Cade searched his eyes for some form of humor, found none.

"I'm just..." He was lost for words.

Sighing and conforming, the devil said, "Fine. Ask anything you want to ask and I will tell you what you need to know-not what you want to hear. I like breaking it to you this way anyway. Piece by piece I will chip away at all you have ever been taught to believe."

Chills sprinted through Cade's body as the devil spoke, the sense of his evil presence seeping into a part of him.

"I want to know who Jesus is?"

Satan laughed. "Who do you think He is?"

Cade hesitated and answered, "Son of-"

"Wrong!" Satan barked at Cade who coward in the wheelchair. "Wrong! Wrong! Wrong!"

Satan paced around Cade who could only listen as he began a monologue.

"The Bible is a beautiful work of art," the devil began. "Notice I say art. It's *artistically* written and thought provoking. So much so that people can't seem to agree on certain parts of the book. Namely, who was Jesus Christ?"

"The center of all debates when it comes to faith."

"Precisely."

"So?"

"So, he says," Satan chuckled, waving Cade off. "So why should I tell you when you have already been brainwashed into believing what you have been taught? *That so?*"

"No, so who is Jesus?"

"Not so sure you can handle the truth. You're not even using your own heart right now. You sure you want to risk that ticker?"

Sucking in a deep, painful breath and releasing it slowly Cade looked off into the sky, wondering what was out there far beyond this world. Was there a higher power that had created and left humans on their own to figure out life as time went on? Had there been groups of people who wrote a book so logical and meaningful that people were now being controlled by it for fear of punishment in an afterlife?

"I'm ready. I want to know who Jesus was?"

Stopping his pace in front of Cade, the devil nodded and went on.

"The Bible is all about perceptions, Cade. Take King David for example. You really think a feeble young teenager killed a ten-foot giant with a slingshot? Or do you think the story is an allegory for the human condition?"

"We've seen stranger things. I think it could've happened."

"Even the strongest believers have trouble with stories in the Bible, Cade. No one can be faulted for having questions, because you can't truly expect to give humans something to read and expect there not to be curiosities and disagreements about the content. Your minds are not built that way. You're all explorers, wanderers into the lands of dangerous and destructive things. Kudos, though, because your foolishness has moved you forward in this world. People have come a long way, only they went the wrong direction."

"Won't dispute that."

"You better not," the devil said before continuing on. "One has to ask questions about the Bible. Only in those pages people can be swallowed by whales and spit out to safety after showing faith in an unseen God. People take it literally. How about the buddies in Babylon, thrown into a hot stove and not once burned? You have seen nothing close to that."

"Just because I haven't seen it doesn't mean I don't believe it existed or happened. I'd never seen you before and still believed."

"You still haven't seen me. This is not my body. I got this from a close friend from a distant time. But if there is *anything* you should believe in, it's me. One thing all belief systems can agree on is yours truly, the magnificent one."

"I hear you."

"Hear this; man has always had reproductive organs. God never had to see that he was lonely in order to give him a mate. He was always with a woman, because he was built to procreate, one of your two true purposes in life."

"What's that got to do with Christ?"

"Everything. From the opening of the book it begins with lies. So, what makes you think that thousands of years later the lies haven't become more elaborate? The bigger the lie-like a son from the highest power coming to save his people-the more people believe it."

"He was God in the flesh."

"So naïve," the devil said as he shook his head and leaned onto a concrete rail. "You have so little knowledge of the stories you read. None more than revelations, the supposed end of times."

"What's that all about, the end?"

"You'll know when it comes. I'd hate to ruin the suspense for you. Now, back to your savior. The man who knows something knows he knows nothing at all, and you would do good to remember that. Leave all these traditions of men in the wind and do your own thing, because it's all a big guess anyway."

"Jesus isn't just a guess," Cade countered. "They have record of him."

"At least that's what they say. But have you seen any attempts to get those records to the public? The answer is no, and you never will. They have people who are smarter than you to put you in place with their philosophies on life. So, when a good theologian comes in and says, 'yes, this is the history of Jesus,' the weak-minded take heed to the bigger brain in a thinking situation."

"I can see that. Too often we would rather take the word of a minister or teacher rather than find the answers ourselves."

"Exactly. It's no different with their lies about Jesus. He was just a man, that's all. Says so in 1 Timothy 2:5. 'For there is one God, and one mediator between God and mankind, the *man* Jesus Christ.'"

"He left in sacrifice and is supposed to come back like a thief in the night."

"Yeah, well, I'm not sneaking in like a thief. I'm here in your face, right now, kicking your door in."

True, Cade thought.

"Speaking of Jesus, don't you think it's painfully obvious no one really believes the story? If people believed He died so brutally in order for them to have this eternal life they'd been promised, you'd think they would appreciate it more and sin much less."

"That would be the thinking on that, yeah."

"I'd say it's a gross misuse of time being a part-time believer. Either go all in on something or don't go at all. You going all in with me, Cade?"

"Keep talking about Christ, then we will see."

Smiling and shaking his head slowly the devil asked, "What else you want to know?"

"Are you telling me Christ was not killed and risen on the third day?"

"I didn't say that. I'm telling you He wasn't the Son of God. Yes, he was killed just like any other great mouthpiece to walk the earth. He was clearly in tune with himself on another level, one the Scribes and Pharisees could not comprehend. Love thy neighbor. Turn the other cheek. The meek shall inherent the Earth. Jesus Christ was raising dead minds rather than dead bodies.

The people knew He was different," The devil went on. "He only knew love in a world of hate. God didn't send Him to die on a cross for a bunch of ungrateful individuals such as yourselves. His so-called death was something the envious did to Him for spreading the Word of Love-the same stuff you see in modern times. They hate to love you."

"You said so-called? He died, right?"

"No. You'll find out when you pass from this earth. You'll get all the facts in the afterlife."

"What about His birth to a virgin mother?"

"God's law says virgins don't get pregnant, Cade. He is arrogant and does not break His rules for any pheasant of a human. Anyone who keeps track of all sins just to throw them in your face later..." the devil shook his head. "Hard to deal with."

Cade sat back and considered everything he'd just heard, tossed it around in his head.

"The whole Christian faith hinges on Jesus being the Son of God," he said.

"Who cares? You have a bunch of different faith groups out here claiming to know the way into heaven, bullying smaller groups. They're nothing more than a bunch of gang bangers. It is all a joke, one big competition. Live life how you want to and stop fearing this hell they created overnight. People who were born centuries after Jesus walked the Earth will foolishly argue about

Him as if they really have a clue. He is the biggest mystery to ever walk the Earth."

"With good reason. When you are God in the flesh that type of confusion happens."

"He never said He was God in the flesh. *Stop that!* I can preach this all day, but you should just read John 14:28, 5:30, 5:37. Check out Mark 13:32. The answers are there for you."

"I don't know if I ever really want to read the Bible again," Cade admitted. "I feel cheated."

"As you should. That's usually the legacy for God's people. If you look around you will see that the people who have everything in the world, they don't even really entertain the notion of there being a God, let alone a Son who was sent to die for their sins. *How dare He save them from anything that would destroy them!*" He quipped.

"You making God out to be a liar?"

"No, I am saying man is a liar-all his choice though."

"Just so happens to have you along for the ride to cheerlead it on, huh?"

"It's my job to. If people want to spread lies and create a bunch of human parrots that will repeat these lies, well, I want to see how it works out. I am the balance, remember?"

Cade nodded, beginning to ease, although skeptical of the words that came from Satan's mouth.

"If God slaughtered His own son and created a place of eternal suffering for not accepting Him, that sounds to me you have been praising an unjust individual, considering all the confusion you have to deal with down here. The mind is very vulnerable, so how can you be held accountable for not being a Christian."

"It's hard sledding, I'll say that much."

"Jesus only preached in certain areas of the world. Why would people of other lands with established beliefs change for a man who was nothing more than a rumor to them? Unless they had some persuading-murder, slavery, maybe?"

"I can see what you're getting at."

"Why make people suffer for not accepting Jesus? God could just leave them out of heaven. Am I wrong?"

"No, you're not wrong. I would think if He were all loving it would be impossible for Him to hold grudges like that."

"Now you are waking up. As you can see, they have created a biased God. Romans 9:18 reads that God hardens the hearts of some while choosing mercy for others. First off, why would God harden the hearts of people? That is stupid. Secondly, what others? Are we talking about a so-called chosen race of people? There is no such thing!"

"You say 'they' created a biased God. Who?"

"That's not something you really want to know. You are not prepared for the level of scandal that is going on behind the scenes. But one day...I may slide you a little something extra. We'll see how well you do.

If God has a purpose for everyone you can't think that that purpose would include any kind of suffering in the end. Not written by Him. I'm telling you to be done with all the foolery and scrutiny that comes with religion. You're better off without it. Live your life, get laid and blow millions of dollars for once in your life."

Cade explained that after the slip ups in the halfway house he was now saving himself for marriage.

"Corny ass dude," the devil grumbled. "Man is meant to have as many women as possible, and you want to hold out?"

"The Bible speaks of one wife in 1 Corinthians."

"Yeah, we'll we don't care what the Bible has to say anymore, do we? But if you want to use that book, you never saw a punishment for Solomon. He had seven *hundred* wives and three hundred concubines, if you want to believe that story. Are you sure you can handle what I am telling you?"

"I'm not so sure what I can handle."

"Whatever you can handle, you do it on your own terms. I live through you."

"Through me?"

"Yes, with all the fame and fortune comes more sin. The more people see you having a good time and doing what you want to do with your life instead of letting the big shots at the top control you, the more they will want to do the same thing. The world is beginning to praise a new God, Cade. All of these powerful belief systems have faded, as will Christianity."

With that Satan turned to move back into the house, beckoning the wheelchair to keep pace with him.

"Let's see that garage."

16

Moving down another long hallway the devil continued speaking as if conducting the last part of a job interview, detailing the smaller things about Cade's new assignment.

Operation: Live Life

"The people you have in your life," Satan was saying. "You need to cut them all off. You can start fresh with a new crowd."

"You mean my family?" Cade said, taken aback.

"Yes, them. The ones who left you hanging while you were in prison. They did not support your dreams, but will be the biggest leaches."

"Let's leave the family out of this-"

"I'm not leaving anything out. You have to hold these people accountable. God's congregation is the weak side, always forgiving everything. *We*, on the other hand, don't cave in so easily. *We* will crush those who oppose us and give slow forgiveness to those who spite us, family included."

"Kind of harsh, isn't it?"

"Not by a long shot. Anyone who ever slighted you, you're now in a higher position than all of them. Your family, people you grew up with...it's your world now, and they are ants marching to your beat. Keep your foot on their necks and give them nothing in return. At the end of the day you had to suffer behind those gates and in that hospital only hours ago alone. Who has your back more than me?"

"Nobody, it seems."

"I've had my eyes on you since you were born. And when you went to prison, I had you in the beginning, but you had a change of heart, sided with the Lord. Usually guys in prison are so caught up with putting on the front of brotherhood they lose sight of my temptations, for a time at least. When they come home, I'm always here waiting for them."

"That's sounds scarier than I think you meant it to be."

"No, it was on point. You should always fear the unknown. Fear is the beginning of respect. Indeed, you should fear me."

They came to an elevator, this one equally mirrored as the one from their previous trip.

"You don't have anything to worry about. You don't cross me and I won't cross you."

"Little white lie?" Cade said with a nervous smile.

"You'll have to see, I guess." The devil replied without looking at him.

"How would I cross you?"

"Going back to God. Do anything you want except that. That's *my* one unforgivable sin."

They rode in silence and the devil could sense something on Cade's mind.

"Ask the question already," he said with a chuckle. "It's killing you to know."

Letting out a sigh of relief Cade smile and said, "Well, it's just that when I was in prison you had all the black factions who always went around saying Jesus is a black man."

"What does it matter?"

"I don't suppose-"

"He couldn't be black? You saying Jesus should be white?" the devil said, his voice tight.

Cade straightened in his seat.

"No-"

"You a racist, boy! Wouldn't praise a black man?"

"No! That's not what I'm saying at all." Cade

stammered. "I'm just curious after all this time. I figured you could add some insight to the situation. You obviously think you know everything else."

They came to the garage but Satan hit a button that left the doors closed.

"I don't *think* anything. I *know* everything, my friend. I know Jesus was a Hebrew, born in a region of darker skinned people," Satan said, his voice calm again. "They hid Him in Egypt-hid Him among dark skinned people, considering that Egypt is in Africa. He and his parents blended in."

"I recall that story."

"I'm just pointing out the negro qualities of your Jesus in the Bible you believe in so much. Especially the fact that he got an unfair trial that sent him to His fate. Sounds like a brother to me."

Unsure whether he should laugh at the last statement, Cade deferred to Satan's humorous response of the situation before joining in.

"Just know that's not Him in the universal picture you've seen in churches, right? They are practicing idolatry-which I just love. Every time they praise it, they worship a false God. The pastors know it, but let it be. Cut ties with the ministers as well, Cade. They are the biggest poison to society."

Cade thought of Gil, his pastor friend, and expressed his feelings for him.

"He left you hanging when you went homeless. Damn him too."

"He's got a heavy situation going on at home."

"And? I stick my neck out against the creator for you. What's anyone else going to do for you that even comes close to that?"

Nothing, Cade had to admit.

"Cut ties and forget the charade. Most people only care for the Lord when something is wrong, or better yet, when my name comes up. They are pathetic victims of propaganda who wear the symbol of their role model's death around their necks, as if the crucifix was a friendly thing in the times when they were used. *The gall of these hypocrites!*

They make up these stories that make you believe in hope and miracles from a great God, but the stories are so far-fetched that when you don't see things like they spoke of in those times you begin to lose faith. They burden you with the fear of a burning eternity if you don't get back on board with the show."

"Religious extortion."

The devil paused, brightened. "I could not have said it any better. I knew you were destined for great things, Cade. So long as you just toss those Ten Commandments out the window and live life as you desire. I will say this though; you do need me to help you succeed in writing."

"I don't need you-"

"Your ambition far outweighs your talent. Trust me, you need my help."

Cade's mind was boggled and he felt an inestimable amount of doubt over all he had been led to believe about the Word of God. Years of studying and serving in the name of the Lord had been turned upside down in only days by the devil.

Had his faith really been weak all along? Had he been fooling himself in order to gain prosperity?

The doubts of self that crept in on him made him cringe.

The devil explained to him that he should not feel so ashamed of his transition. Once he got a broader view of all who truly served the devil while purporting to the public to be great people, he would fall right in line with the rest of those whom had sold their souls before him and were now living it up all over the world.

"None of them have ever tried to expose me or go against me," the devil added. "That's just a warning."

Cade nodded.

"I can bless you financially and give you guidance, but I cannot give you powers like the story of Dr. Faustus. That was fiction. This is real. If you read Genesis 3: 17-19 it's clear that God wanted you to have the finer things in life rather than breaking your back for the things you barely want. I'm just here to raise you up to that level. We got a deal?"

Cade went over everything in his head-his faith versus all that he had been told and shown in the last week by the devil. He questioned heaven and hell more than ever now, and with the help of the devil he would bypass all the coming denials from publishing houses and go straight to the top.

"With all this money you can help your mother see more days on this earth. She's been sick awhile, Cade. Now you can do more for her than you ever have imagined. You can give your daughter a better life and buy her back from the fools that have been raising her all these years. If it makes you feel any better, you can go to the families of the guys you killed and pay them a large settlement. Start a foundation in their names."

"You want me to do to good by people? I figured you would want me to be stingy with my money."

"I do. But that's not who Gabriel Cade is. You don't have to be all the way evil to serve me. But...the more good you do for people, the more the public will idolize you, and adulation is good for vanity's spirit."

"I bet it is," Cade said sarcastically, sensing the devil making even the good of the world something of his own.

Still, the devil warned Cade, this was all about him, and he shouldn't suddenly become some savior of humanity.

"You sold *your* soul. They have no stake in what is yours, " Satan added. "Don't be acting like Joseph of Genesis. You don't have to be so forgiving like him. If left up to me, his brothers would have been fed to the lions for what they did. But hey, everyone doesn't think like me, do they?"

"No, they don't."

"*But they should!* It would all be so much easier. So free, without all the shackles they put on your spirits, all the fear they instill."

Satan leaned forward and pressed a button on the wall, causing the doors to part, revealing an underground garage full of imported sports and luxury cars.

"All the toys in the world are yours. Your wealth is unlimited now."

"How I am going to explain all of this? It's all so sudden."

"Simple. You busted your ass and climbed up the ranks quietly and now you are here."

"No one has heard of me though."

"I'll take care of logistics. You just get well enough to get out of that wheelchair and enjoy some of these blessings I have bestowed upon you."

Rolling into the garage Cade was all smiles as he rode past various names of cars he could only have imagined owning when he was a younger version of himself, let alone his modern self.

This is real, he thought.

Just what the hell am I getting myself into?

Whatever it was, it was too late to turn back, so he decided to do the only thing left to do.

Live!

17

The next four years of Cade's life were a breeze, just as Satan had told him they would be. He had more money than he had thoughts now, and he flaunted it to the world in various ways, including charity. No longer did he worry over things that stressed him so much before his chance meeting with the devil.

He owned the biggest home in Tennessee, along with various other homes across the states. Friends and women came in endless groups, all lining up for a shot at the great Gabriel Cade, felon turned super star, turned exclusive individual.

This was the life of a man worth over half a billion dollars, clearly unprepared for everything that was thrown at him, but handling it well enough.

A lover of the finest clothes and a modern sex symbol now, he slept with the most beautiful women in the world and bought the priciest luxuries there were to offer without thinking twice about doing so. To top it all off he was in the best shape of his life after the incident with the homeless man left him half-dead in a hospital fighting for his life.

He learned quickly how to be a host to the elitist society, flying private chefs in to cater his dinner parties in his massive home that often lasted until the sun came up.

The fame came swift like the wind, his books soaring to the top of the charts and making him a familiar name among high ranking names in Hollywood. Movie deal after movie deal soon followed, making him even richer than he already was when he first started.

Not bad coming from where he was only a few short years ago. And to think, all it took was to make a deal with the devil and forget all that he had praised before their first flesh encounter.

Funniest thing of it all was that the same books no one wanted to read were the same that the world praised now. Followers of popularity.

Once his three-year probationary period ended, he was able to file a petition to have his felonies exonerated, and to his surprise he won the court battle. Apparently being a rich man who willingly did things for the meek was looked upon by the higher ups as enough to grant him the clemency. It didn't hurt his cause to grease the palms of a few politicians who were close golfing buddies of the judge handling his case either.

He was king of the world now.

And he was never going back to prison!

His books were best sellers, all seven in the series, and each had been adapted to screenplays. He owned his own production studio now and raked in major kudos from the movie profits as a movie producer.

It had always been a dream of his to do film, so once the books began to vanish off the shelves, he figured he could do anything he very well pleased. He decided to learn the art of filmmaking and the hobby quickly became the main vein in his body of entertainment skills.

Soon after he landed his first magazine cover, the title reading "FROM BIG HOUSE TO BIG TIME!"

Instant infamy indeed, and now he was the most celebrated person to come from his city, even starting a writing program for young students from every local high school.

Satan convinced him to set the studio up in his hometown of Knoxville, Tennessee, home to nearly everyone who ever doubted him-teachers who told him he would amount to nothing in life, those who called him a loser before and after the incident that sent him to prison. Most of all, any woman who ever played him for less because of his status in life.

Eat your hearts out.

"Most people don't dream when they are asleep," Satan informed him. "You can't possibly expect them to see your visions."

Deep down he despised them all, could hardly stomach the doltish expressions on their faces whenever they were lucky enough for him to grace their presence, which wasn't often. No one had ever taken him serious, but with Satan by his side their attitudes had quickly adjusted.

"You are a star to the world," Satan informed him, "but in the town you are from, you are a God."

Funny how money could make an average individual such as himself a sex symbol, but he accepted the responsibility with opens arms after some coaxing by the devil. In the beginning he was wary of women who so openly chased after him for financial or celebratory gain, but once Satan got into his head he no longer cared.

"You dislike flashy cars and big houses?" Satan had asked, to which Cade shook his head "no". "Good, because the same thing applies to the most beautiful women in the world. You can't have any of that stuff unless you have the money. Treat them like the toys they are."

And that was the end of that discussion. He went from not ever having women in his life to having any he chose; it was a wonder he didn't have a dozen illegitimate children or sex scandals.

Could things get any better for him? he would think at night while bundled up with the newest silver screen beauty or some model from a foreign country. These journeys into the world of seduction and fornicating usually left him empty, feeling shallow and cheapened. Money, he was finding out first hand, could not buy him love-at least not the love he wanted. Nothing was genuine in his new world, but it was part of the game he had chosen to play. What he got from the people closest to him in his present day was the love for his money and stature.

"It can buy you a damn good time though," the devil would debate, Cade foolishly agreeing every time, pushing real love aside for the pleasure of wilds nights and his own fleshly desires.

The women came and went in hoards, making him wonder if he had a sex addiction.

"You're just a man," the devil would assure him. "Take as many women as you please. Take them two or three at a time. You're the king of Hollywood. You are entitled to this life."

Indeed, he was. And all the west coast women loved his "country" accent, which was always a plus for him.

But even though all the new female company was fun, he often woke up the next day after a long night of intercourse feeling unfilled. He wasn't getting any younger, and wanted another chance at fatherhood, and this time, he would be there through it all.

With whom would he share his love? Many had come and many had gone. Friendships had been ruined over sexual encounters, but he was far too busy a man to keep count.

Then there was Lily, his most current girlfriend. She was a sweet-faced twenty-something actress with a struggling career who had been in film since her early teens. Never mind she was young enough to be a friend of his daughter's, he didn't care. To him, she was lovely and artistic, with a personality that could warm a man's leftover pie. After meeting during film festival weekend in Cannes, France a year earlier prior, the two of them had become inseparable. On several occasions Cade nearly popping the question to her.

Satan would quickly admonish him. "You don't want to be with one woman the rest of your life. Think of all the fun you will miss. Not to mention, would she love you if not for the fame?"

With that said, Cade continued to have relations with women outside of Lily. The devil had been right about so many things in the beginning. What made this any different? Cade would constantly ask himself every time he replaced the marriage ring in his pocket. Now it lay dormant on his work desk, a mere thought in passing.

Lily's career was quickly fading to black and waiting for the credits to roll, but he loved her, no matter how much fame she did or didn't have. No matter where her pretty face ended up in the sea of prettier, more famous ones. He was someone powerful now and could have or do anything, including reviving her career, which he was in the process of doing.

I'll write a marvelous role for her and she will be back to the top, he thought.

Her demise had been swift after having fallen from the stars during an interview on abortion in which she supported the killing of innocent, unborn children, denounced religion and God altogether. A hard one to bounce back from,

Cade was in support of her stance, as was Satan, who he knew was the centerpiece of her downfall.

Strangely he understood Satan now, and in that realization, he was sure he had lost his mind. He was delusional, but he didn't care as long as the party continued on.

"Embrace it all," the devil would tell him. "Even the drama that comes with it."

Lily was drama, but she made him feel young, and gave his heart reason other than success to continue beating. But he worried about her. The slide of an illustrious career caused her depression to peak and she was now more on shaky ground than he had ever seen, her cocaine use doubling in the last month.

"Rich white people problems," Satan would say, shrugging it off when the subject was broached.

Asshole!

Does he care about anything other than cash? Cade would think with a frown. Money was all he talked about, and getting it by any means necessary was just fine with the devil, no matter who had to get stepped on in the process.

Step!

On!

Them!

"Because they will step on you, given the opportunity," Satan would constantly remind him.

Even though Cade was revenge in the form of success, he had a problem with that. He could never be as cold-hearted as Satan would like him to be, and this was the biggest problem they had.

The money was great, yes, but having no real friends or family to share it with was a downer. Everything in his new world was about status, a game of "Who's Who" amongst adults that clearly had nothing better to do than compete with one another.

He wondered if someone close to him-from the past or present-would attempt to take his life out of jealousy one day. Envy bred hatred, and hatred bred violence, which could get him killed eventually. Therefore, he invested in the best security team money could buy. It would take a military expert to take him off this earth.

Then there were the bloodsuckers, too many to count. Relatives were the worst, and he now had cousins he was unaware of when he was a dope-using waiter trying to find his way. Who didn't want something from him now that he was an affluent artist? He had plenty to go around and would never go broke again, but one thing led to another, always a sink or a car needing fixing, some event he would not attend in need of financial backing.

All fine, but...he was more than a bank.

Where was the true love?

He continued to celebrate holidays-all the manmade days- for they were the devil's work. Seeing all the fools of the world come together to praise Jesus at Christmas and Easter after long absences from the church was all too humorous, an inside joke he and Satan shared yearly.

He was the ultimate Pagan now.

The world truly belonged to Satan, and God was a joke to him. All the people in the world crying to an unseen Lord who wouldn't help them was something he could vaguely remember comprehending. With everything going on in the world, how could one not begin to wonder if that God even existed?

Everything that humans did-from fornicating to murder-Satan supported. He supported all their fleshly desires, and they rewarded him by serving unwittingly, pushing God to the side ever so slightly. There were even had gay churches now, ironically, considering the act of homosexuality was an abomination in the Bible. All a game of pick and choose.

God was all loving and He would allow all the closest Satanists into heaven, right?

No!

That wasn't what was taught over the centuries. But where did all emotions in the human spirit come from in the first place? Who put the decisions people made-murder, lust, greed-in them to begin with?

God?

Satan?

These thoughts gave him headaches.

His proudest moment in life was putting his mother in a better position to continue living. She was in much better condition now, thanks to him buying her the best healthcare money could find. He even went as far as to hire personal help for her when she was at home and could not get around on her own. Anything for mom, although he still had it in the back of his mind that she, too, had left him for dead in prison.

Satan was always there, just as he had promised, to remind Cade of people's shortcomings...of how they were nowhere to be found in his worst times, but quickly changed their tune upon him becoming famous.

"Most call that bitterness," Satan told him during dinner one night. "I call it *being on your toes*. You should always use the negativity in your heart to drive you to become successful. Most people in your position have done so. If people hurt you once, they will do it to you again. If they can't be there for you in your worst times, you can't allow them around during the best either. You would do best to cut ties with them, but it's your life. Do what you want to do."

"I don't want to hold grudges."

"God does it. Why can't you? They say He brings up your past at the gates of Heaven. Why can't He let it go?"

Cade hated when he talked that way. It had a sense of both rational and irrational thinking, and this scared him more than he would ever admit to himself, although the devil knew.

Still, it was his family he was talking about. There were problems, but that's how it went with blood. He now had unlimited funds, and whatever he wanted to do he could. So, he did, for everyone. His mother, his brother who had kicked him out and left him for homeless; his sister who had disowned him in recent years, and most of all, Jacy and Chance, who still, for some reason was dating Terry.

"Why are you still supporting *her*?" Satan barked.

The mother-of-my-child excuse was wearing thin with the devil and Cade would need a new reason soon.

He'd done his best to rid Chance from her fiendish ways, but she was obviously gone. With the new fame he had acquired the checks she received for child support had grown, as had her circle of friends, which in turn led to a strong heroin addiction that Cade financed, one she had been jailed for more than once.

She was a scandal waiting to happen, an embarrassment not only to him but to Jacy as well, who was now in Bible College, of all things. She was her own woman though, so he supported her.

The irony of it made him laugh aloud.

When she had decided to attend the Johnson City, Tennessee school she expected him to be thrilled, but that was not the case. Unfortunately, this caused her a great deal of strain and confusion. He'd been the one to introduce her to The Word when he was released, and after seeing what a blessing God had worked in her father's life-bringing him from prison, homelessness and near death, to become a rich and successful man- she chose to go full throttle with Christianity.

God was great, right?

Needless to say, they no longer saw eye to eye, and she all too often gave him a verbal chastening for the new, sinful life he led.

Just before asking for money or course.

But she was his child and could get anything she wanted. He'd missed too much of her life to ever deny her desires, and if she wanted to be a faithful little God-fearing minion of the Lord, then so be it.

Ignorance was bliss and she could stay tucked away safely in it for all he cared. As long as she loved him more than Terry and no harm was done to her, he could sleep easy at night. It was safer on the side she played for anyway. The wolves played on daddy's side and she would only be an appetizer for them.

He was done with God, done with all the guilt and rage that was associated with Him, all the tricky ways to con the people out of their money for miracles. No longer did he care who had all the answers to heaven-Jews, Muslims, Christians- they were all just jockeying for position in a powerful ocean of beliefs and dangerous waves of judgment.

It was no secret amongst his new group of peers that he wasn't interested in any religious groups or cults, although they would continuously invite him to social outings since he'd been inaugurated to fame.

Your books are based on the stories in the Bible, they would say.

Yes, that's because religion is so profitable, he would think inwardly, careful not to go as far and deep as Lily had.

Deep down he didn't care what they thought of him. Rich people could do or believe whatever they damn well pleased, Satan had assured him. And so far, he was right.

So why had Lily fallen from grace so quickly? There were plenty of celebrities who denounced God and their careers were hotter than ever because of it. *People loved dirty laundry!*

The darker a celebrity was, the more mysterious they were, adding to their allure and making them more desirable.

Hate was love!

But that way of thinking brought enemies, strong ones with envy and hate driving them to violent endeavors, although most powerful people didn't believe in God. It was all a big front, one that had to be maintained in the public eye.

Satan's work, of course, and very often he would use Cade's own arrogance and disregard for people's feelings against him to simply prove his point.

Oh, that devil was slick, but he knew exactly what he was doing or saying in most cases before the devil could push him over the edge to express some kind of distaste for something that would ultimately send a wash of negativity his way.

He was controversy in the flesh, but if nothing else, his path to success and the belief that, he, not God, had made everything he possessed a possibility was intriguing enough to the folks in Hollywood that he got a pass from the higher ups who would rather see him back in Fountain City, struggling as he had before hitting a homerun with his writing.

He didn't belong, and he could smell the distaste on their clothing, but they would have to stomach him until his day came to pass the torch.

Too everyone else he was a real life 'bad boy' who had survived things only they could fantasize or write about, unafraid to speak his mind on any subject. He was their voice, a living legend and his new heart pumped stronger than it ever had, full of vibrancy and life.

"You are doing more than that old bum would have done with the heart," Satan joked, Cade laughing along in agreement.

Yes, he was worthy, more so than the man who had attacked and nearly killed him so long ago.

Was that very man living it up in hell? He had asked. "Yep, stabbing you every day. Only you die in his fantasy, every time," was Satan's response, which, to no surprise at all, elicited not even the slightest grin from Cade.

He now followed a strict diet and exercise regimen in order to keep himself healthy, his goal to surpass the 33-year old record the nurse had informed him of so long ago. He would have to eat better in order to accomplish the feat, which was a challenge with the depth chart of culinary artists who made decadent dishes that caused his mouth to water.

Participation in drugs and alcohol was a no-no, although Satan had tempted him many times over the years to indulge. To Cade, he was the friend that no one in the circle was too fond of, yet wouldn't get rid of, for if nothing else they were loyal.

The occasional bottle of champagne had its place in his life though, what with all the celebrations, none more important than the upcoming Academy Awards Ceremony he would be attending in two weeks. There would be plenty of bubbly flowing like canoes in a river of beautiful people.

His film was nominated for five major Oscars and was the front-runner for every category. Not since The Silence of the Lambs had a film won all five major awards in one night, and only two prior to that-It Happened One Night and One Flew Over the Cuckoo's Nest.

His film would be next.

He would be legendary.

Only if the boys back inside the prison cells could see him now after all their doubts and snickering behind his back. *Fools!* Only if they could see what they would never be, see what greatness looked like. Especially Ramsey. It still pained him to think that someone he was so close to in his worst time would turn his back on him from the inside. That just didn't happen.

Upon his release Ramsey had contacted Cade via social media, the hardest place in the galaxy to remain anonymous. No response was just as good as "I never got the text" in Cade's book, but the city was small and eventually Ramsey had accosted him in a public place where Cade was doing a book signing. The situation became ugly when he expressed his distaste for his old cellmate, who apparently was strung out on drugs and doing very bad for himself.

No fault of yours, Satan had told him. He could have had a set life had he stayed in touch with you, but he chose otherwise because you hadn't made anything of yourself. Now look at him.

"You think you're better than me now?" Ramsey had yelled in Cade's face, just before his security delivered a rough escort out, leaving him beaten and embarrassed.

Yes, I am better than all of you.

"I'll get you for this!" Ramsey had vowed.

Vultures came in many shapes, forms and relationship statuses, so what made his old friend any different? What gave Cade the idea that he would never turn on him? When he thought about it...*nothing.*

Over the years he had won various awards, book accolades mostly. His personal favorite was "Sexiest Man of the Year" for a very popular magazine. That one still made him laugh every time he thought about it. Sexy was the game in Hollywood, and rich was sexy, which made him to die for in the world's eyes.

"From slum to bum to sum," the devil would remind him. "People love you for your position. They live through celebrities."

So true, Cade thought. He now had a major following on social media and his rock star status was growing by the day. Before fame, no one wanted to hear a anything he had to say, but now they hung onto his every word.

His attitude could be off-putting to some, but he didn't care as long as the majority loved him. There would be no humbling him, and as evil rose in the world so did his stock and his pride-the one sin he felt he contributed most to the evil games Satan played on people right before their eyes, the answer to all their problems so simple if they looked past a few books.

He didn't want to be loved for his celebrity, but rather being a big-hearted man with various acts of good on his side. To him that was more sensible.

He was on the side of the devil, but even the new heart in his body had compassion for the world and all its trouble.

"I think the world is fine the way it is," Satan would say with a big smile.

"I think not."

They would go back and forth like this about everything, but in the end, Cade would do what he wanted to.

"Let the dead care for the dead, man," Satan would advise him. "Some of those people don't even need help. They just choose to mooch."

True, but what about the people of the world who couldn't get a break, the ones who were stuck in their unfavorable position?

"The rich get rich and the poor get poorer. I have a chance to even it up some."

"You could not be any more wrong, my friend," Satan argued. "The rich get richer, yes, but the poor, having nothing to their name, can only go up from their place in life."

True, Cade thought.

So, he began his venture into the world of philanthropy, starting with the families of the men he had killed in the military-a million dollars to each and another quarter of a million to their desired charities. With money as endless as the water in the ocean 2.5 million meant nothing to him.

From there he was off, donating to various causes, seeing the world as he went. These endeavors were never to be leaked, but as things went, they were, making him an instant hit on daytime television, his face appearing on various newscasts and talk shows for acts of kindness.

This is the best thing for us, Satan cried.

"The world is feeding into you being so generous with your money, but the Bible says to keep your good deeds to yourself, for the more you do for the cheer of the people the less you are to Him."

"'Truly I tell you, they have received their reward in full,'" Cade recited the verse. "But that's not what I'm trying to do. It's not my fault anything got leaked in the first place. I'm doing good because I'm not a total jerk."

He was ultra-famous and mingled with the elite, had enough money to call it quits, but deep down he had to admit, he was addicted to this life. It was better than any drug he had ever taken-five seconds of it could truly hook you for life, and he truly believed it was the one thing keeping his heart pumping, the drive to be great stronger than a dying organ.

Unfortunately, all good things came with a downside, and that downside for Cade was a blonde-haired, green-eyed woman. Chance was slim in the waist from a lack of eating, which was the result of drugs and partying, a habit that she would eventual succumb to soon if she didn't change her ways.

She was too caught up in herself, doing interviews and reality television as the mother of a great writer/producer's child, her envy and hate for him guiding the foolish movements she made, unaware that the vultures in the studios only wished to cause drama for the sake of ratings.

She didn't care, they were paying good money to hear any kind of dirt she could offer.

"No such thing as bad press," Satan informed him. "Book of Arrogance, chapter one, verse one."

Right.

The embarrassment she caused he and Jacy was beginning to get to him.

"Kill her," Satan suggested as they sat in Cade's office at the production studio. "Get rid of the bitch."

"No." Cade replied, waving the suggestion off. After a moment he looked Satan over with curiosity. "If I wanted to, how would I do it?"

Satan smiled greatly. "Funny you should ask?"

Gambling was a new hobby Cade had picked up as the years went by, and Las Vegas was by far his favorite place other than home. He was familiar with sports wagering from his time in prison, not only from seeing guys win and lose money, but from over hearing their conversations as well.

But a bet on killing Chance without the trail leading back to him wasn't the closest thing to a sure shot, and those were the only kind of bets he laid big dollars on.

Unless...

He pondered it a few days and planned the perfect crime, one that would seem suspicious but could not be challenged because it was too air tight. In less than a week he would be in Los Angeles for the Oscars, the perfect alibi. He was rich and famous, so no one would suspect or convict him. But in the event that they did, he could simply buy the case, right?

He gave monthly allowances to those he chose to help, and Chance was no different, even though she blew it long before four weeks could pass, often being granted twice her allotted amount.

She was the biggest of the leeches, and having a big heart meant nothing more than an opportunity for her to stick her hands out at him.

Jesus had a big heart and they killed him; Satan always reminded Cade. Never forget that.

But eliminate Chance? She annoyed him, yes, but not to the point of him wanting to kill her, at least literally.

Or did he want to kill her?

His heart was bitter towards her-had been for years-and erasing her could not be topped emotionally in his mind. The euphoria he felt just thinking about delivering a deathblow to her sent chills through him.

It could all be so simple, and she would be gone for good.

So here he was with the devil at the doorstep of a large suburban home he'd practically bought for her in the last years of child support. Somehow, her lawyer had convinced a judge to grant an awarded bonus amount outside of what he owed to her in light of Cade's new fortune, and she milked him for all she could.

Her time was up.

Satan was right. Why the hell was he funding her lifestyle after all she had put him through, the humiliation while he was behind the gates and beyond? This was a long time coming, and there was no turning back now that he was here.

"Get rid of her!" Satan commanded with a hiss.

"She has a small child," Cade said of the blind baby she had conceived with Terry in what Cade could only imagine was an intoxicated tango between two addicts.

"I don't care. The child is better off without her. Do what you have to do."

"Yes, sweetheart," Cade responded.

Her son, Maxwell, was blind as a result of Chance's drug use. He was innocent and had never seen the sin of the world that most had, a benefit for him in Cade's personal opinion.

Chance opened the door to meet them, marijuana smoke wafting up around her. Cade frowned and looked to the devil, smiling in his delight of the situation.

"Got what I asked for?" she asked rudely, puffing her joint.

"Well, hello to you as well, evil," the devil said. She knew him only as Lew, the bodyguard that had nearly killed her presently incarcerated boyfriend who'd found himself in a pickle after trying to sell an undercover officer heroine.

She stood to the side and allowed them in. Amazingly the house was spotless, as always.

"For a junkie you keep a clean house," Cade said, face unwavering. "Too bad that's the only thing clean here though."

He nodded to Satan who chuckled, causing the two of them to burst into laughter. Chance took aim and shot them both with profanities.

"Stop playing games, you two," she whined, sucking away at the marijuana that smelled invigorating to Cade, nostalgia of his old days when he had a healthy heart that could be trusted.

"A puff or two won't hurt you," Satan would tempt, receiving negative responses from Cade.

"Where is your son?" Satan asked.

"Upstairs sleeping. Why do you care?" Chance said rudely.

"Chance," Cade said, settling himself on the pearl couch, another item he couldn't help but notice he paid for, "What are you doing to yourself? Hell, what are you trying to do to me?"

"Do to you?"

"You are an embarrassment," Cade said Heatedly, yet level as he could. Chance's puppy came from the back of the house and leapt onto the couch with Cade who welcomed it with rubs and belly scratches.

"Why you want to do this right now?" she asked, shaking and scratching at the skin around her concealed track marked arms.

Cade looked up at her with disgust, caressing the puppy to keep himself from springing off the couch and slapping her sour face into the wall.

Do as you feel! Satan suggested.

Frowning at the thought, Cade requested privacy for he and Chance. Satan conceded and slipped off into another part of the house.

He stood from the couch and moved over to Chance.

"Let me get you some help," Cade said, receiving a groan in return as Chance moved past him to the couch and flopped down. "There are some good specialist in California. Come with me to L.A."

"What? While you are at the Oscars being praised, I'm supposed to sit in a rehab?" Chance said incredulously. "Ha! You just want to bring me out there so your little girlfriend can see what a loser your child's mother is."

"Why would I do that? No one cares to see you, and I, for one, do not wish to show you off to one single soul-not in this condition."

She scolded him with a frown as she stood and walked back to him.

"What's that mean, huh? I'm not sexy to you anymore?" she leaned into him, ran a hand down to his crotch, causing him to stiffen. "You used to love me before prison. What happened? The rabbit got him a gun and wants to act all different now?"

"Terry and drugs happened. And for your information, this rabbit always had the gun. I just went and got some bullets for it."

"Whatever, smartass. Terry's in jail, so it's out of sight out of mind, right? Isn't that the saying you boys have in jail?"

Cade pierced her with a glare and said disdainfully, "Yeah, that's what they say. Unfortunately, too many people out here make that statement real."

"That's not what happened with you and your friend, Ramsey. He ghosted you from the *inside*." She said with teasing laughter. "Now that's bad."

Cade burned inside from her insult as he thought of Ramsey. The man hadn't responded to a single letter or email he sent him back in those days. The slight was one that Cade-even in his Christian state-had pocketed, bitterness spewing in him when it came to the man he'd once called brother.

Chance's hands began to wander to his pocket as she held his eye.

"Looking for something?" he asked with a sly smirk.

She scoffed and pushed him away. "Let's cut the shit. We both know that I'm a junky, but whatever. I am who I am. Don't torture me with your spiels about getting clean when you're the reason I'm as bad off as I am."

"Me?" a shocked Cade said. "How am I the reason you are strung out on dope."

Her face cringed. "You think that you being away and leaving me to raise a child on my own didn't bring me down to a point where I thought I would never make it? You have any idea what that is like?"

"Oh, here we go with the sad story. Your life is good now, so what's the problem?"

"That's not the point," Chance said, her voice cracking as she looked away from him. "You never see the point. I'm hooked on drugs because of my weakness to the situation *then*."

A tear ran down her face and for a moment Cade could see the innocence beneath the hard exterior of what was Chance. He wished he could clean her up, wished that they would have had a happier ending to their courtship than what was. It was a shame, but life threw things at people.

He could not push one thought away though; if not for losing Chance he could not have gained Lily, and he couldn't accept that. Aside from selling his soul and attaining everything he could imagine she was the best thing to ever happen to him, something he would cherish for life if she would let him. Damn her career, he would finance her whole life as long as she gave him her love.

"Whatever," Cade continued. "You need to clean yourself up. You're killing Jacy."

"Whatever. You always talk like I'm the only messed up person in all of this. Look at you! You've gone and grown your hair out like a woman, wearing all those fancy clothes-do you even know who you are anymore? You have completely changed from the God-fearing man that came home from prison. I didn't like that guy either, but I liked him better than this new Cade. You've practically shut off everyone from your past and it's like Hollywood is your new family. You just went off and forgot the little people."

"Oh, sure, say I'm acting different now that I am rich. That is such a classic line. I'm supposed to feel bad for succeeding in life?"

"Everyone sees it, no one more than Jacy. You think you can buy her love? She hardly ever sees you. You have missed her whole life, you idiot!" She beat him across the chest twice before he slid to the side and sidestepped her, pushed her to the couch.

She looked up at him, a child being scorned by an angry parent. *"We needed you!"*

"What do you want from me?" Cade said, straightening himself. "I pay for your life, even got you into rehab twice, and it's never good enough. Our daughter is in school because of me, never good enough. What the hell do you want from me?"

"You went away and left me in this cruel world to fend for myself," Chance cried.

"That was never my intention, and you know that."

"You asked me what I want? I want you to know what it feels like to have your daughter look at you with disgust, when before she looked at you like a hero. Like you were the strongest person in the world."

Cade pulled air into his lungs slowly, looked to the right and caught a glimpse of Satan leaning in the doorway of the kitchen, eating an apple with great pleasure.

Don't let her guilt trip you, my friend. It's all a game to her. Do what you came to do.

"I'm done supplying you," Cade said. "If you want to go to rehab, I will finance it-"

"Damn your money," Chance growled, "It's all dirty. I wish you were still in prison. You've become a corrupt and unlikable son-of-a-bitch since you got rich."

"Says the one who always needs my money. I can't tell people don't like me. They're always in need and asking for things all the time. You know what," he reached into his pocket and produced a small baggy of heroine, tossed it on the table.

You wish I were still in prison, huh?

We'll see how you feel when you shoot that dope into your blood.

The drugs he had brought to her were heavily laced with Fentanyl, something that had been a problem in Knoxville for some time. Her death would look like any other KPD had discovered.

She would be talked about like a dog, her closest friends the gossipers. He wondered if she would even be missed, if he was doing her a favor by taking her out of a world that was obviously too much for her.

He had a chance to play God for once, and would give her a choice, didn't care if it was a sin. No longer did he have to worry about a God that expected him to forgive all sins while not doing so Himself.

Satan was now his God and guidance, although he had to keep an eye him most times.

In situations like these Cade figured the devil was right. Kill her off, and be done with it. A quick funeral and a few fake tears later she would be long forgotten, the thorn removed from his side finally.

He would take great pleasure in getting rid of her.

"That's the last time I ever supply you with anything. My advice is don't even use it. Clean your life up now and come with me to rehab. You have a choice."

He wondered if she heard a word he was saying as she stared at the baggy on the table, sweat forming on her top lip. She was sick, he knew, but this was her decision to make. It was her life to play with now.

His stomach turned as he watched her. This was real. He was really going to get rid of her. He looked back to Satan who nodded his approval, continuing his apple.

"What's it going to be?" he asked her.

She remained silent, an emotionless expression on her face.

He repeated himself and began to get frustrated.

"You know what, fine," he said, moving to the door. "I'm leaving. I don't care what you do."

A lie, true, but he had to play his role. Everything was about appearance and character to him now. He could not allow himself to be forced out of character by her, could not be pushed into an emotional state.

He would not beg her to save her own life.

The truth was he wished she would decide not to use the drugs and take him up on his offer of rehab.

Why did you care? Satan asked his conscious.

There's no coming back from death, man! Cade replied.

That's a worldwide fact, but what's your point?

What about her son?

What about the little bastard? That child came from two people that gave you hell in your worst situation, conceived by intoxicated lust, and she is living off your money all while thinking of you as a joke. You can get back at both of them.

At the door Cade stopped, looked back at her with pain in his heart. He wanted to grab her, take her to a facility for help, but everyone in life had temptations and choices to make. She would be no exception. God would not be guiding her on the road she chose to take. This life altering decision was solely hers.

He would stand back and watch the show unfold.

18

He touched down at LAX in a time zone three hours behind Knoxville, which meant the night was young. Jet lag would kick in hard the next day, but this was California. He was young, rich, admired and the town was his.

It would be a disservice to himself if he didn't live every moment to the fullest. His party life over the years could be ancient folklore one day, and he wanted to enjoy every moment of it.

There was a verse in the Bible that told of how it would be easier for a camel to pass through the eye of a needle before a rich man could get into heaven. When in the presence of his celebrity friends Cade indeed knew why the verse existed.

Crazy, he would think to himself. At every level of his life he felt the righteousness and truth of the Word, and even though he was far past that now the spirit within him spoke loudly. He was sure the devil could smell it on him.

They would often argue and Satan would assure him that at any time Cade could relinquish all he had and go back to living the way he did before.

"But never forget that the heart in your body is mine," the devil would tell him with a smile. "I want everything I gave you back. Everything!"

Things were good between them more times than not and their energy was great together. Even though Cade knew Satan was a trouble-shooter that could ruin or cost him his life he could not deny his loyalty to him.

What would life be like if he were to fall from the stars? Would losing everything be worse than never having it at all?

All of his new cronies would acknowledge him still, right? His fans, would they look at him with the same starry-eyed gaze of wonder they did now? Surely if he lost all Satan had given him he could bounce back off his name alone, right.

Right?

No, Satan warned him before he got ahead of himself.

"I will smear you into hiding, boy," the devil announced through laughter. "No one will even associate their name with you. Don't play with me."

No one was really his friend anyway, Cade thought. They only tolerated each other for one reason-the mighty dollar. It drove them and they had no shame in it.

But when things hit the fan they would be nowhere to be found, as was the case so many times over.

"When you are winning, you have friends aplenty," Satan coined. "When you are losing, not one of twenty."

Always there with a quick comeback, damn devil. There were times when Cade clearly didn't trust a word the devil was saying, and then there were the gems he would drop on him, the words that made Cade truly feel as though Satan had his best interests in mind.

He wondered if God was having extra mercy on him, waiting for him to come back to his senses and see the error of his ways.

"You don't trust me?" Satan had asked.

"Should I?" Cade responded, the devil laughing heartily.

He moved through LAX, his bags carried by assistants.

The weather for the time of year was to die for, and the sun shined down on him as he exited the airport. He breathed in the California air and smiled at the thought of his privileged position.

"Baby!" came the joyous cry of a woman to his right.

He turned to find Lily in the backseat of her classic convertible with the top down, her driver standing close by.

Career be damn, she was still worth a cool eight figures. Money was not the issue, rather her loss of love from the fans. Sadly, some thespians lived through the ones who idolized them as much as they lived through the celebrities.

Rich people problems, Cade thought with a smirk.

His heart warmed instantly and he could only imagine how silly he looked standing there grinning like a fool. He didn't care though. That's how love was supposed to make you feel.

Goofy!

He moved towards her car with security close by as she hopped from the back and ran to him, jumping in his arms as if they were in a love movie. If fading to black came next he was fine with that, as long as he was with her when the credits rolled.

"I have been in need of you so badly," he said to her, holding her face in his hands.

"You know just what to say to all the women, you trickster," she joked.

"You have to out here. The women will eat you alive."

"I could eat you alive."

They embraced with a kiss, long and deep.

A camera flash caused them to pull apart just as a member the paparazzi took off in the opposite direction, his money made for the day.

"Jeez," Lily said through laughter. "You just stepped off the plane and you get ambushed. They love you."

Looking off into the distance Cade said, "Yeah, they do."

There was pride in his voice and Lilly picked up on it, her attitude changing as she thought of her own failing career.

"I remember those days," she said, her head hanging.

"Hey," Cade said, consoling her. "You took a hit, but you will bounce back from it. "

"How? I haven't had a solid gig in over two years now."

"I'm going to write you a good role. Trust me. I'll take care of everything."

He met her blue eyes as she looked up at him. She puckered her lips for a kiss that he readily delivered to her youthful face.

"I've got something the paparazzi can talk about," Cade said, switching the subject. He reached into his jacket pocket and pulled out a case for an engagement ring.

Lily's face changed to painful delight, her squeal a clear sign of her answer to the question he'd yet to ask.

"Yes?" He asked her.

"Yes!" she cried.

He lifted her in the air with a bear hug, spun around as she expressed her excitement.

Satan came to a stop beside them, clapping with jollity.

Mistake, my friend, he said to Cade's conscious. *I told you not to do this.*

Cade looked into the eyes of the devil, nothing more to be said about the situation. He had spoken and he was now a man with a full plan. He would establish himself with Lily and bring a child into the world that would carry on his name with pride.

It'll never happen, Satan pushed.

"We have three days until the Oscars," Cade said to Lily. "I'm pretty sure we can figure out a few things to do until then, right?"

"Maybe." She smiled up at him.

Just what the hell did the devil mean by his last statement? he wondered as they jumped into the back of Lily's car and sped off.

For the next three days they made love and shopped at expensive designer stores before returning to their swanky hotel for more lust. They had beach side lunches and late-night dinners on rooftops, rode the countryside and drank themselves silly on the finest wines.

Indeed, these were the times for drinking alcohol.

"I love you more than I have ever loved any woman in my life," he proclaimed as they strolled hand-in-hand down Rodeo Drive. "I'm lost without you."

The tears that formed in Lily's eyes were genuine, and it broke his heart to see her torn behind a career that was stagnant.

"We are going to be the king and queen of Hollywood," he assured her as they dressed for the Academy Awards in their hotel suit the day of the show.

She nodded and remained mute, not fully buying into his logic of making a movie with her in it to bring her back to the spotlight.

"I'm surprised people still love you the way they do considering we are still an item," she said, feeling sorry for herself as she always did. "Probably doesn't look good associating with me."

"I'm the hottest thing on the face of the earth, babe," he told her. "If they love me, they love you."

So not true, Lily thought. But she understood his heart and the intentions he had for her, foolish as they were.

The pressure of being his queen was beginning to be too much for her and he could tell. Status was everything to the silver screen elite. How would he look dating an atheist who couldn't get a job to at least keep her career above water?

Pressure.

Once the pursuit of fame began for a person, they would pursue it for life in order to obtain and keep it. When it outran you, it could destroy your spirit, take you into the pits.

Before, in his days of fantasizing about being in the position he was in now, he had imagined himself receiving an Oscar and breaking down with tears of joy on stage. Now that Satan had erased the softer side of him, he had a different attitude toward the ceremony.

He had his acceptance speech ready, burning in his pocket. Since he could not acknowledge the devil on television for fear of ending up like his girlfriend, he had an even better plan in mind.

I want to thank me for getting here! And he fully intended to say it, because it was his world. Knowing that people all over the world would be tuning in for the show made him feel bigger than the Pope.

He would then hold the Oscar high in the air and praise those who called him crazy for thinking he couldn't do anything great with himself.

"I've got your crazy right here!"

It was tempting, and he had more to say than that, so much that the music would start playing-a sign that he needed to exit stage right.

He embraced the flashing lights as they exited their limo at the front entrance to the award show. The two of them were photogenic, she the consummate beauty and he the big man in Hollywood. So many celebrities were miserable, putting on fake smiles for the audience and he wondered how long before he became one of them.

"Living a predestined life would really suck," he expressed to Satan. "I like having control of my destiny."

He acknowledged that none of what he knew as life now was real, but he couldn't care any less. As long he sat atop of his own world, so be it. Better to be rich on this side than struggling and broke on the other, waiting on the promise of a false heaven.

Fame was the most addictive drug he had ever taken in his life, and the high that he got from it was so amazing that he couldn't see anyone attaining it without having sold their soul to do so.

The most important people in the world don't believe in God, Satan preached.

These days Cade walked on air, a level above the rest as he moved about his business making a killing right up under their noses. If they only knew how it all had occurred.

No one would believe him anyway.

Or would they?

At the Oscars he did interviews while Lily garnered no attention from the reporters in attendance, her annoyance with the situation very apparent.

"Katherine," a lady said, coming to a stop beside Lily, startling her "It's so good to see you again after all these years."

Visibly shaken by the woman's presence Lily said, "Yes, it has been too long."

"Not long enough," the woman said, her face tightening. "But we'll catch up soon."

Cade eyed the woman up and down as she turned to walk away. She was regal in appearance, mid-forties at least, and moved with grace, which made him wonder why she would be so threatening to Lily.

"I'm going to the restroom," Lily said to Cade. There was something in her eye that made him grab her by the arm.

"You okay?" he asked with heavy concern as he grabbed her by the hand. "That woman called you Katherine. Who was that?"

"Just leave me alone," Lily said, jerking away violently and causing a slight stir amongst onlookers.

She turned to storm off, Cade watching her hips as she did.

"Even sexier when she's mad, right?" said Satan as he came to Cade's side, dapper as always for these events. He wore a three-piece black suit, trimmed in red, a top hat to match.

"Oh yeah," Cade concurred, looking the devil up and down, admiring his taste. He was the devil after all, so it was no wonder he would show up dressed to impress.

"I know you wish you could make it look so good," Satan said, patting Cade on the back

"What are you talking about? I dressed you."

The two of them laughed as Cade tried to shake the angst he felt for Lily.

Who was that lady? He needed to know.

"She'll be okay," Satan assured him. "All the pressure of being around these bright and shining stars is too much for her, I suppose."

"I suppose. I'd still like to know who that lady was."

"Who cares who she was? You are about to make it into the history books, man."

He had already made history with his books, surpassing many legendary titles that had already been made into movies. But this was movie lore, where the big dogs played, and he was beginning to feel so much larger than life.

An Oscar would cap off everything he had worked for, all the things he sold his soul to have. Still, there was so much more left to accomplish.

Inside they were seated side by side, the empty seat to Cade's left reserved for Lily, who had yet to come back from the ladies room.

Come on, girl, what is wrong with you?

"I'm going to go look for-"

"No, you are not. Sit right here and enjoy the opening ceremony. All the work you have put into this very moment and you want to let someone ruin it?"

Cade held the devil's gaze, contemplated the next move, finally sitting back in his chair.

"Good boy," Satan said, patting Cade's shoulder.

The show began and his stomach turned as he felt himself about to exploded. Satan looked to him and burst into laughter, knowing the situation. Attention in the crowd shifted to them at once and a few dazzling females waved and blew kisses to Cade, which seemed to ease him.

He could not lose out tonight, not with all the hype surrounding his controversial film about young super heroes. Not at this prestigious soiree in front of Tinseltown's finest.

The first awards were given out and still no Lily. He did his best to hold it together, but his mind could not unwrap itself from her.

An hour into the show and there was still no sign of her. He was about get up to begin his search when it was announced that the first award for his movie would be given out next.

"You trying to miss this?" the devil said, noticing his movement to rise up.

"No," Cade responded, sitting back in his seat.

Whatever, he thought. If she wants to throw a fit tonight then let her do as she pleases. This is not her night, by any means.

Something would have to be done with the revival of her career, and soon. He loved her, but was unsure how much more of her blatant need for attention he could take.

"She can be replaced by any actress with a great body and a cute face who is up next for a chance at fame," Satan had said to him earlier in the evening. "Besides, would she be with you if you weren't who you are?"

As far as Satan was concerned Cade was her lifeline, and at any moment he could stop her career's heartbeat.

"She is trying to steal your juice and bring you down, man," Satan leaned over and told him. "Don't you ever forget why she is around."

"Yeah, your probably right."

"Probably? Don't I usually call good money about people?"

"I guess," Cade said with a shrug.

"Don't guess, *know*. Fame will break you when you have it. What do you think will happen to you once you have fallen from the stars? Could you handle that after having tasted this lifestyle?"

Cade was beginning to reconsider his proposal to Lily. It was possible she had been right. Maybe being with him was going to be too much pressure for her to overcome. The fact that he would possibly have to let her go played in his mind, made his heart twitch.

The Oscars for best actor, actress, screenplay, and director fell in place, just as they should have and now it was down to the last, most prestigious, award of the night.

He was four for four so far and the probability of the best film going to him when all the other major awards winners were involved with his movie was extremely high.

He'd gone with a different director for the project, otherwise he would have taken the stage already. What did it matter? The Best Picture award was up next, and that was the one that focused mostly on him.

He was ready to claim it.

Oh, how his vanity had grown.

His anxiety grew as he thought of Lily.

Nevermind her, Satan barked in his ear.

Yes, you are right.

A male actor who had already won an award on the evening and was still riding his own high escorted a young actress Cade had previously bedded onto the stage.

It's Hollywood, Cade would tell himself when all the vanity around him seemed far too much to bear. What else is there to expect?

Holding his breath through the thespian's exhausting preamble, accompanied by the rehearsed laughter from the crowd he was ready to bolt up from his seat to accept the award he felt most deserving of.

This is why I sold my soul, he thought, looking over at Satan who wore a satisfied smirk.

Money could not buy love, but it could buy a spot at the Oscars, and those were taking place *now*.

Make tomorrow happen today. That was his motto.

He'd been a loser in high school, had luckily gotten a judge who saw fit not to send him to prison longer than the time he served, and had battled back from homelessness, even a near death experience. He knew what he had overcome, knew where he had been, and didn't care to give much thought to the past or future, considering they had both been so rocky to him throughout his whole life thus far.

This was his moment, and he didn't have to share it with anyone from his past if he didn't desire to. His family life was in shambles and he hardly ever spoke to them unless it was about money, which kept him away from home. All the work he was doing took the place of them on his list of priorities.

Money had become everything to him now. It bought him the fancy life he lived, made people rave over him, gave him the opportunity to make his dreams a reality.

No, my friend, that isn't the money's work, Satan chimed in. *It's mine.*

Take all the credit then, Cade laughed.

"And the award for best picture goes to..." the pretty actress was saying. The anticipation was heavy. "Expressway to Heaven."

Cade could feel the blood drain from his face as he his heart began pacing rapidly.

He'd lost!

What the hell? This was not supposed to be happening. Not on his night.

He had to breathe slowly to prevent a stroke as he got up to leave, everyone watching him as he went.

Who gives a damn what they think?

He wanted to cry like a child.

If not now, when would he win the biggest award in film? Cade wondered, knowing that his best story to date had been told. *He was now out of Oscar worthy material.* Writing stories that won everyone but himself an Oscar was not exactly his plan for the night, or for his career for that matter.

He had stories in mind that would make him hundreds of millions more, but would they win an Oscar?

There were plenty of stars in Hollywood who didn't have an award from the academy, but their fame was greater than those who did, some even having starts on the walk fame.

Damn that! He wanted that Oscar!

The Oscars, the money, the fame-he wanted to be a triple threat.

He sucked in a deep breath when he finally made it out of the building, turning to look up at the bright lights he felt had betrayed him.

"Better not start crying out here with all these photographers," Satan said, coming up beside him.

Only a few hours ago he felt big enough to knock down the Sears Tower, but now he felt empty, hollow enough to be taken away by the smallest of gusts.

An Oscar would have solidified him amongst the legends that had come through the ranks in the great land of fantasy, but now he would have to retreat, go back to the drawing board and figure out how to bounce back from this defeat.

A fire burned in the pit of his stomach and in an instant so many bad things that had happened to him over his lifespan came rushing in like an assault team. Funny how the subconscious stored those memories for times like these-times when Satan would turn up the heat.

"Shut up," Cade fussed, as he turned to walk to his Bentley, around looking for Lily along the way. Vernon stood by at the ready to take him to any requested destination.

Where is she?

"Don't get pissed at me because the people have spoken," Satan said to Cade. "Apparently they think you stink and the other guy makes better movies. Who cares?"

"*I care!*" barked Cade, who stepped into Satan's face. "*I deserve that award.*"

Satan leaned against the car and smiled. "Such conceit. I like it."

"I'm not in a playful mood," Cade said, boldly sticking a finger in Satan's face as a warning.

"Not like I care. Shake it off. Let's go get some drinks."

"No," Cade said, stepping away from the car. "I don't want to be around anyone tonight. They'll all ask the same question."

"*'How do you feel?'*"

"Exactly. How am I supposed to feel?" He let out dark laughter. "Not to mention I have all the people rooting for me to lose that just can't wait to hear how I *truly* feel after the loss. That'll feed their gossip hunger for months, won't it?"

"So, you don't want to go for drinks?"

"No," Cade groaned, slapping the hood of the car. He was a defeated man. "Do I look like I want to celebrate losing?"

"It's not so bad. When you break it down and look at it from the right angle that really matters, it's like a win."

"And what angle is that? I'm dying to know what you come up with this time."

He was past tired of the devil always having a comeback and logic for everything that went wrong. Maybe it was because it usually made sense, the things he was saying, or maybe Cade would just rather sulk in misery for a while before settling back on solid ground to think straight.

"You are getting all worked up over a hypocritically acclaimed movie. Every voter who made that film a winner tonight is on the fence about their beliefs in God. It spoke in favor of sinners making it to heaven, and that's why they truly made him the winner. They felt comfortable with the movie. All the great people out here-the rich and powerful-are my people. They're all hell bound and delusional about a trip to heaven when their breath of life elapses. The bible says that only a few will make it to heaven. *What the hell makes any of them think that they are the ones who will get there?"*

"You should have made them vote for me."

"Only if I could."

"Lame answer. You can persuade."

"It's the world you live in, my man. It's changing. You lost because people honestly think they are rooting for God when they are truly rooting for me. They don't even see it, and that's the funniest thing," he added with laughter. "It's a glorious and wondrous feeling to know that I am getting so close to overthrowing Him."

"You'll pull that off before I win that Oscar!" Cade spat.

"Don't be so hard on yourself. You have something deep inside that can produce an even better film. You are high priority to me, and I am going to make sure that all of your dreams come true."

Cade looked the devil over, searching for any kind of lie within him. Whenever he did that, he highly questioned his own judgment about life, being he thought he could squeeze the truth out of him-the devil.

Finding nothing Cade said, "Right."

They got into the car and left, nothing more to be discussed.

19

In many opinions the Oscar for best film hardly ever went to the actual "best movie," or the one that smoked all the others at the box office, so Cade shouldn't have felt so bad.

At least that was what the devil told him. Cade on the other hand wasn't about to let this one rest any time soon. He was already plotting his next move. One thing about being in prison was it taught you to always be on your toes and expect the worse, to be ready to make your next move at any given moment.

Inside the hotel lobby, along with Satan and his security team he moved to the elevator holding a cell phone to his ear, reaching out to Lily who still wasn't answering her phone.

"I want to be left alone," Cade said to Satan as they rode up to the suite. "This night turned bad quickly."

"Yes, it did," Satan agreed, sighing.
The cart came to a stop on the eighth floor.

"See you later, my friend," Satan said with a wave as he stepped from the inside. "Let me know if you change your mind about coming out for drinks."

Cade rolled his eyes as the doors close and the ascent continued.

In his suite he cut the lights on and swept the rooms for any trace of Lily. Her bags where there, untouched and he could faintly smell her perfume.

"Lily!" he called as he moved through entranceways. Nothing, no reply.

What is going on? he wondered as his mind raced back to the mature lady who had approached Lily at the Oscars. She'd called her Katherine, and suddenly her attitude had changed, darkness overtaking her aura and forcing her into hiding.

Hiding where though?

He raised his phone to call her when the blare of his own ring tone sounded.

Jacy.

He'd been ignoring her calls all night and now that he had lost out on the Oscar, he was even less enthused about talking to her-especially since every conversation led to her telling him about Jesus and the blessings he could reap if he came back to the good side.

Whatever that meant.

He loved her, but she would have to miss him with all the talk about God tonight. As soon as she started, he would hang up on her.

"Yes?" he answered his daughter.

She was hysterical on the other line and her words ran closely together like marathon runners bending a turn on a track.

"It's mom!" she screamed into the phone. *"They found her overdosed!"*

His heart rate spiked and sweat formed at his brow as he thought of Chance, needle in arm with no life in her body. The sick side of him smiled inwardly at the thought she would never be able to bother him again. The other side wished he hadn't done what he had done.

Taking advantage of her weakness didn't give her a fair chance at more life, but at the end of the day she made her final decision, and it had cost her.

Feeling sick and numb all over, he doubled over as he sat on the couch, forehead touching the glass table in front of him.

"I'm so sorry, Jacy," he offered condolences.

"You should be," Jacy said, coldly. "I know that she has been getting her supply from you, and the doctor said that the drugs she used were laced with more Fentanyl than they had seen in most cases. *Where you trying to kill her?*"

Trying?

Was Chance still alive? He thought with an inward groan. "I don't know what you are talking about," he said, wiping the tears from his eyes and recomposing himself. "You're talking non-sense right now."

"It's not non-sense! You tried to get rid of her. Just admit it."

From his experience with the judicial system he knew better than to admit anything. He was rich, and money bought the best legal defenses, so he was innocent until proven guilty.

Something told him that the courts would not be so quick to prosecute him-a prominent individual-just because of a junkie's death. And even if they did, the jury wouldn't convict him.

He would be okay. He was on top of the world, in the clear, an untouchable man.

"I think you need to get your head together," he opined sternly, maintaining his tough aura. "You're making some harsh allegations right now. I'm your father."

She rebuked him again, accused him of trying to murder her mother and vowed to make him pay for it, just as soon as Chance came out of her coma and could tell police what he had attempted to do to her.

"It's over for you!" she said.

"Whatever you want to believe, fine, believe it," he was saying when he heard talking coming from the outside.

Was someone out on the balcony? He wondered as he slowly moved toward the door that led out to the dark of the night.

Jacy was saying something he was not privy to as he noticed the door was open slightly enough to allow a breath of air through. His stomach turned as he placed a hand on the handle, hearing a familiar voice come from outside.

Lily.

"Jacy, we will continue this conversation another time," Cade said distantly, almost inaudibly.

"We will continue this in court, when they send you back to prison where you belong."

"Sweetheart-"

She hung up, leaving him with his thoughts. He had to admit she won the opening round and had exposed him, letting it be known that his darkness was out in the light.

But how would she prove it?

The first round would be the only round she won.

What would this do to their relationship? he thought with a frown, stepping out onto the balcony to discover Lily standing on the rail, teetering with a deathly fall.

"Don't take another step," she said, stopping him in his place.

They shared a moment of silence, the wind the only sound, a haunting whistle that slipped into his most hidden spaces.

"I feel so free out here," she sang distantly. "I feel like I can fly. Do you want to fly with me?"

She was high, he could tell. Maybe off of cocaine, maybe off of pills-she liked a bit of everything, but she was no addict like Chance.

He thought of the mother of his child, struggling to live. If she woke up...

Whatever Lilly was on had her in the wrong mind. Did she even know what she was doing? Where or who she was?

"Babe, how 'bout you come down from there and we can talk about this."

"There's nothing to talk about. What is done is done." She looked down on him with dead eyes, her face gaunt behind her hair. "I am done."

"Don't do anything stupid."

Her laugh was like a gargle, a choking sound that was otherworldly.

"Nothing I could do now compares to the things I've done to get to this point in my life. A thirty-story fall for me may be the best thing. At least I can say I took matters into my own hands. I will leave this retched place on my own terms. How many people can say that they took the most precious, delicate thing known to us and decided its fate? Death is a beautiful thing..."

Lily sounded so sad and broken. She was at the end of her rope, Cade knew, and it was very possible she would let herself fall from the ledge. He thought of the best way to defuse the situation but found nothing in his head to resolve the problem.

Damn it, he thought, cursing the devil in his head.

Leave her be, man! Leave her alone! I'll do anything you ask! he pleaded.

This could be negotiated somehow, he was sure. But he was getting no response from the devil, and this worried him. Very unlike him. Even when the answer wasn't the one Cade wanted to hear there would be an answer.

"I wrote you a letter..." Lilly said. "I want you to know some things about me that will make it easier for you to understand my troubles. I will always love you, Gabriel Cade. You have been the best thing a girl could ask for, and I wish things could end better for us." She held up a hand with her engagement ring.

End?

What was ending?

"Don't talk like that," he pouted, his spine turning to ice as she pointed to the table where an envelope sat with his name on it.

"Take it. Open it," she told him.

He held her gaze a moment, knowing what was about to happen, wishing there was something that he could do in order to prevent it.

Damn you, Satan.

Then again, he knew the game and Satan's wicked ways.

The thought of rushing to Lily and pulling her back to safety crossed his mind, but he thought better of it. There was no way he could reach her before she leapt to her demise.

Is that what she wanted him to do? Show some effort? He took a step forward.

"Don't do it!" Lilly warned.

He wasn't so sure he wanted to understand the devil anymore. In less than a week he had attempted to kill Chance he wasn't even a killer- and he'd lost out on the biggest award of the night- of his life.

Now this.

Lily was the best thing he had going. He couldn't lose her as well, not the only real thing in his collage of an existence.

"Okay, babe," he said, slowly turning to get the letter, keeping an eye on her best he could. "But I think you should come down from there, don't you? Maybe it's a little safer."

He would remember her the way she looked in that moment, glaring down at him as if from the heavens. He would not remember the good times when he wanted to spend the rest of his life with her, times when she his everything.

There would only be that look, the darkness sweeping over her and taking the love of his life away from him forever.

No sooner than when he turned his back, he felt her presence evaporate, causing the wind to stop blowing for just a moment as he listened for her to land down below.

Turning to discover her gone, a beat later he heard the loud crash of her body hitting a car, people screaming hysterically.

"Lily!"

His insides felt as if they had been shaken like a can of juice as he moved to the edge of the balcony to look down at the street.

"Oh...no," he cried faintly as he took in the scene happening beneath him. Pedestrians were circling around, taking pictures that would surely land them some kind of profit off of her death.

Vultures! he raved in his mind as tears streamed down his face. *All the devil's work.*

"Don't be blaming me for this," Satan said, stepping out onto the balcony. "Everyone has choices in life. She made hers just as you make yours."

"I can't believe this is happening," Cade said, falling to a sitting position on the ground. His voice wasn't his own as he cried. "Why did you do that to her! This was not supposed to happen."

"The man who knows something knows he knows nothing at all. I have told you this before. People have new problems arise every day and sometimes they just don't know how to handle them. So, they turn to the things that make them feel best. I, the good guy, want nothing more for them than to live out their fantasies. Drugs, sex, alcohol..." he pointed to the rail. "Suicide. For some reason you still have a problem with this, even though you say you understand me. You will never understand me."

"Suicide is not a fantasy," Cade barked.

"Oh, so you've got all the answers now? You know more than me?" Satan asked, insulted.

Cade got to his feet and faced off with Satan who invited the challenge with a smile.

"You're pushing it." He pointed in the devil's face.

"Is that right? You're tough now, Cade? Do something about it."

Pausing, knowing he could do nothing to the devil, Cade turned back and looked over the rail, down at the chaos that had started around Lily's body.

"Told you the marriage between you and her would never happen. She had way too many problems that would hinder your success. I could not let that happen."

The sickness that overtook Cade was unbearable. He wondered if Lily was at peace now, in hell with other spirits who had taken their life or lost it in the process of sinning.

"She's fine," Satan assured Cade. "The Bible says that death is a beautiful thing. I agreed with her on that."

"As if you care about what the Bible says?"

"I do. I have to know it in order to use it against people," Satan said with a smirk, tossing his hands out at his sides. "The body and spirit never really die-nothing can, actually. The body goes to the ground and the spirit moves on."

True, Cade agreed in his thoughts, but he wanted Lily's body and soul there with him.

"Like I always say, you can give all this up and go back to where you were if you don't like the way things are going."

"Maybe I should. I sided with you from a lack of faith, not persuasion."

"Easy there, champ. You won't last too long without me," Satan added, tapping his chest a few times, reminding Cade of the heart in his body. "You want to see just how beautiful death is so soon?"

What am I doing? Cade thought.

He was a slave to his own celebrity and could not let it go for anything, not even his sanity. He could not remember all the love he had now when he was incarcerated-even if it was fake love. People were infatuated with him, but no one wanted to offer him a home to lay his head when he was released from the penal system.

Money.

Funny something so common as wood turned into flimsy paper with ink on it could control people the way it did. But he could not be mad at them, for the money had changed him as well. He was no saint by any means.

The love of money is the route to evil.

Or was it truly the lack, as Satan had enlightened him years ago? His mind was always at war with itself, and the devil enjoyed every minute of it.

"You going to read that?" Satan asked, pointing to the letter in his hand as sirens could be heard down below.

Hesitantly Cade lifted the envelope, looked it over before walking in to the suite and cutting the lights on. He tore the paper open, pulled the letter out and began to read, the breath in his body leaving the instant he did.

The first words on the page hit like a cheap shot, taking him by surprise and leaving his thoughts disoriented.

I sold my soul to the devil.

This couldn't be real. Or could it? Satan had come to him, so why not Lily? Why not every person that participated in the Academy Awards?

The most powerful people in the world don't believe in God.

Looking at the devil with a harsh look, he read on, his heart twisting with each word.

Lily revealed to him that she had met the devil when she was a teenager, just before coming to Hollywood to become a star. She had been an overweight loner growing up and was teased by her peers when all she wanted was to love and have her emotions reciprocated.

The devil had come to that girl in the form of a stylish, middle-aged woman who would be a mother figure to her-something she never had due to her biological mother, a rape victim, dying giving birth to her at the age of fourteen. She would be bounced around from various homes until finally landing in a group home where she would be molested and raped herself, bullied and defeated, on the brink of suicide at age eleven.

It had been an uphill battle from the beginning but finally she-Katherine Mays, of Wichita, Kansas-made it to the big screen and became an instant hit by eighteen.

With everything she could ever dream to have in hand things looked very promising for her future. But in her bold arrogance the devil convinced her to speak out against God in an interview two years earlier, causing her career to dissipate like fog in a progressing day.

He was pulling her down with depression because of the loss of fame, tempting her to end it all, which he had become successful in after many attempts. He had tricked her into destroying the thing she wanted most, a happy life with plenty of love to keep her warm in a cold world.

She was dead at the foot of a building now, the centerpiece of what would be a crazy magazine cover the next day.

The letter she wrote to him was a suicide note and confession, the latter she had been dying to let someone know for years during her worst times. But who would believe such a claim? People didn't buy devil stories, but yes, they were real, and she had no one to talk to about the situation.

Cade was different, she knew. He wouldn't look at her strangely for the claim, which was why he held the letter in his hand.

He knew everything there was to humanly know about the devil, and even though he understood him, he was like the cigarettes killing millions of people around the world yearly; They knew the smokes were bad for them, but they sparked the tips and sucked away regardless of the consequences. Same was the case with anything people were addicted to that was bad for them. The pleasure made their judgment questionable.

Hence the current situation of his life, similar to the one that had taken such a precious soul from him, one that was detached from the lovely vessel lying broken from a fall only ten minutes ago.

Still, one question lingered in Cade's mind.

"She went against God for you," Cade said. "Why did you take her out like that? She was loyal and you chopped her down."

"That's what you say," the devil said, taking a seat on the couch. "Here's a lesson you should learn, and fast. Everything is about perspective. How you see things versus how I or anyone else sees them. It's up to you to make decisions in life based on what makes you happy. Who cares what others think?"

"What is your point?" Cade erupted, pacing the floor. "You always want to get philosophical at the wrong times."

Satan watched Cade closely as he continued to pace the room, his hands moving erratically.

"You don't ever listen," the devil said. "You never see the point. Chance was right about you."

Cade stopped and stared at the him.

"Don't do that," he said. "Don't you dare use her against me. She's lying in a hospital-"

"Barely holding onto life. Yes, I know. I helped put her there, remember? You can look at her as a victim, or you can look at her for what she really is-a fool who destroyed herself and is now paying the tab on all her actions. Again, perspective."

Cade said nothing as he stood with his hands on his head.

"It wasn't even that serious," he finally moaned. "She didn't deserve that."

"That's not what you need to be worried about right now. If she wakes up out of that comma, you can kiss everything that we worked for good-bye."

"We? That *we* worked for? You serious?"

Satan tilted his head, a patient father listening to his child. "Everything that we worked for, like I said. *I* gave you everything. Damn right it's we. It's *we* until your spirit leaves that body. And that's what that little bitch fiancé of yours didn't respect."

"Watch your mouth!"

"You got a mirror?"

"Fuck you!"

"You're really not at all my type, Cade. Although I do support homosexuality."

A massive smile appeared on the devil's face, knowing he was getting under the skin of his pupil.

"She wanted to go back to God, or at least

pretended to," the devil reasoned. "She figured it would get her back in good graces with the people. *Perspective*. She must have forgotten that was a big no-no."

"So, you take *everything* from her? You break her down mentally? You kill her?"

"She killed herself-"

"You killed her!"

Shaking his head, the devil said, "I am not about to have this conversation while you are leading with your emotions. You know better than to say something like that. The best thing you can do right now is figure out what to do about Chance. You need to finish the job."

Cade held his eye, searching as always, finding nothing as always. Satan was right, if he didn't do something quickly about her, he could very possibly end up back in prison with nothing but hard times and heartache. He knew what was to come, and he would be damned if he let that happen to him again.

"What you got in mind?"

Chuckling the devil said, "My man."

20

Cade hated himself, but more than that he loathed the fact that the devil had such a strong hold on him-despised the thought of it.

The night of Lily's death he had wanted to storm out of the room and run downstairs to be beside her dead body, but instead he sat in the hotel suite with the lord of flies constructing an idea on how to get rid of Chance as the starlet's body lay lifeless, rigormortis setting in.

"Think it will work?" he asked Satan when he had what he figured was the perfect plan.

Money talked, and he could get to anyone if he wanted them badly enough. Money, power, and position was what he had now. With all three he could move a mountain if need be.

But I can't win an Oscar?

"You will, trust me," Satan assured him that night in the hotel. "I see next year being the most pivotal year of your life."

"Really?"

"Absolutely. You're my main man."

Cade realized he couldn't fully trust Satan, but the fact remained he had been there for him when he was down, when he had nearly lost his life living as a homeless man. He had taken him from the mud and molded him into a strong brick of a man, made him prosperous.

There was no one walking the earth he could say the same for-not even God-so he decided he would stick with the devil and not cross him, no matter if he had taken the love of his life away from him.

No, she killed herself. It was her choice.

But Satan had influenced her, so it wasn't like she killed herself all her own.

So, did that mean he did kill her?

The confusion of it all drove him crazy, and with all the many other distractions he had in his life, he tossed the idea of anything other than success out of his mind. So many things could and would distract him from putting a film together that would win him an Oscar.

He could not buy true love or fulfillment, but his money could buy him the happiness of winning that award he coveted so deeply. And he had plenty to spend, especially since his latest book was set to come out in a matter of weeks.

"This could be the one," he had told Satan. "It's better than the one that actually went up for all those awards."

"I agree."

"You're just telling me what I want to hear?"

"You know me all too well."

Pride came before the fall, and he knew his was eminent for the things he had done in the last week.

$50,000 had bought Chance's life only hours after he had received the news of her survival from the drugs he had given her. Being rich and famous had its advantages that made it easy to convince a nurse to slip into the hospital room and smother her without causing too much curiosity or mystery, keeping the attention off of him.

And then the nurse had to go.

Rather than continually have people killed by people who would only have to be killed themselves for fear of their mouths running, he pulled the trigger himself when he delivered the money to the man who killed the nurse.

He was now responsible for taking five lives and considered himself 'the black hand of death,' a man who could not be reasoned with. The men in the military definitely counted towards the body count. He could hardly look at himself in the mirror, the anger and disappointment in himself crawling over his body like spiders.

Still, anyone who crossed him would have to go from that point on. No questions asked. They would be dead and gone, forever.

Let the Lord deal with them.

Never could he have imagined being so cold, but the fame and fortune he had acquired was something to be protected, and he would do just that, even if it meant killing his own daughter to keep her mouth from running and sending him back to prison for life.

She was on the fence with the accusations she had shot at him when she delivered the news about her mother's misfortune, unsure if the man who had introduced her to Christ could be so cruel.

If you only knew, my precious child, he thought as he dropped a flower onto Chance's coffin, slowly descending six feet in the earth.

Good riddance!

Initially he felt bad about what he had done to her, but after some thought and much talk from the devil, he didn't feel that pang of guilt anymore.

"Didn't she have it coming?" Satan asked.

"I guess so,"

"Don't guess, *know.*"

And he did know. She did have it coming, for far too long. Terry, out of jail on bond courtesy of Cade, stood off to his right beside Deborah, head down and whining like a baby as the casket dropped.

Don't fret, my friend, you will be reunited with her soon, Cade thought, reminiscing about the time Satan choked him. I'm going to get you as well. Why else would I bail you out?

Dead man walking, he smirked, looking at Terry, the two of them making eye contact.

Terry looked rougher than he had when the two had first met, and even though he was doing what he could to clean his life up as he struggled through addiction, Cade felt he was responsible for Chance depending on filth to get by.

Cardinal sin, one that was punishable by death.

I am the black hand of death. I determine who lives and dies. It was all out war now against the people who wronged him, and he was playing for keeps.

Jacy stood to the other side of her grandmother, holding her younger brother and avoiding eye contact with Cade, refusing to look his way. Her heart had been ripped to shreds over her mother, and the prospect that her father could be the reason she was no longer breathing had caused her to lose countless hours of sleep.

The preacher had been a damn fool, going on about Chance's spirit being at peace with the Lord now, fully knowing that she had died from drug use.

Amazing, Cade thought. *Not everyone is going to heaven, you imbecile.*

He hadn't read an obituary in his life that said someone was with the devil burning in hell for misdeeds in life. No, it was always heaven, the place everyone wanted to go when they died-the unanimously popular place to be.

But did they have the slightest clue that heaven may not have been the place to go? He figured people enjoyed being lied to, that they truly felt safe in their beliefs and were too scared to explore anything other than what they had been taught.

Not me!

Still, he had his doubts, and Satan could see them. They would wrestle back and forth over it, Satan never taking offense. Second-guessing came with the job..

Chance's funeral was a far cry from Lily's, which had been a sideshow only two days prior in L.A. It had been filled with gossiping celebrities networking and doing business as she was laid to rest, no one truly caring about her untimely death.

Cade hopped a flight home soon after to make sure Chance would go into the frozen ground as planned. It was February, and his heart was colder than the month itself as, knowing his true valentine lie stiff in a coffin back in California.

In attendance to pay their respects to Chance were a few friends and family, the small group who felt obligated to come see her off to the next life, wherever that may be for such people like her. He was sure she hadn't gotten to any heaven they had heard of.

The media was having a field day with Cade's troubles-the mother of his child and the starlet he would marry both dying within days of each other. There were even whispering rumors that he himself, in a fit of rage after his Oscars loss, had pushed Lily to her death.

The media.

But...whatever kept him in the tabloids was good for the ego, and his was like no other in Hollywood. Who could stop him other than himself?

"Chance killed herself," Satan had told him. "You gave her the choice."

That I did, Cade thought. But who was he to play God with anyone's life? It was far too precious for man to make to the final decision, and clearly humans needed something else-a higher power-to take the wheel in life because they were too unstable. Eventually they would wipe each other out.

I love it, the devil would tell him.

"She never meant you any harm," Deborah said to Cade upon his arrival, wrapping him like a blanket with a strong hug. "There were problems in her life that she just didn't know how to deal with. But she always said you were the one that got away. You were her one true love. She was proud of you. We all are."

The words tore at him as he remembered better times with Chance, tears filling his eyes until the levy broke, allowing them to run down his face like sprinters.

This was no act on his part, for he was truly torn about the act he had committed. Still, what was done had to be done.

Or did it have to be?

Maybe in haste he had overreacted. Then again maybe he had done Chance a big favor by taking her out.

Stop being a baby! Satan barked in Cade's conscious as he wiped the tears from his face.

No one suspected him of any foul play, and with the show of emotion Deborah had shown him, he knew Jacy wasn't telling everyone what she thought of the situation.

That's daddy's girl.

He was unable to get through to his daughter, the cold shoulder she gave him freezing his lips closed before he could get a word out. Deborah took notice of the action and appeared to be curious but said nothing, figuring Jacy was simply depressed and being antisocial given the circumstances.

If only that were the case, lady.

When the casket was lowered people began to retreat and he once again tried to speak to Jacy.

"I'll meet you at the car," his daughter said to her grandmother, handing her brother to her who looked hardened with age, her heart heavy with the stress of losing her only child.

She'd been forty when she finally was able to conceive a child, a sign from God that it was her one and only chance, hence the name she had given her daughter. Now that one and only chance was gone.

Jacy crossed her arms and held herself tightly beside the grave as she looked down at the coffin, avoiding eye contact with her father. When her grandmother was out of earshot she gave her father a harsh look.

"Sweetheart," he began, struggling to find the words to break the ice.

"Don't call me that," she said, looking up at him with red, teary eyes. "Don't even call me your daughter anymore."

"Don't say that."

"I liked you better when you had nothing to your name but a dream and were staying in my grandmother's house. I detest everything that you have become since you got rich. Tell me, is there *any* good left in you?"

Her words pierced his heart and caused his throat to tighten as he held back tears at the thought of his only child disowning him.

This was not the way things were supposed to be. She continued.

"Money and fame have corrupted you You've lost your way. I use to be a brat to you at first, when you came home, but little did you know you were the most inspirational person I ever knew. Seeing what you had been through and survived gave me hope. All the work you were putting in to make things right with your family by creating a way to provide for them-even though mom, God rest her soul, was making it as hard for you as she could. It was all so inspirational. But now I don't know who you are."

"I'm still the same person you knew-" Cade said.

"No, you are not. I don't know who you are anymore. What happened to the man of God I used to know?"

I got wise, Cade thought.

"You can't buy your way through this life. You will have to face the Lord for your actions."

Whatever, Satan mocked.

He placed his hand on her shoulder and she slapped it away, saying nothing as she looked up at with him fury.

"You okay, Jacy," a voice came from the side.

Terry.

What did he want?

He was skinnier than before, the drugs having taken a full toll on him in the years leading up to now. His eyes were yellow and his skin was pasty, hepatitis eating away at his liver.

"Yes, I'm fine, thank you," Jacy said. There were only the three of them standing by the grave now, and Jacy stepped into Terry's arms for an embrace, burning Cade's insides as he took it in.

Looking off to his right he saw Satan leaning against his car with Vernon close by, both dressed in their funeral black. The devil smiled and shook his head.

"You want to get out of here?" Terry asked her, disregarding Cade's presence.

"Yes," she replied.

"I'm not done talking to you," Cade said to his daughter.

"I'm done talking to you!"

"Leave her alone, man," Terry said.

"Stay out of this," Cade warned, his patience already as thin as the man was. He could not wait to see him in a six-foot hole. In due time, he thought.

"I'm already in it," Terry said, gently guiding Jacy to the side of him, squaring up with Cade. "Been in it for years."

"This is not the time or place for this."

"That's right, back down like you always do."

"You two stop it," Jacy said.

Terry raised his hands in surrender. "I'm sorry, sweetheart. Your punk ass daddy is right. This is not the time." Terry smiled an ugly, mocking smile that made Cade want to kill him on the spot.

"Thank you," Jacy said, hanging her head low.

Cade's face screwed up, wrath boiling inside as he once again looked to the devil whose head was tilted in a questioning way.

He can call her sweetheart, but you can't?

Cade expressed this and Jacy let out an exasperated sigh.

"Yeah," Terry said, "She feels safe with a real man. You think all that money you making now makes you a man or a father, boy? Takes more than that."

"Don't worry about the money I make, you bum. What the hell would know about being a father anyway, sitting in jail all the time? You're a junky just like she was," he pointed down to the coffin in the ground.

Jacy's eyes widened with insult.

"Watch your mouth!" she exclaimed.

"It is what it is, and they are what they are," Cade growled, stepping closer to Terry, so close he could smell his stale breath. "You ever call me boy again, I will kill you. Understand me?"

His clinched his fist tightly, ready to pounce. The threat wasn't called for-*he was going to have him killed in due time anyway*. In fact, in that moment he decided he would do it himself. It would be more pleasing to the devil in him.

Laughing, Terry said, "Well, now, look who grew a pair of balls out there in Cali. Too bad you couldn't do it in the places where the real men roam. You were weak in the military and weak in prison...*boy*."

Cade's body tensed as he imagined all the vile things he wanted to do. He hated Terry, not just for his relationship with Jacy, or even the fact he was the man that Chance chose to be with in the years leading up to her death.

He despised Terry's kind, had his whole life, and if he could rid the earth of one more piece of trash then society was all the better for it.

Get him! the devil encouraged.

Thoughts of Cade's past rushed in like defensive lineman, reminding him of the pain he had suffered in his short time breathing. Tears welled in his eyes, air filling his lungs as he heaved, his stomach tightening as he prepared to pounce.

Do it!

Suddenly Cade grabbed Terry by the ears and head butted him, cracking his nose and drawing first blood, causing Jacy to squeal. He wasn't done just yet, drawing back and connecting with a solid shot to the gut, dropping Terry to his knees.

Jacy grabbed him and pleaded with him to stop but was thrown aside to the cold ground as Cade tried to punch a hole in Terry's face, blood covering his fist as onlookers stopped to watch.

Knocking Terry to his back, Cade could hear Deborah demand that he "stop" as he blanketed the fallen man with punches, dishing out the pain of ten men.

The devil smiled his delight and Vernon gave a thumbs-up as encouragement for Cade to finish the job.

Jacy turned to see Satan just as he yelled, *"That's right, kick his ass!"*

Just as Terry got to his knees Cade spun on one leg, kicking his victim in the head with his free foot, sending him into the open grave with a loud thud as he landed on the coffin.

"It should have been you in this grave!" he yelled, pushing one of the two gravediggers on site to the side and moving for a shovel in the mound of dirt that was to be used for Chance's burial.

Now she would have company, Cade thought, scooping the dirt and hauling it into the hole.

"Stop!" Jacy yelled as people began to scurry back to the site to stop the madness. *"You are crazy!"*

"I know!" Cade barked as he showered dirt into the grave. To Terry: *"Who's the boy now?"*

He felt himself being grabbed from behind by Jacy. *"Stop!"* she ordered. *"Stop!"* Others rushed in to stop him from doing something he would regret later. Standing back with the shovel in hand he looked down on Terry and spit a large wad of phlegm at him, a show of disrespect that would have cost him his life in prison many years ago.

But he wasn't in prison anymore. No longer a peon, he wasn't someone to be taken lightly. He was on top of the world, and if he wanted to push someone into an open grave and attempt to bury that person alive then he damn well would.

Oh, the media would feast on this for weeks. He'd caught a few members in the distance with their cameras, reporting his every movement.

You like the show? Are you entertained?

Although he loved the attention he received from fame, there was still something inside him that wanted his privacy.

Some things weren't to be shared with the public, and this family event was one of them. He expected media for Lily's funeral, had accepted the fact that being a celebrity brought that on. But Chance's funeral?

Show some damn respect!

Throwing the shovel into the grave with the last of his rage he instantly changed his demeanor, his calm taking Jacy by surprise.

Cade said to her. "I've given you the world. If I'm not satisfactory enough for you then this will be where we part ways. You need me more than I need you."

Jacy was lost for words, her face masked with pain as she stared at him

"I can't believe you would say that," she said, her pain evident.

"Jacy," he said, stepping closer to her and placing a hand on her should, "I'm sorry. I didn't mean that."

It was too late; the damage had been done. Violently she pulled away from him and said, "*I hate you*. You have changed so much, and not for the good. Things have not been good ever since *he* came into the picture."

She pointed to the devil, a childish grin on his face as he waved to the small crowd only thirty feet away, not caring how the gesture would be taken.

"Who is he, really?" Jacy asked.

"That's not something you should concern yourself with," Cade said, avoiding eye contact with her.

He looked around at the familiar faces of people he had known in a past life, lost souls he didn't care to associate himself with going forward.

The gravediggers worked to help Terry out of the hole as Deborah said, "You have completely lost your way. You've sold your soul to the devil for money and fame."

"What do you know about selling a soul to the devil?" Cade asked her. "Huh? You tell me, since you have all the answers."

"Don't speak to me that way, young man. I gave you a home to stay in when you had nowhere to go."

"You want a reward, lady? Can you toot your horn any louder?"

"Stop it!" Jacy said.

"No, she needs to hear this. I appreciate everything that you did for me, truly. But it's not like you haven't reaped any benefits from my success. In my eyes, we are even as even can be."

"Well, we all see what path you are on, don't we?" Deborah said, tears in her eyes.

"Yes, the same path your dead daughter was on."

Deborah's face turned to a painful frown and she gasped, holding her chest. Cade, unaffected by her show of emotion went on.

"You may not like me, but you will respect me," he announced to the group, jabbing his index at each of them as his rant went on.

That's right, the devil cheered. *Tell them all how you really feel.*

"What happened to all the Christian stuff you were talking when you came home?" Jacy asked.

"It's all bullshit! Lies!"

"It's not lies. You need to reconnect with the Savior. You need God."

"I am my own savior. *I am God!*"

A haunting silence fell over them all.

"Just leave..." Jacy said, exasperated. "I don't want to see you again until you change your ways. You can take me out of your will as well. Your money is dirty."

He remained silent as he held her eyes, wondering if this was really happening to him at the moment. Admittedly he could be crass, but enough to make his daughter want nothing to do with him?

So be it. She made her choice.

Terry moaned as he was pulled from the grave. "You broke his collar bone," one of the diggers was saying.

"Someone call the police!" Deborah ordered.

Hearing this, Cade walked past her and the rest of the people gathered around, never once glancing back at them. He would not sit around waiting for the cops to place him in cuffs for assault. Instead, he would call his lawyer to clear the situation up.

The power of money worked wonders.

I am God!

"Ready, Mr. Cade?" Vernon asked when Cade made it to the car-a shiny, brand new Bentley.

"Let's get out of here," Cade responded, getting into the car and pulling the curtain on the window closed.

21

After assaulting Terry at the funeral and all but severing his ties with his daughter, Cade found himself in a new court situation, one that would be easily handled, but a headache none-the-less. It was a nice to have money to make things like the funeral assault go away, unlike his first go around with the law so many years ago.

His lawyer was the best money could buy, a sly devil himself who would stop at nothing to win a case, even if it meant sliding the judge a few bills to make things go his way.

The devil was alive and well in the world, and even though they didn't see eye-to-eye at all times Cade was fortunate and more than thankful to be on his side. Seeing the benefits of money from a distance was one thing, but once his soul belonged to the devil, he was allowed into the underworld of how it all truly went down. Where the money was present the winners were as well.

Get the money, get the girls, and get the life you want, along with everything that came with it, including freedom in the court system. A crying shame, but he didn't care as long as he was on the right end of it all.

Oh, how things had changed.

Mediation was a favorite word of his now, and through it he agreed to pay Terry's hospital bills and participate in anger management classes, something he had no intentions of doing. He would simply pay his way through it, just as he did everything else in life.

But he couldn't buy his daughter's love.

After all he had done for her since becoming affluent, the best she could do to repay those deeds was accuse him of killing her mother and being nothing more than a devil, a lover of self and finances?

All true, but she could keep that to herself as far he was concerned. He didn't need anyone-especially someone he supported financially-throwing his mishaps and shortcomings in his face.

Who the hell did she think she was? he thought, burning internally. If she only knew what he had to do to ensure she lived a comfortable life.

She would berate him even more! He laughed inwardly.

He shook his head in spite of himself. How could he win with people when they were never satisfied?

In the weeks after he buried two women who held a special place in his heart-he could never fully hate Chance, because after all, she gave him a child-he focused only on winning an Oscar. He would not allow what happened only a month ago happen to him again.

He vowed to win the next one.

Satan assured him of this, and that stroked his ego just enough to get him back into the studio and working again.

But the devil had said he would win the last one as well, so what was he to think? It was no secret between the two of them that Satan would tell him anything that he wanted to hear rather what he needed to be told. At times Cade was thrown into the pits of confusion when things did not go as he had planned.

"Your ambition far outweighs your talent," Satan had told him. "But, as long as you think you can do something, I won't hold you back from doing it."

The devil was there for the pleasure of his flesh, prompting him to live his life the way he pleased, no matter if it were right or wrong.

His family life was sliding more and more by the day as he distanced himself from them, avoiding their requests for money every time they asked, which was as often as they possibly could. They brought all their problems to him, whether directly or through his mother, whom he had limited contacted with.

Money-money-money, that was all anyone cared about. Their wants weren't too different from his, of course, but the money they wanted was his, and their relationship should have been based more on love than money. He had no problem helping those he had known his whole life, but the least they could do was let him do it on his own terms instead of begging and giving themselves away all the time.

The beggar's outnumbered roaches, only they didn't hide in the light-they made no bones about sticking their hands out.

Sell your souls if you really want some money, fools.

No, they could not handle the pressure of riches and fame. He was made for this, the devil assured him. Whatever came his way he could handle, even watching the woman of his dreams fall from a thirty-story building to her death.

His mother's health was fading and getting worse in his absence, her diabetes killing her slowly and leaving her in bed most days, unable to move around on her own. Her days were numbered and his heart ached for her as he watched her near the end from afar.

He could never be prepared for the loss of the woman who carried him in her womb for nine months, the woman who sacrificed so much for him as a young nineteen-year old college student. Her life had been put on pause as she prepared to give birth to him, and eventually she and his father, a young military policeman, settled in fountain city where they raised Cade and his siblings.

She endured many years of mental and verbal assaults at the hands of his father who, in the early years of their relationship had developed a drinking problem, eventually leading to their divorce just before Cade entered the service.

He hated the air his father, Gabriel Sr. breathed, so much that he refused to use his own first name. Whenever people called him by it, he cringed at the thought of becoming his old man. More and more every day his anger built up for him, and at one point his name had been added to Cade's hit list.

The thought of killing his own father had crossed his mind more than once, especially when he visited his mother and received worse news than his previous trips from the in- home nurses he paid thousands of dollars per month for.

He had to be careful with his thoughts because Satan would only push him forward rather than talk him out of it.

Kill his own father?

His mother, in all her depression from the abuse she suffered at the hands of his father, had developed a drinking and smoking problem of her own, which, partnered with stress-eating habits and an excess of weight from birthing three children had been the cause of her sickness. Her kidneys were failing and her heart was in terrible condition.

His father was the reason she was going to die before her time, or so he used to think.

No such thing as dying before your time, Satan would tell him whenever he got down and out about the inevitable.

No one had a death date, and he was fully convinced of this now. Why would there be a God hovering above mankind deciding who lived and died each day? Years ago, he was convinced that was the way the Lord operated, but now it was a laughable thought to him-pure foolery.

Everyone made decisions of their own in life and that included his mother, whom he loved dearly. No matter what his father did to her she had a choice, and her choices, born from years of the abuse she suffered from him, were not the best ones.

But the devil was her tempter, right?

"Yes, but she has the first say," Satan would say, reminding him of free will and his roll in it all. "And the final say. I'm just a guy along for the ride."

So true, Cade thought, wondering why his mother would continue to destroy herself, knowing her days were only being shaved down to the bare minimum by continuing her actions.

Her weight had ballooned from the fried foods and alcohol, and Cade could only blame himself for enabling her with the finances she used to procure the vices that were slowly but surely killing her as her family sat back and watched.

Why do people do those things to themselves? He often wondered.

Why would anyone sell their soul? A voice would come back to him just as often.

Self-pleasure was the simplest answer to the question.

He sat with his feet up on an expensive desk reading a newspaper in his office, Satan sitting across from him grinning.

"What the hell you cheesing about?" Cade asked.

"I'm jubilant just thinking of how far you have come."

"You mean how far away from God I have gotten since I met you in the flesh?"

"Aren't we saying the same thing?"

Cade pointed at the devil with the newspaper. "You could say that. It wouldn't be possible without you though."

"On the contrary, my friend. You gave to me, and in turn I gave to you. We are a team, and you should never forget that."

"You filled a void in my life. I wouldn't do that."

"Sure you would. It's human nature to bite the hand that feeds you."

Sitting up in his seat Cade asked, "Where is this coming from?"

"It's coming from you. I see your heart, and I know you have doubts about me. I know you second guess my intentions for you-always have-but you feel it's too late to go back to where you were spiritually."

"Whatever."

"Whatever then. The fact remains you don't trust me fully, and that's fine."

"Should I?"

"No, and I can handle that. But as I have told You before...if you go against me, I guarantee you'll come out a loser."

"Yeah, yeah, yeah, you have told me that before. Do we need to go into this right now? I have a book signing to go to today, and I have to stop by my mom's house to check in on her."

"As if I don't know this," Satan said.

"It's bad enough I have family there to deal with as well."

"I'm just keeping you honest, my friend."

"Do it some other time. I just want to see mom and get to the mall and do this book signing."

The devil gave him a thumbs-up, done with the issue.

"And how about you don't tempt my dad to say anything stupid that will provoke me, Cade said. He'd only spoken to his father by phone since returning home from prison, avoiding confrontation with the old man for fear of an encounter that could get physical.

He wasn't a young, naive teen anymore, and would have loved to break the man's face. The fact remained he was his father, and Cade hated to imagine laying a hand on him. So, therefore, he took the high road and stayed as far away from him as he could.

There had been some good times in his childhood and Cade held onto those, trying his best to discard all the bad for fear of an internal explosion that would lead to a physical altercation.

Honor thy mother and fa-

Who cared what the Bible said! The prince of darkness drilled him.

His father had been to his mother's home much more lately in the wake of her failing health. Death's knock at the door had a funny way of pulling people back together after years of turmoil. Misdeeds were forgiven and all was well.

"I can't do that, and you know this," the devil responded. "If daddy has something on his mind that he desires to share with you then that is on him. They're his thoughts. You know my role in all of it."

Cade ignored the devil and went back to his reading. There was a reason he took it upon himself to continually remind Cade of what he had done for him and what would happen if he turned back God, but he hadn't figured it out yet.

I know what will happen!

At least he thought he did.

Cade's favorite part of the paper, eerily, was the obituary. Here he could see who had died, and who hadn't that he felt deserved to. A lot of people needed to be in this section, he would joke.

More than that he entertained himself with the write-ups the families had paid to put in them.

Oh, how the people of blind faith believed their loved ones resided in the kingdom of heaven with the all mighty God. It was terribly sad in his opinion, and he wondered how folks could be so blatantly blinded by their own love of those who lived lives of sin, thinking that everyone was in heaven when clearly that was not the case. It most certainly wasn't preached in any church.

He wondered what would be said about him when he died, wondered who would come to his funeral, other than celebrities. He had shunned his whole family, so why would they make an appearance?

He truly was a man alone, every smiling face that got close to him synthetic in makeup. His spirit was broken, shackled by the need for fame. He wondered how he could stray so far from the man he once was.

Questions like these lingered in his mind constantly. There was something tugging inside his soul that made him want to make things right with everyone before his day with the reaper.

But why?

To hell with them, he would think, shaking back to himself, realizing that he was having a moment of weakness.

That's to be expected, the devil enlightened him. The mind was vulnerable, and whatever had been programmed in him prior to their chance meeting on a dark street was still in there, leaving him with a good conscious the devil was trying to eliminate in him altogether.

It was a work in progress, but they were close, *almost there*, if he could only keep Cade's mind focused on the negative things of the world instead of turning back to God's way. Satan could not allow that to happen.

In fact, he had long ago decided to take his servant out. It was time for Gabriel Cade to die. And he knew just how to get it done.

22

Upon his arrival at his mother's beautiful two-story brick home Cade was immediately thrown into a dark mood at the sight of family member's cars parked in her driveway and lining the street. A large truck with mud tracks on it was the most noticeable-his father's vehicle.

"Jeez," he moaned with exasperation. "Do they all have to be here at once?"

One car that was not present was his daughter's, and he felt the slightest reprieve because of this. She and his father together would give him a conniption.

He wasn't on the best of terms with any of the people inside the home, although he had helped a few of them substantially since becoming rich. It would linger on his conscious if he supported charities and not his own family, but once they had gotten greedy, he was quick to cut them back, causing a rift.

They just love you for your money, the devil constantly reminded him. You would have never heard a word from any of them if you were still broke and struggling.

But they are family, my blood.

Blood doesn't make you family, was the devil's motto.

Family was nothing more than a word to Cade now, and if they wanted to use him for his money, they had another thing coming to them. Not a single one of them had earned a dollar from him, hadn't made a deal with the devil that he was now second-guessing.

Vernon opened the door for him and he gave the order for his security team to wait outside.

"I won't be too long."

He needed to get to his book signing, and though his mother was the priority of the moment he didn't want to deal with his family for any more than half an hour, if that.

They would all have to be here at once, huh?

He knocked on the door and was met by his mother's sister, Candice, a chubby, red-faced woman of about sixty with closely cropped, salt and pepper hair. She grunted upon seeing him, stepped to the side without a word, allowing him access to yet another home he had bought.

His family was gathered in the living room, all of them falling quiet as his feet met the hardwood flooring. The reason for the gathering today was to say their final good-bye's to his mother, but in his personal opinion she was not going to die. At least the devil had convinced him to think that way.

It wasn't over until it was over. They are exaggerating as always.

Cade wasn't so sure about that, which was why he had to stop in to check on her periodically to make sure that the fear of death that had everyone in the room on edge was a false alarm.

He tossed his head side to side, cracked his neck. "How's everyone?" he said, clearing his throat.

He didn't plan to be here long. He would say his hellos, see that his mother was in better-than-deathly condition, and bid his family farewell in orderly fashion. There was nothing that he could do for his mother other than what he had already done, which was pay for her healthcare.

The rest of the family could stay for moral support.

"What good does sitting around mourning do?" the devil had said on the way over. "That's doesn't benefit anyone, and it's not making you any money."

Point taken.

He didn't exactly want to do the book signing, but of course it was always a good look to appease the crowds of fans that flocked to him whenever he did such things.

His siblings sat together on a couch, avoiding eye contact with him as aunt's and uncle's stood around, a few of his cousins milling about throughout the rest of the home.

"What's up guys?" he attempted to break the ice.

The energy in the house was pure negativity and he wondered if turning around and walking back to his car would be the best option.

I can come back when they are gone, he thought, calculating his escape.

"Well, if it isn't the one and only Gabriel Cade. You come home to see your momma off to the heaven's?"

The voice of his father came from the right. Cade turned to see his old man leaning on the doorjamb, a beer can of the cheapest brand in hand. His face was screwed up in disgust of his first-born child.

Cade knew this moment was coming, but he couldn't have been prepared for it if he had lived it ten times already.

"Or do you just come around to show off how big you are now?" his father added. "Cause you sure are pretty in your little pink polo. *Look at you!*"

"Hello, Gabriel," Cade said, looking through the man. "I see you're still anal as ever."

"Gabriel, huh? Since when am I Gabriel and not dad?"

The tension seeped into the room like gas, and at any moment a spark would blow the roof off the house.

A nurse came from the upstairs and acknowledged Cade. He had personally done all the hiring for his mother's hospice care and the blonde had been one of his favorites, for reasons unrelated to the medical field.

"Would you like to see your mother?" she asked softly, tears in her eyes.

"Yes," Cade said, turning to take the steps. "I'll only stay for a minute. I just want to check in on her."

"What?" Cade's brother said. "You're leaving. Everyone's staying for a while. It's time for family. What else could you have to do?"

"I have a book signing in less than two hours," Cade explained, receiving moans and sounds of distaste from his loved ones.

"Your fans are more important to you than your mother?"

"Never said that. I'm here, aren't I? Can't recall any of you paying for any of these medical bills."

"Oh, excuse us for not having the wealth you have. A lot of help that has done for mom, right?"

"Could your jealousy be any more obvious? Why do you all always have to bring up my money in arguments? I don't think I am better than any of you, but I am not about to settle for less if I don't have to. As far mom goes, sitting around here moping won't get us anywhere. Whatever is going to happen is going to happen, regardless of what we do at this point."

"You know it all, huh?" his father said sarcastically.

"Old man, you and I have nothing to talk about," Cade said calmly, fighting the urge to step across the room and kick his father in the chest. "I would rather you not speak to me. I came to see my mother, not you."

Eyes growing with rage at the show of disrespect from his very own creation, Gabriel Sr. stepped from the doorway with a drunken stagger and came closer, causing Cade to tense up.

"Who you think you talking to, son? I made you, I will end you."

Cliché.

This was it, the moment he would deck his father right on the chin and shut his lights of as if he were late on an electric bill. He clinched his fist tight, his blood rushed and he felt light headed from the adrenaline.

"Dad!" Cade's sister barked. "Now is not the time."

She did this more because she didn't want to hear the ruckus between the two of them. It most certainly was not in defense of her brother whom she detested most days, and Cade knew this.

"You're right, sweetie," The elder Cade said. "You're right. But I tell you this much," he added, pointing a finger at his son, the wondrous Gabriel Cade. "I don't care what we've been through as a family, how you feel about me, or how much damn fame you acquire. I will not tolerate that cocky ass attitude you have."

"That seems to be the common theme amongst you people," Cade responded, causing eyebrows to rise at the statement.

"You people?" his aunt Candice asked. "Just what is that supposed to mean?"

"It means he thinks he's better than the rest of us since he sold his soul to the devil," Cade's brother said, suddenly rising from his place on the couch.

Cade's heart skipped a beat and he caught his breath, a move noticeable to all who were in the room.

"What did you say?" Cade said to his brother.

"You heard him," his father broke in. "You sold your soul for riches, and now you think you better than the rest of us small people. You've let all that money go to your head, son, and that isn't you! What good does it do a man to gain the world and lose his soul?"

"Miss me with the scriptures, *dad*! You are no saint by any means, and the whole room knows who you truly are. As far as me being better than everyone in here, I am."

"You just said you didn't think you were better than anyone," his sister interjected, her face screwed.

"I had a change of heart just that fast. The more you all talk the more I realize the differences between us. You think I wanted the life I had? You think that was living?"

"You were blessed," his brother said.

"Blessed?" Cade said, incredulously. "I was dejected and homeless. Remember kicking me out?" He pointed at his brother, who shook his head in disappointment. "Tell me, which of you that I have supported with *my* money came to see me in prison or while I was in the hospital fighting for my life?"

"What does it matter where you were in life?" his aunt Candice said. "You are rich now."

"That's not the point," Cade said, instantly remembering the conversation he and Chance had before her death, similar to what was just said.

The tide had been turned on him, and he felt foolish. Maybe he really never did get the point.

His mind moved to Chance and he realized that he missed her deeply, more than he would admit to anyone.

"Bitterness is eating you alive, young man," his aunt said. "Let the past go and forgive the people you think have wronged you. The Lord was obviously taking you through something so you could truly appreciate what you have now."

Cutting his eyes to her Cade said, "That's the dumbest shit I have ever heard, woman. My past is what made me run to where I am now. *I'm never letting it go.* It made me the success I am today. The moment I forget where I come from is the moment I fall back to your level in life. I'm not bitter, but you must be stupid if you think I'm about forgive anyone?"

Her husband, a burly man whom Cade always respected, stood and said, "You might talk to your daddy like that, and you may be rich and powerful...but you ever talk to my wife like that again-"

"I have a security team with big ass guns on them outside this house, Jessie. I'd choose my next actions very carefully if I were you."

"It's like that?"

"You damn right it is. I would hate to show you what kind of power money has really bought me."

Jessie looked around the room at everyone before saying "You think they can get in here to save you before I break your little ass in half?"

Cade said nothing, lost for words as he looked around the room at his family, their snide expressions confirmation he was not well taken inside the walls of the house he had paid for with his soul.

His father took a drink and cackled. "Same old punk ass son I raised. Never amounted to what I had hoped, that's for sure. Figured the military would've straightened you up, but you ended up in prison anyway. Then the justice system was supposed to do the job, but you came home to be an even bigger piece-of-shit. No matter how much you have accomplished, you never amounted to the son I thought you could be-and that's a good man. What the hell happened to you?"

"A good man? You're the reason our mother is in the situation she is in now. *You are a terrible man!*" Cade growled, choking back tears at the thought of his mother laying on what could possibly be her deathbed.

But he would not fall for the devil's temptation to charge his father, although it would feel so good to do so. Satan was at work in this house. Even though he could not be seen. He was hard at work, urging them to push his buttons and force him to lose his cool.

It's my job! The devil's voice echoed in his head.

"Sure, blame me for everything." Gabriel Sr. said. "What do want from me?"

"I want you to die," Cade answered too fast, taking the room by surprise. "I want you to go upstairs and take my mother's place on that deathbed."

The air left the room and the two men eyed each other, waiting for the next move, but instead of charging his son Gabriel Sr. raised his hand to his head and combed through what little hair he had left.

"I'm sorry you feel that way, son."

"You should be."

Suddenly Gabriel Sr. startled everyone by throwing his beer can against the wall in a fit of rage, or so it seemed. All eyes were on him now as he began to cry, and in that moment, Cade could honestly say he felt sorry for the man and the pathetic existence he lived in.

"I'm sorry for everything that I put you and the family through all those years, son. I was controlled by something I can't explain." He pointed to the beer. "I still am. But it was never my intent to hurt any of you," he added, looking to each of his children who all had trouble keeping eye contact with the man they had known to be so hard in their childhood.

To Cade he said, "I swear I didn't mean any of the things I just said to you, son. I couldn't be any prouder of the man you have become. Coming from where you were to now..." the tears flowed heavy now. "I'm just glad you made it home alive. You have become a much better man that I ever was or could be. If I die today, I just want you to know that."

Tears formed in Cade's eyes and his chest became tight. His father wiped tears from his own face and stepped closer to his son, pulled him in for a strong hug, something Cade could not remember him doing since his childhood.

He stood frozen in the man's grasp, his arms at his side, unsure of how to respond to the gesture.

His father was not a soft man by any standard, and to hear him speak like this brought a wave of guilt upon him. Everyone had demons, and his dad was no different. There wasn't a single person breathing who was exempt from the trials and tribulations of the world-especially the temptations of the devil. Some people drank themselves to death, and others sold their souls for riches and fame in hopes of escaping the pain of life they faced daily.

It was tragic, but so true, and in this moment of emotion shared between father and son the devil was completely blocked out by love.

He could not imagine the day he would hear his father apologize for the abuse he had bestowed upon his family, but when the words "I love you, son" spilled from his mouth Cade forgave him in that moment without a second guess as he wrapped his arms around his father.

That was all he wanted to hear. All he would ever need.

"I love you, too," he told his father, squeezing him tightly, just a vulnerable child in need of his father's love.

Only if he could say he made his father proud doing the right thing in life. Everyone was amazed by the facade he had put on in order to hide true actions.

They had no clue, and never would.

"Go upstairs to see your mother," his father said. "She's always excited to see you. Never shuts up about her pride and joy. You really have made the family proud."

Only if you knew, old man, Cade thought. Only if you knew what had to be done in order to attain the success you see.

To the rest of the family Gabriel Sr. said, "Let's cut this guy some slack. He's been through more than any of us. The fact that he was able to pull himself out of the mud..." he held Cade's face in his hands, smiled proudly. "I'm honored to say I'm your father."

Heads nodded their agreement, and one by one Cade's family members came to him with gestures of love, which he readily accepted as the tears flowed.

This was all so sudden, so unexpected. Something was wrong, and he knew it, could feel it. Why was this happening? His father stood back and raised his hand to his head in salute, a soldier's way of showing respect. The two of them may not have gotten along over the years, but the bond they shared in service could never be broken.

Wiping tears away Cade mirrored his father's action, and he had to admit it was the proudest moment of his life. Nothing compared, not even the birth of his daughter, which was strange. It was more than a salute. In that moment he had achieved one of the ultimate feats of life.

Forgiveness.

But deep down inside he knew something was off. There was a reason it was put on his father's heart to make amends with him. He just didn't know what it was.

And he was afraid to find out.

23

His mother lied motionless in bed when he walked through her bedroom door. It pained him to see her this way, so weak and vulnerable when she had been so strong and vibrant before his federal vacation. He remembered tails of her archery skills that had gotten her into college, and could still see her shooting in the back yard at her targets on the trees when he was young.

She was so strong in those days before the fall.

As a gift for her birthday a few years earlier he had bought her a gold bow and arrow, custom made just for her and she had been thrilled.

"This is the best gift ever," she had squealed, running her fingers over the beautifully handcrafted razor-sharp tips on the arrows. He was sure she would never shoot it in her condition, but the thought was what mattered, right?

Time passed quickly and parents became dependent upon their children, but in the back of his mind this was not the way it was supposed to go.

She was only fifty-seven with so much life to be had at that age, and yet hers was slipping away from her by the second.

Meeting his eye, she said, "Hey, sweetie. You came to see me."

"Of course," he said as he moved to his mother's side. He kissed her forehead and took a seat beside the bed. "Had to come see my favorite girl in the world."

"I heard fussing downstairs," she said, her voice weak and fading. "Your father must be drinking."

The two of them laughed at this, knowing how true the statement was. He told her what happened only moments ago and she smirked.

"Getting soft in his old age," she joshed. "If you would have kicked his ass, I would not have minded."

Cade laughed and said, "Something had to break him down."

"Yeah, well, it sure wasn't me."

"It's very becoming of him, the whole soft thing. I never could have imagined it."

"Not in a million years, my child." Her expression changed and she asked, "What troubles you?"

He tried denying the fact that he was weighed down with stress, but she was his mother and knew better. She expressed condolences for the losses of Lily and Chance.

"Talk to me, son. We may not have many more moments like this."

So painfully true, he had to admit.

She sounded weaker than she looked, her voice barely above a whisper and he had to lean in to hear her. These meetings were always gut wrenching, but he had to be strong in the expectance of her coming death. He was, in his opinion, the leader of the family, the strong one who the rest of the family would lean on for relief.

His mother's heart and kidney condition along with his own organ problem shaped his motivation to treat his body like the temple it was.

I will not go to the grave in this manner, he promised himself. No matter the temptation he faced daily to put himself in position to do so.

The devil had done a number on his mother, and Cade loathed the fact that he was in cahoots with such an evil, confusing individual as savvy as Satan.

"How do you feel?" Cade asked her.

"You're looking at how I feel," his mother responded, her eyes half open. "But, it's ok. I have made peace with God over this situation. I am at peace."

Cade turned his head, unable to look at her, his soul at odds over how he felt about what she had said. He knew the devil would do anything for him, yet would take him out any given chance each day of the week. For some sick reason he accepted this, even though he didn't fully comprehend it.

God, on the other hand, was a different story entirely. The things that the devil had implanted inside his head so many years ago still stuck and made so much sense to him, leaving Cade wondering what was really true.

Had the devil told him just enough truth to get him to believe his lies? It was said that the devil's greatest trick ever played on mankind was making them believe that he didn't exist, but Cade begged to differ.

The biggest trick the devil could play on mankind was making them think he was their friend.

Now, with all that was happening in his life he began to wonder just how bad he had been duped.

He loved the money, embraced the adulation that he received from hordes of fans, but now he was beginning to wonder if it was all worth it.

He'd lost his fiancé, his daughter disowned him, and Chance was gone. To top it all off he and his family had been at odds for years without any just cause.

All the devil's work.

"What's bothering you, son?" his mother asked.

He denied there was anything wrong but she knew, still saw through him as if he were her precious little baby crying after a day of being picked on in school. There had been many of those days, but now he was someone powerful, an important figure in the world, and it would never happen to him again.

Unless, of course, Satan was the one doing the picking.

No matter how much he had acquired over the years his heart was still troubled because the devil was one entity that had the ability to bully him with his own selfish ambitions and fleshy desires of the world that entangled and suffocated him, causing him to push everyone he loved aside in order to attain his wants.

"I had a disturbing dream about you last night," Cade's mother said, piquing his interest. "I saw you as a beautiful bird, flying high towards the sun and all its glory. Suddenly you took a nosedive and crashed into the ground, breaking your wings. You lay there, not dead, but a crippled beauty that could no longer be what it was meant to be. When the weather changed you were unable to hibernate, forcing you to die a slow death if you didn't."

Cade's face fell to a frown as he continued listening.

"But you were not out of the fight completely. Even though you could not move to a warmer location with all the other beast of the air, you got on your feet before it was time to move and hobbled to the next location, hard as that was. You met your fellow birds there where you healed and returned to the air soon after, a warrior in their eyes. Do you know what this dream means?"

Cade nodded, knowing the dream was a parable of him flying towards God when he came home. Selling his soul was the reason he had crashed into the ground. And now he was the cripple bird that would have to hobble back to glory.

But how could he do so when the devil owned his soul?

Would God see fit to forgive him and give him a second chance? Or was he condemned now, doomed to the fire he had read about in the Bible, the one preached about around the world in so many churches?

The devil would have him believe there was no fire, but with everything he had witnessed in recent months-death and pain, he wondered if he had been fully deceived as was to be expected of the devil.

How could I have been so foolish?

"The devil can't get to you if you have the blood of Christ on you, son?"

She could not be any more wrong, and Cade hated to admit it. He had been a devout Christian upon his release, was all in with God and had the blood of his savior on him. But when the devil came to him in the flesh his cunning ways had been far too strong for him to resist, and he had been hoodwinked into selling his soul.

Ramsey had once told him, "Jesus came to heal the sick and the devil came to hurt the healed. When you are doing the righteous will of God, Satan will come to destroy you at all cost. He is the negative of everything. Don't lose sight of that."

Sadly, he had lost all sight of it when he laid his eyes upon the riches of the world.

He missed his best friend and would do anything for them to fix their relationship. Ramsey may have forgotten about him like the rest, but his words were always uplifting, and deep down, Cade knew the man would never hurt him. He was wrong for having his friend manhandled the way he had.

He would find Ramsey and help him.

But what he wouldn't do was admit the deal he had done with the devil to his mother for fear of sending her into a diabetic shock. She was already in bad enough condition and if he stressed her it would only cause her to want the things that had put her in the bed she lay in now. The devil would be there to tempt her to do as her flesh desired.

How could one defeat their fleshy desires? he wondered, his mind traveling back to a book on Buddhism he had read in prison during his spiritual search. In the book there was a paragraph speaking on the issue-The desire in life should be to have no desire.

Desire and ignorance lay at the root of all suffering, the book went on. The cravings of pleasure, material things and immortality were just a few of those desires that man would never be able to satisfy. True wealth was not of the pocket, but of the heart and mind.

In those days he could understand what he was reading, but experiencing them was a whole different beast, one that would sink its teeth into you, sending venom through one's body, leaving them untamed and lethal as they chased full satisfaction of the flesh.

Unattainable, Cade now knew.

"I left you alone while you were in prison for a reason," his mother said, grabbing Cade's attention. Finally, she was going to tell him why she had been so distant with him while he was away all those years.

"Why, mom?" he asked. "I felt so hurt that I hardly ever heard from you. I figured you didn't love me anymore."

"That was never the case-could never be the case. But you are stronger than your brother and sister. I knew I didn't have to baby you the whole time you were there. If you needed me to coddle you, I would have, but you didn't. I knew you would make it home, so I left you there to find yourself. And you have done a splendid job. I am so proud of you."

That is such bullshit! Satan cried in Cade's conscious as tears streaked down his face. *If you fall for that line, you are a fool!*

Cade shut him out, listened to what his mother had to say as he fought to control the wave of emotions crashing into him.

"I know you were hurt by our lack of love, and maybe we could have gone about things a different way..." she paused to cough. "You have to make things right with everyone. You don't have to forget anything that's been done, but it's on you to forgive. Money is material, and you can always make it back. But you will never have the same family back once they are gone."

Nodding his agreement Cade expressed to his mother the need to make things right with his daughter. Jacy was very close to her and he was sure the two of them had talked about the struggles they were having in their relationship. He could only hope Jacy hadn't brought up Chance's murder.

"I'm losing all the most important women in my life," he cried, laying his head across his mother's bosom as she smoothed his hair with her fingers, as only a mother could.

"Well, when she gets here you can make things better," his mother said.

Cade raised his head. "She's coming?"

"Yes. We spoke earlier by phone. I prayed last night that I would be able to get both of you here, and praise God, it will happen."

Praise God? Had the Lord really brought him here for a reunion with his daughter?

"That's great," Cade said. "When will she be here?"

"Soon," his mother said. What she said next took him by surprised. "Pray with me, son."

He was hesitant, knowing he would be violating the devil in doing such a thing. She took him by the hand.

"Pray with me..."

He nodded, knowing he might be throwing everything he had away.

They closed their eyes to pray, but before his mother could speak the sound of a car horn sounded twice in succession. Cade stood and moved to the window to see that his daughter had indeed arrived with her boyfriend, a young man she had met in Bible-college.

"She's with her guy friend?" his mother asked.

"Yes," Cade answered, turning to her. "I haven't met him. You knew he was coming?"

"Oh yes, it takes two to make a big announcement."

"Big announcement? What announcement?" Shrugging childishly his mother smiled a smile he could remember from his childhood. In that moment he felt a connection between them that had been lost over the years. He couldn't remember exactly when their relationship went bad, but at the moment it didn't matter.

Today was a good day-he made amends with his father, siblings and now his mother. Jacy would be icing on the cake.

He moved back to the window to see that his brother and father had moved to the outside to greet the two young lovers.

Announcement, he thought with a smile. What were these two up to? Whatever it was he would accept it, for as long as his daughter was happy, he could be just as thrilled for her.

But it was not to be.

His face turned to a mask of horror and his thinking evaporated as a speeding car came to a screeching halt in front of his family members who were now congregating in the yard, all smiles as they greeted one another and accepted Jacy's boyfriend.

The driver's side window rolled down and a hand gripping a pistol appeared, thunder exploding from the barrel, bullets striking his father in the chest, killing him instantly.

Panic set in, sending them scattering in all directions, desperately searching for cover, finding none as neighbors scurried into their homes. The open space made them all sitting ducks, and the man in the car was the duck hunter.

Cade's brother was next to go down, clutching a wound in his leg, pulling himself away in hopes of safety as Jacy and her boyfriend attempted to make it to the house.

His mother screamed from her bed as Cade raised the window and yelled, *"Jacy, run!"*

Two shots ripped through the back of the young man running with her, a young man Cade would never have the pleasure of knowing.

They had an announcement to make!

Jacy fell to the ground and grabbed him by the shoulders, pulled his bloodied body towards the house as the security team moved into action, returning fire at the car. The assailant sped in reverse, spinning the car sideways and blocking the road.

Pushing the door open, the driver fell to the ground unleashing fury from his weapon and Cade could see that he wore a mask along with body armor that covered his torso. He moved to the back door on the same side, retrieving a menacing looking assault rifle.

Who the hell was this psycho?

Quickly, the man popped up and aimed the rifle at the security team, ripping off a series of automatic shots that trumped their handguns, sending them into hiding behind Cade's car, chunks of paint and metal flying all around them as Vernon was hit in the back, dropping dead on the scene. And then another one was dropped dead.

"Jesus Christ!" yelled Cade as he ran downstairs yelling, "Everyone get down!"

Shots came through the front of the house as the words jumped off the edge of his tongue. His aunt and uncle lay on the floor beside his sister and Jacy who was streaked with blood and covering her head with her arms.

Thank God she is okay, he thought.

"Stay down!" Cade order as he moved to the front door, the sound of shots echoing outside as the man continued to pick people off one by one.

He pulled the door open to see that the shooter had made his way into the front yard past his father's motionless body and was now taking aim at his brother who crawled in effort to escape.

The brother's locked eyes in what would be the last time Cade ever saw his sibling alive.

Pop! Pop!

"No!" he cried out for his brother. Only moments ago he had made amends with his father and brother. Now they were gone.

The shooter aimed at Cade and let off two shots just as he let his body fall to the left side of the door on the hardwood floor.

Shots came from the street, as the one remaining security guard engaged in a shootout with the masked man, taking cover behind Cade's bullet-riddled car as they traded shots.

Two bullets connected with the masked shooter's legs before the guard was shot down, removing all hope Cade had in getting out of this situation alive.

This is chaos.

A thought crossed his mind.

The devil is loving this!

And then there was silence, no sign of life left outside "Gabriel Cade!" the shooter called out with a familiar voice. "Face me like a man without your security!"

The voice belonged to Dalton Ramsey, his old cellmate in prison, the very man who had taught him the things he knew about God.

Also, a military marksman, and it showed.

"I can get to anyone," the devil's voice sang in Cade's head. "You messed up going back to God, my friend."

I never did! Cade responded in thought.

"You would have."

Cade instantly thought back to the day in Market Square when Ramsey tried to approach him and have a conversation. If he hadn't treated the man he called a friend years ago so badly, the bodies in the yard and street would still be full of life.

I've got all of them now, Satan echoed in his head. And for your information, they aren't happy with what they are experiencing.

Shots rang out again causing pieces of the wall to implode as Cade curled up, doing all he could to dodge the bullets.

"No more!" Cade cried out, waving his hand in the doorway. "No more!"

Without hesitation Ramsey aimed the rifle at Cade's hand and sent a bullet soaring through his palm.

Screaming in pain Cade clutched his wrist as blood spilled onto the floor. Quickly he ripped the sleeve off his shirt and tied it around his hand to stop the bleeding before he got light headed.

"Ramsey!" he called. "Stop! Just stop!"

At the mention of his name, Ramsey yanked off his mask, sucked in a deep breath and spit on the ground.

"Not so tough now, huh?" he called out over the distant sound of police sirens fast approaching. "That's some fine security you got. Look at them now. *All dead!*"

"Stop!" Cade pleaded.

"All I wanted was for you to help me."

"I still can!"

Ramsey let out a demonic laugh and fired more shots off at the house. "It's too late for all of that. Don't you hear the cops coming? We're all dead!"

He slowly moved closer to the house, rifle ready to fire.

Inside the house Cade was taken aback to see his mother on her feet, moving painfully into the living room, her bow and arrow in hand, the string drawn back tightly. Frantically he waved her back upstairs, but she shook her head.

"How many more have to die?" Ramsey yelled.

He was moving closer, Cade could tell. What to do, what to do?

He looked his mother in the eyes, and in that moment made a decision to act. He nodded and twirled his finger in the air, giving a single that he hoped she would catch. This would take some doing, and a lot of teamwork, but if they did it right, they would get out alive. That was all that mattered to him at the moment.

His father and brother were gone, his security team had been wiped away like a smudge on a windshield, and his daughter was now covered in her boyfriend's blood, traumatized by the event.

This was their last chance. Taking a deep breath, he put his plan into action.

Rolling across the floor to the other side of the door Cade dodged the bullets that Ramsey sprayed at him, taking his focus away from anything other than him, allowing his mother to step into the doorway with the bow.

Her aim was impeccable, he knew, and as she raised the arrow in Ramsey's direction Cade hoped that he had done enough to give her a clear shot.

"Fucker!" his mother hissed as she let the arrow fly, fast and furious in to Ramsey's neck, sending him staggering backwards.

Go mom! Go!

The victory was short lived as a series of shots exploded into the house, hitting his mother in the torso, her body stiffening then convulsing where she stood before falling to the floor, blood spilling from her mouth.

"Mom!" Cade cried, hurriedly getting to his feet and rushing to her side, peaking over his should through the doorway at a stricken Ramsey who lay in the front yard, one hand on the arrow in his neck, his chest barely rising.

He would die a moment later.

His family was gone as was his security team.

The devil had made it loud and clear that he was out to kill him now.

So, Gabriel Cade, convict turned celebrity did the only thing left to do in his current situation. He dropped to his knees and begged the Lord to forgive him his transgressions.

24

He was discharged the next day from the same hospital he had his heart transplant in a few years prior. Oddly enough the same nurse who had been so kind to offer him a Bible greeted him before he left.

"Do you remember me?" she asked him. She was a bit grayer, but Cade could tell it was the same woman.

He nodded, saying nothing, too traumatized by the event at his mother's home. The loss of so many lives at one time left him in a daze.

"I will pray for you, young man," the nurse said, tears in her eyes. "I am truly sorry for your losses."

Finally, Cade spoke.

"I can't be prayed for," he replied, turning to walk away. Before he could bend the corner, the nurse walked him down.

"There is nothing that is too big for the Lord to handle," she said. "Give it all to Him, the good and the bad. You will see what happens. But you have to believe in it. That's the only way it will work for you."

He nodded and turned to leave.

Darkness had fallen over him the previous day as his family members were covered in white sheets and eventually taken to the morgue, never to be heard from again.

Two detectives interviewed him in his hospital room about the killer, Dalton Ramsey. It was revealed that he had been seen a few days prior with a man in a flashy suit and they questioned if he could be connected to the crime. Cade wanted so badly to blurt out that the devil was the man in the suit, the real culprit behind the whole event.

But how would that be taken?

Most people said that they believed in God and the devil, but when it came to things Cade could testify to, they would look at him crazy, although the devil came in the flesh to many people in the Bible.

So why not him?

False believers, all of them.

His assistant, Claudia, picked him up from the hospital and they drove in silence on the way to his mansion, which he still owned, surprisingly. In fact, his bank account was still full as well, which was odd considering he figured the devil would have taken everything from him by now.

Strange, but what did he care? His family had been wiped out in one violent act and his daughter was without a fiancé now.

Their big announcement was that they were getting married, something Cade had expected, but still would have loved to have heard from the two of them. He would have loved to have seen the expressions on their faces when they told him.

So much joy had been taken away by a careless act.

He shook his head sullenly, all cried out. His tears were now replaced with rage and he could not wait to see the devil in person. There was a hole in his hand now and the meds he had been given at the hospital relaxed him to the point where he could think level, but he was unsure of what he would do once he saw Satan.

Looking at the wound he realized his hand would never work the same, but even that didn't bother him right now.

He wanted revenge!

But how could he get that when the devil was a spirit?

"You can leave," he told Claudia when they pulled up to the mansion. She nodded and was gone a moment later.

Inside the house he found all the lights off and moved to the wall and flipped the switch.

"And when there was darkness, Satan brought forth the light," the devil said, sitting at the top of the stairs waiting for Cade. "Hello, my friend."

"We are far from friends," Cade replied coldly.

"Oh, come on, man. You took that shit yesterday personal? I was just playing," Satan added standing and throwing his arms out at his side. "We're still cool, right? I left you all your possessions. Haven't touched a thing that belongs to you."

The nerve of him, Cade thought, his stomach sinking at the thought of Satan thinking the two of them would be on friendly terms after wiping his family out.

"I don't want anything from you."

"Ah, your stupid *and* ungrateful. I love it. Tell me, why did you come back here if you don't want anything that I have for you?"

Cade eyed him without a word.

"Figures," Satan said. "I know you want revenge, but you know that won't happen. So, how about we work this whole situation out and move forward?"

"There's nothing to work out, you son-of-bitch."

"Are you sure you want to curse God like that?"

Cade gave thought to what the devil said and shook his head, his internal organs steaming with rage.

Satan smiled and slowly began to walk down the steps. "You brought all of this on yourself, Gabriel," he said, a hurtful look on his face. "You got soft on me. We were having such a great time and you ruined it by having a good conscience."

"I came to my senses about you," Cade said. "You were out to get me the whole time."

"You are your own worst enemy. You have been out to get yourself since the first time you discovered sin. Why else would Ramsey want to kill you? Is it because of something I did or something *you* did?"

"I suppose you played no part in that..."

"I played the biggest part, but you opened yourself for me to come in. *You know that!* It takes a real fool to think I wouldn't push a person to the kind of chaos Ramey caused yesterday once it's in their mind. You don't think I wanted to see that? I'm the devil, *the* anti-Christ. And if I get a chance to do it again, I will. I helped kill most of your family, and eventually I will get you also. And *you* can't do shit about it. Just know that."

He came to the last step and turned left, moved into the massive living room as Cade followed closely behind, his eyes piercing him the whole way as he silently prayed to God, asking that He would allow Satan to be human for five minutes.

"You don't want those type of problems with me," the devil called over his shoulder, obviously reading Cade's thoughts. "But you may get a chance soon. A little quid pro quo never hurt. I may just have the deal you are looking for. If you accept my offer, I will grant you a chance to avenge your family."

"You lie," Cade blurted. *"You lie!"*

"I have never told you a lie. I gave you everything, as promised. You knew long ago how this game works, and you still think I'm that other guy you used to worship."

"I don't want to do any kind of deals with you."

"You sure about that?" the devil asked, turning to face Cade. "Don't you want your soul back? I can grant that wish."

"You're telling me you will give my soul back?"

"I'll do you one even better. You can keep everything I have blessed you with and go on about your life. It's the least I can do with all the losses you have taken in recent weeks-and there have been so many," the devil mocked, his dark laughter seeping into Cade.

This was funny to him? Cade thought, shaking from anger as he thought of all the death associated with him recently.

Lily, Chance, the nurse and her killer, Ramsey, his parents and his brother, Jacy's fiancé, his bodyguards-twelve total!

Satan had the gall to laugh?

Without much thought Cade leapt at the devil in an attempt to tackle him, missing and grabbing all the air available when the prince of darkness evaporated. He landed hard on an expensive glass table, cutting a forearm deep and letting out a cry. The sound was more from despair than pain, knowing what a foolish move he had just made.

But he didn't care!

Quickly Cade got to his feet and found Satan standing behind him. He charged the devil once more, this time stopping short and throwing a sharp hook to his face that knocked him down.

What?

He pounced on him and began to pummel Satan, his head turning violently with each blow, blood spewing from his mouth and nose. The pain from the hole in his hand was good pain now.

Yes! Cade thought as he released rage on the cause of all his problems. But was the devil really the creator of his angst?

As the thought processed, he looked down and realized he wasn't in fact punching the devil, but the floor.

"When will you humans learn?" the devil said from behind Cade as he looked at his hands, bloodied and broken from attacking the linoleum floor. "It's not me that you are fighting against-it's yourselves. You all love the pleasure you get from doing what you do, but when the results of your actions are pain and struggle, I get the blame. If you are led to water, it is your choice to drink it."

Cade stood, his hands shaking as he turned to see the devil wiping his bloody face with both hands, restoring himself to new. He spit a thick wad of blood the floor that became a clan of hideous spiders, speedily crawling towards Cade and covering his body as he fought them off.

He screamed with terror; his fear of spiders evident in that moment as Satan doubled over with laughter.

"Get his ass!"

"Make it stop! Make it stop!" Cade begged, the spider bites getting worse as he did. They crawled under his clothing and on his neck, biting harshly as he fell to the ground kicking and swiping his body with broken hands to get the bugs off of him.

"Please!"

And then it was over, just as quickly as it had begun.

"You are a pathetic beggar," the devil said, coming to

within a foot of Cade and looking down on him. "I don't know why I even deal with you, or any other human for that matter. All of you are beneath me, so fearful when I only live in your heads because of that very fear which grips you and won't let go. You don't know real fear-haven't even seen it. But I can show it to you."

He pointed to the large wall to his right with various paintings on it just as the house began to rumble fiercely like the empty belly of a whale.

Cade began sweating profusely as the room warmed to a high temperature, the large wall he had been directed to look at crumbling and falling away like shattered glass. He now laid his eyes upon the most gruesome sight he had ever seen in his life as he slowly got to his feet and moved toward what was now an open space.

Thousands-possibly millions-of people of all races and sizes hung from bloody crosses that jutted out of a burning ocean as flames licked at each of them. They wore masks of fear and pain, each just as helpless and mauled as the beaten soul next to them, their cries for help unanswered as maggots exited their snake covered bodies.

The sands were replaced by a stretch of smoldering magma rock, it's cracks filled with boiling lava that burst and landed in small explosions.

"That, Gabriel, is fear," he could hear Satan saying as fear coursed through his blood.

Cade's heart was stuck in his throat and he could not respond, hypnotized by the site in front of him as the heat continued to rise, enveloping him.

"Don't worry, there's plenty of room for you there. You should have no problem getting in."

Finally, Cade turned and spoke. "Is this what I think it is?"

"It most definitely is," was Satan's reply. "That is the big party I have been telling you about for so many years."

"This is no party."

Satan was thoughtful. "Ok, I might have lied about the fun part, but hey, there's a bunch of people there, just like I said it would be."

No one was supposed to be in hell until the judgment, Cade could remember reading. This was a scare tactic and he boldly expressed as much.

"Oh, you think I am trying to scare you?" the devil chuckled. "You want to be scared?"

At the snap of his fingers a massive dragon appeared from beneath the flaming ocean with a roar and stood above all the helpless souls on the crosses, wings outstretched as its head rotated wildly, throwing flames all around and scathing a third of them.

"This isn't real!" Cade cried as he took a step toward the devil. "It's not real!"

He turned back to see the dragon huffing smoke over the people on the crosses, covering them in soot as hot lava dripped from its body, flames bursting all around.

"Oh, it's real, and about to get realer," Satan warned as the ocean began to retreat. "I was good to you and all you did was take me for weak! I allowed you to do as you pleased, and all I asked in return was one thing-don't turn back to God! You brought this on yourself."

"You are always so concerned about me going back to God. What would it matter? You already got what you wanted, didn't you?"

Or had he?

It was then that Cade had a Eureka moment and began to laugh uncontrollably.

"You are weaker than I thought. I gave you way too much credit, ole trickster you. You never had my soul!"

"Oh, I have it. It's mine. I gave to you and you gave to me. Fair trade."

"Fair is where they judge pigs, *bitch*!" Cade said, feeling emboldened to step into the devil's face, never once paying attention to the receding ocean of fire.

Cade was constantly warned against betraying him. It had been beaten into his head that there would be punishment for doing so, as Lily had found out the hard way.

Sadly, she had been tricked out of her life. At any time, she could have gone back to God. but the devil had convinced her that she would never be able to do that.

Satan never purchased his soul in the first place. If Cade decided to go back to God then he could at any time he so desired. Satan could not have that, so he tried to have him killed.

"I live through you," the devil had told him multiple times. "The more you sin and show what a good time you are having, the more people will want to do the same. It keeps me alive."

In reality he couldn't buy his soul, but if Cade would have lived and died in sin the devil could close on the deal that was brokered.

If Cade went back to God...

"You wanted so badly for me to die in my fleshly sin before I got smart and ran back to God," he said. "So, you brought Ramsey back to kill me. But you wanted to cause as much pain as you could if he didn't get me."

Satan smiled. "Got it all figured out, you think?"

"I do. No deal!" Cade growled, pushing the devil to the side and moving past him. He twirled a broken finger around. "You can have all of this back."

"Oh, you think you can just quit me?" Satan barked.

"Tell me, Satan. How does it feel to know that you have so much potential but aren't strong enough to defeat an unworthy human such as myself?"

"You don't think I can't defeat you?"

"That's right. I'm done with you. What are you going to do about it?"

"Funny you should ask," the devil replied with a smile.

The devil had said those words so many times over the years, but never had they been so eerie.

Satan nodded his head toward the fiery ocean, directing Cade's attention back to the horrible scene just as the dragon's head tilted back, fire blazing from its mouth toward the red sky with the most horrible roar assisting the flames.

To his dismay the ocean was receding, revealing more black rock and demons with pig faces chained by the neck, struggling to break free and charge him.

He's trying to scare me! Don't fall for this!

Easier said than done, he thought as the fiery water rose high above those on the crosses. There could only be one result of this action, and his bones began to shake with fear as he looked to the devil wearing a look of anticipation.

"You are not about to do that," Cade said as the house began to shake violently.

"I believe I will."

He's a liar and always has been!

Cade searched Satan's eyes for the lie, found nothing. Cade turned his attention back to the demons and the dragon. They had to be at least a hundred feet away, but he could see the pain in their eyes as they fought to break free from the suffering, jerking and crying as their bodies burned.

"I figured if you go back to God," Satan said, "then I would at least be the one to send you to Him. Say goodnight, Gabriel."

Sensing a real threat of danger Cade looked to the devil and back to the horrific scene as every cross began to burn harshly, the cries of the damned piercing him.

He was sweating profusely and his skin was beginning to cook.

This is real! He thought, turning to run away as the blazing water came crashing down into a raging wave, sending the home up in flames as it chased him back to the staircase where he took the steps two at a time just as the lava moved into the open room.

Fire engulfed the stairs and walls, burning hot on his heels as he pumped his legs harder in an attempt to avoid being set afire, the steps falling into the flames beneath him and exploding.

With a dry mouth he screamed in fear and launched for the hallway floor at the top of the staircase. Surrounded by flames he tried to devise a plan as smoke crept into his lungs. Pulling off his shirt he covered his face he to avoid passing out.

Down below spirits appeared out of the fire and reached out to him with cries for help as the water began to rise, bringing even more heat along with it. So many souls, so much pain. The pig faced demons surfaced from below and began pulling most of them back under, a massive flame replacing each captured soul.

He could see Chance among the damned. Ramsey was there as well, along with his father and so many others he had known in his lifetime that had gone...before their time? Was any of this been predestined for man? Could God ever write this in someone's story?

Or was man the creator of his own path and destination, deserving of any punishment he received for denying the Lord and following Satan?

Too much to think of. Besides, what did it matter now? The walls were on fire and he had nowhere to go, no choice but to stand there and burn to death.

Would he wake up in eternal fire? he thought as he fell to his knees. His skin was red from the heat and the tears that ran down his face left streaks as he felt his body being taken by the flames.

The dragon appeared in the open area, surrounding all the remaining spirits and incinerating them with a sweep of the head. His focus then turned to Cade, the one he truly wanted.

Arms outstretched Cade called to God in heaven to forgive his trespasses and deliver him from evil. Sensing this, the dragon became more incensed and roared, slapping its wings into the water and splashing fire. Rising and elevating through the caving roof, it hovered above Cade, ready to vanish him from the earth when suddenly there was thunder in the sky.

Cade looked up just in time to see the clouds parting in the morning sky, heavy rain falling into the house. The raindrops were larger than any he had ever seen and they brought along a chill in the air

The dragon twisted and fought against the rain midair until it could take no more, quickly retreating into what was left of the fire down below. The rain continued to fall and Cade opened his mouth and took it in, the taste purer than life itself.

What is happening? he had to wonder.

Deep down he knew.

This was the power of God at work. His spirit had been spared, and he felt like the prodigal son in the Bible, coming home to where he was supposed to be after having squandered what as most important-his salvation.

He began crying uncontrollably and realized that letting go of things with no merit was the only way he could place his vision back on God after having being blinded for so long by the devil.

He looked around at the home now that the fire was completely out, hearing fire engine sirens in the distance. The place was charred, completely destroyed, and he laughed to himself inwardly.

Who cares!

Suddenly he realized the pain in his hands had subsided. Holding his hands out in front of him he was tickled to see the hole was now closed and fully healed. Turning them around to marvel at the miraculous blessing he was taken aback to see writing on his palms.

His hands trembled, not from fear, but excitement at what he was reading. He had a new task in front of him now, one that would cement his place in heaven next to the king on the throne.

Yes Lord! I will do as you ask!

Standing quickly, he looked down below at what used to be a spacious room with a lovely staircase and piano. No longer was this home the same, and it never would be, but it didn't matter. Possessions came and went.

He had a mission to complete, one that had come directly from God Himself. And he would accomplish it, even if it cost him his life. It would be well worth it.

Outside and shirtless he let the rain cover him and cool his body, washing his sins away in the holy water. Why the Lord had decided to spare him and place such a heavy assignment on him he would only be able to find out when he departed his life.

For now, he had to focus on God's agenda for him.

Looking down at his hands, he once again read the message.

On the left hand: THERE IS A YOUNG VIRGIN WHO IS PREGNANT WITH THE ANTI-CHRIST. YOU MUST FOLLOW THE STAR TO FIND HER. PROTECT HER SO THE CHILD CAN BE BORN. POWERFUL PEOPLE WILL COME AFTER YOU, FOR THEY DO NOT WANT THIS CHILD TO BE BORN. THEY HAVE SUCCEEDED MANY TIMES IN KILLING THE VIRGIN'S OVER THE HISTORY OF MAN.

On the right hand: YOU MUST ENSURE THE CHILD MAKES IT TO THIS WORLD. IT IS THE ONLY WAY TO SET THE PROPHESIES IN THE BOOK OF REVELATION IN MOTION. YOU HAVE THE CHANCE TO DESTROY THE DEVIL AND VENGEANCE WILL BE YOURS FOR ALL HE HAS PUT YOU THROUGH. I BELIEVE IN YOU. SINCERELY, GOD.

"Won't happen," came the familiar voice of the devil from behind Cade. "You read it yourself-I have killed so many virgins who tried to get that child here. I will not allow you to accomplish this mission. That girl and that child will die, and I will continue to reign here on earth."

Shaking his head, Cade said, "I will defeat you and vengeance will be mine."

Laughing, the devil looked up to the sky. "Are you serious, God? Is this the fool you have called upon to save the world from *me*?"

Clapping, he returned his gaze to Cade. "I have killed better men than you that have taken on his task. Stronger and more cunning. Tell me, what makes you think you will succeed in this?"

Cade simply looked up to the heavens and into the rain. In doing so he was amazed to see a bright and shining star in the clear sky.

You must follow the start to find her.

"Let the games begin," Satan said. "You're a dead man."

Cade turned and began to run, following the star.

He had no clue what he was getting into, but he would sacrifice himself for the Lord.

His Father in Heaven in had spared him.

Made in the USA
Middletown, DE
31 October 2020